playing it cool

by Ariel & Joaquin Dorfman

Burning City

playing it cool

joaquin dorfman

Random House New York

Copyright © 2006 by Joaquin Dorfman
Jacket and title page photo ice image copyright © Daniel Smith/zefa/Corbis

All rights reserved.
Published in the United States by Random House Children's Books,
a division of Random House, Inc., New York.

RANDOM HOUSE and colophon are registered trademarks of Random House, Inc.

www.randomhouse.com/teens

Educators and librarians, for a variety of teaching tools, visit us at
www.randomhouse.com/teachers

Library of Congress Cataloging-in-Publication Data
Dorfman, Joaquin.
Playing it cool / by Joaquin Dorfman. — 1st ed.
p.   cm.
SUMMARY: While tracking down the long-lost father of his best friend Jeremy, popular eighteen-year-old Sebastian calls on a network of favors and debts and begins to question his way of life.
ISBN 0-375-83641-1 (trade) — ISBN 0-375-93641-6 (lib. bdg.)
[1. Interpersonal relations—Fiction.   2. Fathers and sons—Fiction.]   I. Title.
PZ7.D727477Pla 2006
[Fic]—dc22   2005022660

Printed in the United States of America
10 9 8 7 6 5 4 3 2 1
First Edition

For Angelica

playing it cool

Prologue

Far as I'm concerned, it began with a sophomore intent on taking a dive from the second story of his parents' suburban home.

Paul Inverso, fifteen. Brother of Jenny Inverso, eighteen.

Then again, I could start a few weeks earlier with Jeremy King. Coming to me after his mother revealed a secret hidden for well over eighteen years. Shocked to learn that his real father was not the one who had raised him. A lifetime of assumptions over and done with, there was now another man out there responsible for his birth. The second half of his genetic code. Someone who, from all that Jeremy had been told, could not be found.

Or I could start with the investigation that led us to Jeremy's real father. Using all my connections to gather the necessary information. All inquiries and research pointing toward the coast of North Carolina. The town of Wilmington, just 150 miles from our own backyards.

All of which, of course, led me to you.

But I know I don't want to start there. Don't even want to

think about it just yet, not ready. The contrast is too stark, almost painful. How things were, what they became, how they are now. Trying to keep things simple as I retrace my steps, now knowing full well that there was never anything simple about it. Never once considering what lay beneath, even as questions raged out of control that week, brought me to my knees. Too certain of every last thing I had come to believe. Too confident in every last move I made. The world on a string and truth be told . . .

. . . I could start any number of places before March 12 of 1998, but as far as I'm concerned, it all began with a sophomore intent on taking a dive from the second story of his parents' suburban home.

Paul Inverso, fifteen. Brother of Jenny Inverso, eighteen.

Although starting an hour or so before that certainly wouldn't hurt. . . .

PART ONE

THURSDAY

1. Only If It's an Emergency

Cesar dropped us off at my house.

It was four in the afternoon, and spring was making its presence known. Sun at a flattering angle to the neighbors' lawns, single-story houses laying low beneath clear blue skies. Slight humidity, birds engaged in sweet-sounding conversations. Regenerated trees rustling with a little help from the southern breeze. Smells of a nearby cookout, kids reclaiming the streets with their bikes, music from an open window filling the gaps of activity.

Train whistle in the distance.

All the deceptive makings of a small town in North Carolina.

I got out of the car, shut the door to the passenger's side.

Jeremy got out of the backseat. Headed for the house.

Cesar kept the engine of his rust-red Pontiac idling. Earnest seventeen-year-old face looking up at me through rolled-down windows. First-generation Mexican American, eyes still remembering where he came from. Genuine hope displayed in a smile of well-intentioned teeth.

"You really are something, Seba," he told me.

"You're the one who asked her," I replied.

"I didn't think Nicole would say yes."

"Waste of a good worry, Cesar."

"There's still tomorrow night."

"Come on, Bastian, let's go!" Jeremy called out from behind me. Waiting by the curb, fidgeting impatiently. A long-established habit of his.

I ignored him. A long-established habit of mine.

"Tomorrow night's taken care of," I told Cesar. "I've made reservations for two at the Mezzanine."

"The Mezzanine?" Cesar was back to worrying. "I can't afford a place like that. Ten-dollar soups, the catch of the day's the same price as the boat they used to catch it—"

"There are ways around money."

"I don't have anything to wear."

"I'll take care of it."

"My mother needs the car Fridays," Cesar mumbled.

"Just tell Nicole to meet you at the restaurant at eight sharp. I'll be by your house to pick you up at seven."

"And after the date, I'm just supposed to ask her for a ride?"

I shrugged. "It's the nineties."

"So were the eighties."

"Don't worry about it."

Cesar sighed. Nodded, put the car into first. "I hope you know what you're doing."

"I always know what I'm doing."

Cesar knew it, too. Drove off without another word.

I watched him go.

"I'm glad you know what you're doing," I heard Jeremy say. "Because I don't have a goddamn clue."

I turned and saw that Jeremy had sat himself on the curb. Brown sweater and khakis hanging uncomfortably off his scrawny frame. Sneakers tapping against the ground, body bouncing slightly. Blond hair stopping just short of blue eyes that were always thinking two disasters ahead of everyone else. Top set of teeth nervously working on his lower lip. Fingers toying with each other.

I walked past him.

Jeremy stood up and followed me. White aluminum siding accompanied us around the house, through the backyard. Sneakers cutting through tall grass, swishing sounds with each stride as he started in. "We leave the day after tomorrow."

"Excited?"

"Try unprepared."

"We're all the way prepared."

I opened the back door, and the two of us made our way through the small kitchen. Down a dark hallway, floorboards creaking.

"*You* may be all the way prepared." Jeremy's words were starting to gain momentum. "But this is all happening very fast for me. I need to go over this at my own pace, I need details. Contingency plans. We leave the day after tomorrow, and this was supposed to be our day to work on things, get our stories straight. And so far, what . . . ? After school, we dropped Sara off at the clinic, paid Mr. Wallace a visit, fixed Cesar up with Nicole—"

"Your father's probably just as nervous as you."

Jeremy took a moment to find his breath. "Which one?"

"The one in Wilmington, what do you think?"

Another door open, and we were in my room. Nothing special to look at in there. I was never one for decoration. Typical posters and teenage paraphernalia replaced with my own view of the world, simple and clear-cut. Personal touch abandoned in favor of only that which was necessary . . . a bed, two chairs. Bookshelves and a wardrobe. Squat, second-hand desk.

Answering machine.

"I think," Jeremy collapsed in a chair, "that what my . . . father thinks isn't for you to say."

"He's waiting for you with open arms," I assured him. Went back over familiar territory as I took off my jacket. Leaned against the desk with my arms crossed. "Waiting for both of us with open arms. That's got to count for something."

"Won't count for much when we get to Wilmington only to have your switch blow up in my face."

"It's *our* switch, Jeremy. And nothing's going to blow up."

"What are you doing?"

I stopped, my finger inches away from the answering machine. "Checking this message."

A miserable look crossed Jeremy's face.

"It's just one message," I told him.

"Doesn't make me feel better."

"Jeremy—"

"I don't even need to hear that message." Jeremy was talking fast again, repeating himself. "Don't even need the details to know what's going to happen next. You *promised* me today's our day to get things done, smooth out the specifics, and now we're going to end up going off on some other—"

"Jeremy . . ." This conversation was a familiar one. "You asked for my help. You'll get it. But right now I need you to shut up and control yourself. Otherwise, I walk away and you can face your father on your own."

Jeremy stared up at me. "Not likely."

"Not likely, what?"

I returned Jeremy's stare. Trying not to let a lifetime of friendship interfere with what had to be done. Never letting a trace of struggle come to the surface, despite recurring doubts about whether it was Jeremy who couldn't live without me, or possibly the other way around. . . .

"Just check the message," Jeremy conceded, leaning back and crossing his arms.

A moment later, and the tape was playing back Sara's voice for me:

"Bastian, it's Sara. . . . I'm still at the clinic. Oh, God, you're not going to like this. . . . My mother's outside, and she's got around twenty of her friends with her. They've all got signs protesting the place. They're not going anywhere, Bastian, and the clinic closes at six. . . . Please think of something. I can't stay in here forever. . . ."

End of message.

Sara Shaw, fifteen years old. Daughter of Esther Shaw, head of the North Carolina chapter of the Concerned Women for the Right to Life. If Esther caught her daughter leaving that clinic, questions would lead only to unfortunate answers. Shocked onlookers. Resulting punishment that would most likely stretch itself out over the rest of her life. Sara Shaw, who had always struck me as a different breed of high school girl. Strangely in touch with her surroundings, brief conversations between us that revealed a sweet sort of kindness. None of that naïve certainty that dictated every teenager's mindset and attitude. An innocent, despite her many mistakes, and I didn't want visions of her tear-streaked face anywhere near my thoughts. No time to panic, no room for hesitation under the glare of those four, poker-faced walls.

I was already at the door to my room. Jacket on, doorknob waiting for a twist, when I heard Jeremy say something. I turned, saw that he hadn't budged from his chair.

"What?" I asked, impatiently.

"The clinic closes at six," he told me. "It's four. In sixty minutes, it'll be five. Can we at least spend this one hour getting our plans straight?"

"This is important."

"So is my father."

I let a couple of thousand thoughts play out in my head.

"You're already halfway to figuring how to get her out," Jeremy continued, watching me with intent eyes. "I know how your mind works. Those protesters aren't going anywhere, and neither is she. So come on, Bastian. Let's, just please, get something done today."

His words reached out from across the room and took hold.

I let my hand fall from the doorknob.

Jeremy nodded, sighed. "All right . . . good."

The phone rang.

Jeremy bolted upright. Sitting position, body tensing all

over again. Waiting for that second ring, silently praying that maybe the first one hadn't even happened.

It didn't work, and the phone continued to ring.

"Don't answer that," he told me.

"What if it's an emergency?"

"We've already got one of those."

"What if it's another one?"

Jeremy hesitated, maybe because he already knew.... "Only if it's an emergency."

The answering machine came to life: "Hey, this is Sebastian's phone. Keep it simple."

A beep.

Then, Jenny's voice:

"Bastian, this is Jenny, pick up. Pick up, pick up, pick up.... All right, I guess you're not there. Here's what: Paul's going to kill himself and he says he'll only speak to you—"

Jeremy: "Damn it!"

I picked up the phone. "Yeah, Jenny, I'm here...."

A whole slew of words on the other end, dramatic display of panic in each one. I cut through them, just the facts. Paul. On the roof. Legs dangling over a redbrick patio. No idea why. No response to conventional questions....

"He'll only speak to you, Bastian," Jenny finished. "Mom and Dad will be home in an hour."

"I'll be there in twenty minutes."

I hung up and strode to the door.

This time, Jeremy followed. Feet dragging through the hallway, into the kitchen, and back out into idyllic afternoon light. Circling the house again, once more on West Knox

Street. Sounds of a distant train whistle floating through the air as we stopped in mid-stride . . .

Hopscotch court on the street where my car should have been.

"Bastian . . . ," Jeremy managed. "Cesar dropped us off."

"Yes . . ." I nodded a few times. "Yeah. I think this is going to get complicated. . . ."

It was ten past four in the afternoon.

2. What About Wilmington?

Big Niko was a round, pugnacious bastard.

A living, breathing pile of pumpkins. Bulbous nose and a mustache far more prosperous than the hair on his oversized head. Proud owner of a rapidly growing pizza chain. Three in Durham, one out in Raleigh, another in Chapel Hill, branching out into Charlotte and the Carolina coast. Ran his business with an iron fist, and his employees saw to it that nothing stood in the way of expedient service. Those who took the orders got the details down to a tee, so that those who made the pizzas couldn't blame mistakes on them. Those who made the pizzas made sure that each pie was up to standards, so that those who delivered them would never have to worry about customer complaints. . . .

A tightly run ship, and Big Niko saw to it that things ran smoothly.

Smoothly, though Big Niko had his own problems. Had himself a bad habit of making time with any number of women other than his wife. Infidelity at its worst, he was the only man I'd ever known who somehow found time to cheat on his mistresses. What they saw in him, I was never too sure. Admiration for a man with his own business, that's what Big Niko had always told me.

His own explanations, the lies handed out left and right to his wife and the women he romanced, those were always short of satisfactory. Niko's mind for management seemed to regularly fall short when it came to social subtleties. Strange contradiction for an individual so bent on seeing that things went right. Strange that I constantly found myself righting wrongs with the help of a man who'd been in more hotels than the Gideon Bible, but after years of telling myself this was how the world worked, I had finally come to believe it.

And, finally, there was no denying that even complete bastards could be men of their word.

"Big Niko's Pizza," came the voice at the other end of the phone. I recognized the Greek accent immediately, even as the background roared with the sound and fury of a dozen orders called out, prepared, sent off.

"Yeah, Big Niko?" I put a finger to my other ear, thinking it might help. "It's Sebastian."

The clock on the kitchen wall read 4:15.

"Hey, Sebastian!" Big Niko's voice turned ecstatic. "How you doing?"

"Interesting you should ask—"

"Did my brother send you the report you needed?"

"Yeah, the Wilmington stuff is on its way—"

Jeremy ran in from the kitchen, half-empty glass of water in his hand. "What about Wilmington?"

I shooed him away as Big Niko continued. "You be sure

to look my brother up when you and Jeremy get to Wilmington this weekend, all right?"

No more time for pleasantries, and I pressed ahead. "Look, Niko, you remember Cindy?"

"How could I ever forget?"

"Remember Laura?"

I could almost hear the drool form on leering lips. "You know I do."

"You remember who saved your ass when you double-booked them at the same hotel?"

There was a long pause. Someone in the background called out for a large pie with pepperoni.

"All right, Bastian. What do you need?"

Music to my ears.

Moments later, Jeremy and I were outside my house.

Third time in a half hour, and the streets were already starting to lose their exuberance. Kids grudgingly retreating to their homes, doors locked in anticipation of a sunset more than an hour and a half away. Acoustics of an abandoned block making room for Jeremy's next question:

"Is there anything about Wilmington you feel like sharing with me?"

"Don't worry about it," I told him, scanning the street.

"That's what I told my mother, and here I've been lying to her for the past couple of weeks."

"She's been lying to you your whole life—"

"I shouldn't be lying to my mother—"

"And didn't she tell you she's been lying to you for your own good?"

Jeremy frowned. "Yes."

"So this is no different."

"I'm lying to her for her own good?"

"You're lying to her for *your* own good. Just how she wants it."

Seconds later, a compact car came screeching to a halt in front of us. Gaudy colors and the words BIG NIKO'S PIZZA EMPORIUM stenciled on the side. One hubcap gone missing.

Jeremy and I slid in, closed the doors.

The driver was Olaf. A twenty-five-year-old with a calculating look, ropy forearms resting on the steering wheel. Didn't really know his story. Hard life, hard times, a tough customer who had spent most of his years working whatever angle he could. Every bit the lean troublemaker with charm to spare. Pale skin and dark hair. Blue eyes that could pierce Kevlar.

"I'm not a goddamn chauffeur," he said, gunning the engine. "We just lost an order thanks to you."

Sure enough, the car reeked of an anchovy pizza Jeremy had just sat on.

"Big Niko knows what he's doing," I told Olaf.

"What about you?"

"I always know what I'm doing," I answered, picking up the car phone and dialing. "You mind if I use the phone?"

Olaf didn't answer, just hit a left turn.

3. Maybe You Don't Have a Choice

First two tries on the phone didn't bring me any luck.

I redialed and secretly crossed my fingers.

We were driving along West Chapel Hill Street. Rundown part of town, Durham's zoning between poor and prosperous didn't always believe in transitions. Dying gas stations, windows sheltered by dull iron bars. Streets decorated with bottles, sidewalks broken and indifferent to the trudging steps of low-wage workers. I looked out the window, phone to my ear, as residents leaned in doorways and watched cars make their way to better destinations. . . .

The same receptionist picked up on the other end. I asked for Anita's desk, *just try one last time*, and she put me through.

My mother had been with the *Durham Observer* for about as long as I could remember. Had worked her way from division to division. From receptionist to personal assistant, from layout to copyediting to low-level reporter. Not bad for a single mother of thirty-six. She was the one that kept it all going, hanging on, and it was more than either one of us could have ever hoped for back in Chicago.

When she picked up the phone she seemed almost ready for my question.

"Your car's in the garage," she told me. "There's no way you were going to make it to Wilmington this weekend unless I had it fixed."

I shook my head. "When were you planning on telling me this, Mom?"

"Something wrong?"

Olaf was speeding along at a decent clip now, headed toward Forest Hills.

Jeremy in the backseat, looking sullen.

"I need to get to the clinic," I told my mom.

"Clinic?" Her voice registered immediate concern. "Why? Did something happen to Sara?"

"Her mother's outside with an army of pro-lifers ready to pounce on anybody who goes in or out that door."

"Best-laid plans, Seba."

"I'm not joking."

"Neither am I. This puts me in an awkward position."

"Right now, Sara's in an abortion clinic that's under siege by her mother. *That* is an awkward position."

I caught Olaf throwing me a sideways glance.

Shit.

Over the phone, I heard my mother shout out to somebody. Something about a reliable source, then back to me: "You got Sara into this, and now you're going to have to get her out of it. I'm sorry, but I've already done too much for that girl. You're just going to have to think of something else."

"All right," I told her. "All right. . . . See you tonight, Mom."

"See you tonight, Seba."

I hung up.

"Your mother's named Anita?" Olaf asked.

"Yes," I replied. Started dialing again.

"Italian?"

"Latin American."

"I always figured you were Middle Eastern."

I took a quick look in the side mirror as I finished dialing. Olive skin, dark eyes, thick eyebrows. Nose somewhere between lengthy and flat. Dark hair cut close. Unassuming . . .

A nurse picked up on the other end, voice calm and clinical, well-trained.

I asked her if I could speak to Sara Shaw. Fifteen, pale face, strong features. Red hair, probably sitting in reception. A second or so later and Sara was on the line. Voice shaky and low as a strange, almost unwelcome affection threatened to overtake me. All at once, remembering the yellow sundress she had been wearing the day she first approached me for help. Standing on my front porch, breaking new ground in what had been a casually distant relationship till then. Sandals with pink painted toenails peeking out . . .

But it was never good to dwell. Bad for business, so thoughts of floral patterns and Sara's overcast eyes were shoved aside by her breath rasping in my ear. I dealt with what was now, and talked her into a state of relative comfort. Told her to hang on, promised I would be there in a half hour.

"What are you going to do?" I heard her ask.

"When it happens you'll know," I replied, sent the phone back to its cradle.

We drove on, suburban greenery sprouting up out of nowhere. A few stoplights' worth of silence before Olaf finally said it:

"So, Sara Shaw got knocked up."

"That's none of your business."

Olaf kept his eyes on the road, but he might as well have been looking right at me. "Guess it must have been your business, then."

"I'm just trying to help her out."

"Yeah? Maybe I could use a little help myself."

That very self-assured voice. Icy-blue stare of someone who's grown used to just that sort of temperature. Demanding without making it clear just what he was asking for.

"Well . . ." I tried to keep things in the roundabout. "Maybe I can help you."

"Maybe you don't have a choice . . . ," Olaf replied. Plain and simple. No need to mention Sara again. No need for an immediate follow-through. He'd talk when he was ready, and in the meantime, I had more pressing things to attend to.

A suicidal fifteen-year-old. A fence of protesters ready to tear into any employee or patient coming in or out of that clinic. A disgruntled Jeremy in the backseat, less than two days from meeting his real father for the first time.

Headed toward our first stop under the navigation of a twenty-five-year-old with a hard and calculating look.

4. It's Not Me, Man

Forest Hills.

Home to the vastly wealthy and their prosperous secrets. Lazy, winding streets and manicured sidewalks flanked by luxurious mansions. Multiple floors, lengthy driveways, sweeping lawns, both front and back. Separated from the rest of us by an expansive golf course and a thick slipper of towering trees.

Olaf dropped us off at Paul's. Broke his vow of silence just long enough to let me know what he needed and by when. Topped it off with a crystalline wink and sped off without another word.

I filed it in my head under *temporary nuisances*, and wiped the slate clean.

Jeremy and I went up the front walkway. Stones set in soft ground, trimmed hedges on either side of us giving room for flowers to take in the changing seasons. Jenny waiting for us at the oak door, dressed in a swashbuckling pirate outfit. Loose pants, blond hair partially pulled back, tattered white shirt halfway unbuttoned. Heavy makeup around the eyes. Brown shoes with brass buckles.

Jenny Inverso, the future gem of the silver screen.

No denying that there was once an attraction there. When we were younger, a schoolboy crush. Watching from a corner desk as she took notes, eyelashes meeting to kiss every few seconds. Heart murmurs, the thrill of anonymous longing; it all seemed like a long time ago. Heartfelt sentiments now forgotten, because chess players may value their queen, but they don't send her love letters. . . .

"I didn't think you were going to make it," she told me, took us through the threshold.

"Ta-da."

Jenny's father was an optometrist. Their house was the result of three generations upholding the family business. Two living rooms, eight bedrooms, four offices, two pool tables, exercise room, sauna, swimming pool, thirteen bathrooms and only four bladders to fill them all. . . . Jenny led us through room after room, through hallways and doorways, rambling all the while.

"I just came home from rehearsal and he was there. I tried to get him down, but you're the only one he's interested in talking to. Wouldn't tell me a single thing. I don't think he's stopped taking his medication, but you know how those things are. . . ."

Jenny led us up a flight of stairs.

Through a room lined with endless costumes, ranging from hobo to government clerk to Arab sheik. Wigs of all types and textures. Jenny's lifelong collection of disguises, each one hanging obediently in its place. Standing at attention.

Waiting to be filled for any number of theatrical occasions. One or two catching my attention as we breezed past, and I made a few mental notes.

Possibilities.

"Are we there yet?" Jeremy muttered.

"This way." Jenny motioned with her head, through one final threshold. . . .

Paul's room was awash with posters. James Dean, Jack Kerouac, Paul Newman, Humphrey Bogart, Richard Roundtree; the essence of cool plastered over every available space. Even the blue carpet and stainless steel furniture had their own wishful detachment, rejecting the afternoon sunlight as it poured through a pair of windows at the far end.

One of them half open.

And through that window, Paul Inverso.

His back to all of us. Sitting on the edge of the roof, surrounded by rough shingles. Gray jacket shrouding slumped shoulders. Head of dirty-blond hair tilted downward, toward a possible destination.

"Jenny, wait for me downstairs."

Jenny didn't move.

"Go on," I said. "Jeremy will keep you company. . . ."

Jeremy offered her a thin-lipped smile.

Jenny nodded. Grabbed my hand and let her eyes fill with tears.

Drama student.

Wasn't my kind of thing anymore.

Jeremy took her by the hand and led her away. Threw me an irritated look over his shoulder that I could do little about.

Back to Paul. . . .

23

I went up to the window, took a breath. Climbed through and got my grounding on the 45-degree slant. Cleared my throat.

"Paul?"

Paul didn't respond.

"I'm clearly not your sister, Paul, you can stop doing that."

Paul sighed. "Hey, Bastian."

"That's better. . . ."

I inched my way down to the edge of the roof. Sidestepping. A few loose branches scattering along with my black, mock-leather shoes. Got to Paul's side. Looked down and caught sight of that redbrick patio. Swimming pool a few yards to the right, tennis court a hundred yards to the left. The house was built on a slope and Paul's second-story room turned out to be a good three stories above impact.

"So what's the deal?" I asked Paul. "This seat taken?"

Paul shook his head. Drew his knees up to his chest, sneakers resting on the roof.

I sat down, tentative. Let my legs do the same, felt the damp slime of gutters trying to seep into my pants. I pulled out a pack of cigarettes, offered one to Paul. Paul accepted. I handed Paul a lighter, child safety locked in place. . . .

Paul didn't smoke. Struggled with the lighter, focusing. When he finally did manage to generate fire, he sucked in every bit of hell that was everybody's first time. Began to cough and retch. I instructed him to lay back, keep his feet where they were.

I let him find his breath, took care of some things myself.

He sat back up, wheezed once or twice. Took another

pull, didn't inhale this time. The two of us continued to smoke. Not saying anything, and I let this silence drag itself out for as long as the clock would allow.

"You want to tell me what this is about?" I finally asked.

"You must think I'm a complete loser, calling you over like this."

"I don't think you're a loser."

"You do."

"Moreover, who cares what I think?"

Moot question. Approaching rhetorical. Paul was an admirer, an ardent one. I'd been told by Jenny and others that Paul had some sort of goal to be me. I didn't entirely know how this happened, didn't know why it made me so uncomfortable knowing there were followers around every corner. I only knew that Paul had attempted suicide before and his parents' attempts to curb this depression had clearly been unsuccessful. Were they to show up and find him on the roof, even if it turned out to be a mere threat, there was no telling what might happen. More medication. Treatment. An institution in place of school. Jenny, as always, blamed for everything that went wrong in that house.

All these possibilities making me cringe, because I didn't want to be the last resort that failed either one of them. But there was no time for second thoughts, because all these possibilities were less than fifteen minutes away. . . .

"I've got a backup plan, Paul," I told him. "I've got a backup plan to get you off this roof in one piece, but I'd rather take care of this the good old-fashioned way."

"How's that?" Paul's voice was trapped in a flat line.

"Worried about your place in this world?" I asked.

Paul took a moment. Looked out to the vast empire of mowed grass, trees. "It'd be nice to be like you. . . ."

"How's that?"

Paul took another moment, each one adding its weight to the second hand of my wristwatch.

I cleared my throat. "Paul?"

"You always seem to know what you're doing," Paul explained. "You have direction. It's like you understand who you are, and I don't understand what's wrong with me that I can't do what you do."

"Maybe because I'm supposed to be me," I told him.

No room for uncertainty.

"How do you do it?" Paul asked.

Despite my best efforts, I let heartfelt honesty make a guest appearance. "I don't know."

"Then what am I supposed to do?"

"Paul . . ." I flicked my cigarette over the edge of the roof. Hoped Paul wouldn't be joining it anytime soon. "If I could help you with that, then maybe there is something to what you think about me. But I can't. I can't tell you what you're supposed to do. You know what that means?"

Paul shook his head.

"It means that, as Paul Inverso, you don't want to be anything like Sebastian. Because Sebastian can't talk you off this ledge. And Sebastian can't tell you who you are. You see what I'm saying?"

Paul nodded, but it was going to take one or two more lifelines.

"What Sebastian can tell you is that your mother and father are coming home soon," I continued. "And we both know they understand this even less than you do. They'll take one look at this situation and draw conclusions. Make decisions with or without your blessing. Now, you're a special guy, Paul, but this is every teenager's curse, so who do you have to rely on? It's not me, man. . . ."

Paul sighed.

In that one breath, I saw something I recognized. A smile approaching his eyes. Maybe not there yet, but getting there. Working through the present situation. I let myself relax, and let Paul do the rest. Any further words would only reset our progress, and I didn't have that kind of time.

Paul turned to me. "It's just hard."

"Tell me about it."

"I don't want to be an optometrist."

"Nobody wants to be an optometrist."

Paul let out a short laugh.

"Put out your cigarette," I told him.

Paul smothered his cancer stick in the gutter. Extinguished.

"Thanks for helping," he said.

"Well, nothing in this world's free, Paul."

Paul raised his eyebrows, curious. Curious because, despite a crisis averted, there was still the undeniable fact of his admiration. His eagerness to please. Suicide attempt assuaged simply by the fact that I had bothered to assuage it. Might come back to this again someday, but for the moment, one step at a time.

One step closer to five o'clock.

And from there, one hour closer to six.

"Sebastian?"

"Yes, Paul?"

The danger now passed, Paul seemed almost casual. "What was the plan? Your backup plan to get me off of this roof in one piece?"

"Blackmail," I told him.

"Blackmail?"

I pointed downward. Paul followed my finger and took a good, long look. Didn't grasp it at first, but slowly came to realize just what lengths I had been willing to go. A crazy sort of compliment, that's how I figured Paul would take it.

"Oh," Paul said.

"That's right."

"When did you manage to tie our shoelaces together?"

"While you were lying back, hacking out your lungs."

Paul thought about it.

"Another good reason not to be me," I told him.

"Good enough reason to help you, though?"

"If you don't, *I* just might have to jump. . . ."

Paul laughed again, and the afternoon grew cool out there on the roof.

5. Services of a Different Kind

A quick search through Jenny's private collection yielded excellent results. A brown jumpsuit and a few other accessories were pulled from the wall of disguises. Crunch time, we got Paul dressed up and ready to go.

Took Jenny's car, a sweet-sixteen BMW.

I drove, Paul riding shotgun, Jeremy in the back.

Made our way along downtown streets. Redbrick tobacco factories long since shut down, small businesses left in the lurch by faraway strip malls and suburban enterprises. Concrete structures whose purpose nobody even remembered. Municipal buildings sensing an end to their service as we parked a block away from the clinic.

Even from that distance, we could hear the outraged cries of the protesters. Saw them clustered outside. Twenty or twenty-five, hard to tell. Signs held high. Television crews documenting the story for the evening news. Extra surveillance adding insult to injury. Not a pretty sight, and I could sense Paul's resolve slipping.

"Is it too late to kill myself?" he asked.

"Way too late," I told him.

Paul tugged at the ill-fitting jumpsuit. "Just feels like a bit much. Too risky, even for you. It's not like Sara's your girl-friend."

"This doesn't leave the car," I told Paul. "Sara's not of age to get an abortion on her own. I got someone to forge her mother's signature on the parental notice form."

"Shit, Bastian—"

"If Sara's mother finds out about this, her life is pretty much over. I'm not proud of what I did, and I don't want to do this any more than you, but—"

"What about the father?"

"Sara won't tell anybody who he is," Jeremy spoke up from the back. Annoyed. Trying to cut through the foreplay, get the show moving. "And Bastian hasn't had any luck find-ing out, either."

Paul's eyes lit up. "Well, I bet I could find out."

The last thing I wanted was more outside involvement than was necessary. Before I could say anything, though, Paul was already badgering me. Insisting that he could find out in a day or two. His eagerness to please overwhelmed the mo-ment, and I finally relented.

"Do whatever you like on your own time, Philip Mar-lowe," I told Paul, handing him a brown cap and a blond wig with long pigtails. "But for now, services of a different kind are required. . . ."

Paul sighed. Slipped the wig on and tossed the pigtails behind his back.

"I hope you know what you're doing, Bastian."

"I always know what I'm doing."

Paul adjusted his outfit. Nestled the cap onto the wig and drew the rim over his eyes. Took a deep breath and stepped out of the car. I handed him a brown package through the window. He placed it under his right arm and stalked off toward the clinic. I watched him go. Saw him approach the protesters, saw them begin to crowd around him. Held my breath as he ran through his lines, told them that he was just a delivery girl doing her job. Thought I saw Sara's mother, Esther, calling for the rest to let Paul through. Saw Paul disappear through the front door as the mob regrouped behind him.

Phase one complete.

Hardly had time to let out the relief, when I heard the back door open and close.

Jeremy leaning through the front window. "I'm out of here, Bastian."

"Where are you going?"

"Home."

"We haven't even talked about your father."

"Whose fault is that?"

"Look, I promise, tomorrow you'll have all the information you want."

"Tomorrow?" Jeremy's voice cracked with anger, now well beyond exasperation. "Were you even planning to discuss anything with me today?"

"Jeremy—"

"Save it for your next goddamn customer, Baz. . . ."

Jeremy stalked off toward the bus stop, one enraged footstep after the other. Hands stuffed in his pockets. Easy to picture that hurt and confused expression on his face. Half his lower lip disappearing between his teeth, biting down hard with all the world's frustration. I lost my bearings for a moment, reached for the door handle. Was about to call out after him when I heard the passenger door open and close.

Turned and found Sara there. Dressed in Paul's messenger outfit, blond wig, brown cap, and all. Thoughts of Jeremy were wiped clean and it was back to the business at hand as I asked Sara if anyone had recognized her on the way out. She shook her head and took off the wig. Red hair cascading over her shoulders, matching the flush of her cheeks. Hands shaking.

I hesitated. "You all right?"

"A little nauseous. . . ."

I nodded. "Put your head between your knees and breathe."

Sara complied and began to talk, muffled voice pouring onto the floor mat. "It's okay, Bastian. I'm okay. . . . I'm okay, it's just . . . really basic what they do to you in there. Almost medieval . . ." Sounded like she was crying. "I knew going into this what would happen, but I guess I just wasn't prepared. God, you can actually feel it happen—"

"All right," I told her. "All right, it's done, just breathe . . . relax."

Her breathing slowed. Slowed.

I watched her back rise and fall.

Moved to put my hand on her shoulder.

Stopped myself, fingers frozen in the air between us.

Unable to do anything.

Watching her breathe.

Sigh.

Relax . . .

Someone jumped on the hood of my car with a tremendous yell.

Sara bolted upright with a surprised scream, only to see Paul splayed over the windshield. Terrified eyes spread wide, pursued by the protesters as he yelled for me to *Drive, drive, drive!*

I started up the BMW and hit the gas. Made a sweeping U-turn, Paul hanging on for dear life. Left leg dangling into oncoming traffic, screaming the whole time as the protesters closed in on us. Right tire popping up onto the curb, fender narrowly missing a parking meter. I jerked the wheel hard left, somehow managing to straighten out the car as Sara began to laugh hysterically through rapidly drying tears. . . .

"Bastian, you're a genius!" she cried.

"Guilty as charged," I told her. "Hold on. . . ."

I put on a burst of speed and left the rearview mirror to worry about the mob.

By the time I stopped the car to let Paul back in, it was six o'clock on the dot.

Just in time to get home and check my answering machine.

6. Interlude 1

Way I heard it from Dromio was this. . . .

Round about the time Paul dropped me off at my house, the sun was headed to sleep on the coast of North Carolina. Well past yellow, now orange, contemplating red as it dipped toward a skyline of oceanfront houses.

Only a remote citizen or two left on the beach. House after house watching over the few who hadn't given in to the dinner bell. Scant joggers, strollers, the rare person or so who would never take sunsets for granted. Miniature birds darting back and forth with the lowering tide. A wave washing up an unusually large conch shell, resting at the feet of Dromio Johansson. . . .

Round about late forties. Face betraying a nose that looked as though it had taken its fair share of right jabs. Thin lips, eyebrows arching over eyes that had somehow grown younger with wisdom. Every gesture vague and open to interpretation, even as he bent down to pick up the seashell, straightened up, and brought it close to his watchful eyes. . . .

"This shell's probably been around since before the

South Atlantic rift opened. Saw the dinosaurs come and go. Matter of fact, the iridium in this shell could probably tell you if it was a meteor that—"

"Dad . . ."

Hesitant voice, directly to his left. The timid interruption of a sixteen-year-old girl with close-cropped black hair, petite figure. White tank top and a pair of jean shorts. Braces hidden by pouting, inherited lips. Brown eyes turned catlike by oval frames, the wildly intelligent features of a girl named Matilda.

"Dad, you're avoiding my question," she said. Homing in with an expectant stare. "You are avoiding my question."

"He's your brother, Mattie—"

"Jeremy's not my brother."

"Like it or not, he is."

"By virtue of genetics. I prefer to think of family as something beyond DNA or possible kidney donors. . . ." Matilda stared down at the sand. Dug a few toes in. "Truth is Christina is the closest thing to a sibling I've got. And if Jeremy's going to be staying with us, then I don't see why Christina can't spend the week here as well."

"Maybe if you got to know Jeremy as more than a pair of kidneys—"

"You just don't like Christina, Dad." Matilda's murmurs were almost lost to the wind. "That's the only reason you don't want her around."

"You've already decided not to like your brother. . . ." Dromio kept looking out to the ocean. Shell in one hand as though weighing it for value. "That's the only reason you want Christina around."

"I want her around because I need a friend."

"You mean *ally*."

"I mean someone who *understands*...." Frustration threatened to overpower her breath. "I want someone around who realizes that taking in an estranged son, *and* his best friend for the week, is not normal. You may be prepared for this, but it's happening very fast for me.... Jeremy's your son, and you can't be here for both of us."

Dromio stepped back from the conversation for a moment. This is what he told me, stood back from the edge of it all and wondered in different ways than I would in the upcoming week....

"Mattie," he ventured, "I've been here from day one. Every year since you've been born. You've had me your whole life, so at least bear in mind the courage it must have taken for Jeremy to ask for just *one week* of mine."

Matilda was deflated. All aggravation subdued, held in check by her father's words. Shoulders now slanting. Eyes downcast once more. Mouth twitching over armored teeth, and she retaliated the only way she could, determined to win at least one argument that evening:

"Iridium is found in sedimentary rock, Dad... not shells...."

Dromio looked down at Matilda. Recognized a small part of himself caught somewhere in that curious, genetic traffic jam. "I swear, if it weren't for the braces, I might never remember you're only sixteen. How many weeks in sixteen years, can you tell me what that is?"

"Eight hundred thirty-two," Matilda mumbled. "And a half, I guess, if you count the four leap years."

"How about in forty-seven years?"

"Two thousand, four hundred and forty-four, give or take."

"So it's no small wonder the value of a week doesn't hold the same for me as it does for you. . . ." Dromio weighed a few scenarios in his head, then smacked his lips together with a conclusive pop. . . . "Yeah, I suppose there's no real argument anywhere to be found here. Way to stick to your guns, sweetheart. Christina can stay for the week."

Matilda's mood switched, all at once. Bright eyes wide behind her glasses. Threw her arms around Dromio and laughed. Pressed her face against his yellow shirt, nuzzled blue palm trees etched into rayon. Dromio's smile landed close to her ear as he added:

"But you are going to get to know Jeremy."

Matilda stepped back and regarded her father. "Do I have to like him?"

Dromio shrugged. "Not as long as I get to keep disliking Christina."

"Deal."

Matilda slapped fives with her father, Dromio Johansson, who had something in his eyes that resembled a plan. The closely guarded workings of a mind that never quit. Always moving. Looking out onto a beach that would set the stage for an unexpected visit from the past, taking note of every dying wave as though he had already thought of them first. . . .

At least, that's the way I heard it from Dromio.

7. Last Paragraph

The sun went down, replaced by abandoned streets and nine o'clock shadows.

I sat alone at my desk, accompanied by the soft yellow of a 45-watt bulb. Radio turned to the public jazz station. Traces of Miles Davis filling in the vacant space left behind by the day's activities.

I typed out a few more sentences, one paragraph away from completing my midterm paper. I stopped. Listened to some more Miles. Shifted in my seat, wheels squeaking quietly over the uncarpeted floor. I glanced down at the keyboard.

Looked over to the phone.

Answering machine no longer host to anyone's problems.

I waited.

Turned to stare out the window. Caught a single lamppost out there offering up a small white spotlight. I watched a stray cat wander into that glowing circumference. Prowling, paws trudging on with calm grace and lost thoughts. . . .

Cat stepped back into the shadows.

I watched it blend.

Tried to go back to my paper. Blinked absently along with the cursor on the screen, stuck between the words *psyche* and *content*.

I typed out a row of 2s.

Erased them.

Tried the same with the number 3.

Erased that.

Looked at the phone.

Shook my head clear and stood up, swivel chair rolling back against the wall with a light tap.

Left my room.

Down the hall and into the kitchen.

My mother was sitting at the thick wooden table. Hair pulled back in a mass of jet-black curls. Sweat pants and a black T-shirt. Sorting through bills, brown skin smooth under the casual stare of a lazy overhead light.

Alongside the sink, a fluorescent tube hummed. The pale green refrigerator joined in, and I sat down across from my mother.

She glanced up. "Hey there."

"Hey."

"Study break?"

I nodded halfheartedly. "My mind's wandering."

"Nothing wrong with that, Seba. Happens to everybody."

I gave an uncomfortable shrug. "Last paragraph."

"Don't let it get to you."

I nodded again.

"You want a little rum?" she asked. "Got some Coke, too. A little Cuba libre?"

"Cuba libre's made with Cuban rum."

"You want to swim there and get me some?"

I smiled. "Cuba libre sounds good."

My mother went into the kitchen and poured two rum and Cokes, each in its own plastic cup. Served them without ice, the freezer had been busted for around a week.

I took a sip and tasted someplace I'd never been to.

"Sara told me today that she doesn't want me to go to Wilmington," I ventured.

"If I were her, I'd like to have you around."

"She's worried."

"Everything went fine, though, right?"

"She's still worried."

"Sara's very lucky to have someone like you standing by her."

"Working on bills?"

My mother reached for her drink. Took a sip. "Taxes. Bright side, though, I'm going to deposit that last check of yours soon."

"Mm."

"Should bring you up to around twenty-six thousand, last time I checked."

"I don't want to go on student loans."

"I know."

"I know it's a service, but there's no excuse for the way they treat people."

"It's business, Seba. You've said it about yourself many times."

"That's different."

"Mm . . ."

My mother pulled out a pack of Basics. Offered me one, lit them both. Smoke curled around the unfinished conversation. We remained quiet for a minute or so. I drank my rum and Coke, occasionally marveling that my mother was only eighteen years older than me.

"You know what's strange?" I asked.

"What?"

"Most kids I know think it's the most amazing thing in the world that you let me drink and smoke. Right in our own house, too."

"Well . . ." My mother finished her drink. "You're probably the only one of them who wouldn't take that as a cue to kick back a fifth of Boca Chica and pack a bowl."

I grimaced. "Pot's for goddamn losers."

My mother laughed. She had a perfect laugh. Even in the midst of high-pitched hysterics, she could bring it all home, note after finely tuned note.

I stood up, rounded the table, and gave my mother a kiss on the forehead.

She closed her eyes and smiled. "Thanks."

"I'll be in my room if you need any help with this nonsense."

"You're a good kid, Seba. . . ." She looked up in all seriousness. "You know that, right?"

I paused and threw her a smile that shouldn't have been there.

Winked and left my mother to figure out her share of our life together. Went back into my room, now home to the voice of Dinah Washington, reminding me what a difference a day makes. I sat back down at my outdated Macintosh and read the marquee scroll across the screen a few times:

ANY DAY NOW . . .

I jiggled the mouse, confronted once again with the final paragraph of my essay. Thought about every last essay I'd ever written, always done with on the day it was assigned. Thought about reaching that last paragraph. Thought about nights that followed, trying to finish those last few sentences. Night after night trying to complete something that had previously come so easy. . . . Worried about what might be left after all things came to their tidy, inevitable conclusions.

Same as it was that night. Growing more aware of my immaculately bare room with every word closer to the final thought. Listening to the voice of Dinah Washington, who turned even the sweetest of moments into wistful reflection. Ever-increasing glances toward the phone, waiting for a call.

Waiting for the next emergency.

Secret hopes of a conversation with someone, anyone, in the middle of this silent, well-meaning town.

PART TWO

FRIDAY

8. Have a Good Day

I woke up with the ring of an internal clock. Eyes opened, looking at the ceiling. Shook off my dreams, thoughts organizing, already grouping together. Let scenarios play in my head as I went to the bathroom, showered. The heat cut out halfway through, and I leaped out with an embarrassing shriek. Wrapped myself in a towel, dried off, and dressed.

Went to the kitchen in time to find my mother rushing out.

"Finish the paper?" she asked, slinging a purse over her shoulder.

"Didn't have much of a choice."

"Will you be home for dinner?"

"Unlikely."

"Good, I've got a date tonight. Have a good day."

"You too, Mom."

The door shut behind her. Silence and gray shades of morning filled the house. I fixed myself a cup of coffee, sat down, and drank it on my own. Routed out my day, unfinished business nagging like a housewife who could have once been a dancer. One day before Jeremy and I were due in Wilmington, and I was fighting off an entire legion of doubt. Stared across the table, imaginary boardroom letting me know that this move would put the entire company at risk. Our Sara demographics were still uncertain, Cesar's love life was still under development, and Olaf was muscling in on trade negotiations. . . . Funny little drama as I networked in my mind, prepared myself.

This was going to be one of those days, and I knew it.

The rush brought a guilty grin to my face, and I went back to my room. Printed out my paper, double-checking for mistakes. Packed a few books into my book bag. Dropped my coffee cup in the sink with the rest of its family.

Made a call to Federal Express, checked on a package, and grabbed my keys.

I was out the door and into my car.

The engine purred and Friday was now well on its way.

9. Wasted Worries

Pulled into the parking lot, found my space.

Walked up to the main building of Brookside High. Brick infrastructure sprawled out over a couple of acres, students dotting the scenery like ants. Rushing, wandering, chatting away. Spring fever spreading, an exuberant sense of glee as everyone pooled together for the last stretch of the race.

I got respectful nods and greetings, left and right, from students and teachers alike. Handshakes, swift pleasantries, the occasional favor here and there. I took care of what I had to, all the time striding down wide corridors lined with lockers and banners of scholastic encouragement. Roar of a train station in that jumbled mess as the first bell rang.

I opened my locker, interior plastered with yellow Post-it notes. I scanned them, took down a few I'd already attended to, sorted, and cataloged. I closed the metal door with a slam and found Jeremy standing next to me. Expression no different from the last time I'd seen him. Possibly more panicked as deadlines approached their limits.

"It's tomorrow now," he told me.

"That's funny . . ." I looked around. Students headed toward their first-period classes under the clock's commanding mandate. "I could have sworn it was today."

"You owe me some information."

"Hey, no kidding, Jeremy, I really *am* sorry about yesterday. I didn't know things were going to get that out of hand."

Jeremy didn't say anything, waited for more.

"I mean it, Jeremy." And I was pretty sure I did. "I was sitting at the table this morning, and thinking about tomorrow. This isn't just problem-solving, this is the real thing we're doing here. I don't have a father, either, and if I was going to meet him for the first time, I'd be scared, too. This is *your* father, and even still, *I'm* nervous. *You'd* be crazy not to be, so I understand, and I'm sorry. . . ."

Jeremy felt it out, eyes always trapped between conflicting thoughts. "Your heart's like a hologram, you know that?"

I opened my mouth.

Closed it, opened it again. "Is that a compliment?"

"I'm not sure."

"Jeremy—"

"All right, all right . . ." We began walking toward our first class. "Mean it, don't mean it, evidently I have a right to be on edge."

Something new in the way he was talking, and I asked him what was wrong.

"I think my mother's on to us," he said.

I tried not to roll my eyes. "How could she possibly know?"

"She had that look on her face this morning. That mother's look."

"All mothers have that look. It's what makes them mothers."

"She wants to meet with you today."

The late bell rang as we stopped in front of the door to room 203. Students streamed in between us. I waited for a break in the flow before asking, "Why does she want to meet with me?"

"She knows why we're going to Wilmington."

"Wasted worries, Jeremy."

"Some promised information would make me feel a lot better."

We were late, and, once again, schedules got in the way of conversation. "First period, all information will be delivered in substantial material form. Until then, I don't want to hear another word out of you."

I left Jeremy standing in the doorway, only a moment passing before he followed me in.

10. What's in That Package?

"Here's the scenario. . . ."

Mr. Wallace paused, acted as though he had only just come up with his lesson.

It was my business to know all about anyone there was to know, but I never did find out how a thirty-nine-year-old Glasgow card shark ended up teaching American history to a bunch of North Carolina kids. Wild red hair tied back in a ponytail. Well-fitting suit, pants tucked into a pair of combat boots, wide frame, and sweeping stride. It somehow never quite fit the picture.

Quite the showman, though. Very well-placed sense of space, stringing along all eyes as he wandered over to the window. The day was once again sunny, gray skies on hold as he turned back to the rest of us:

"Say you're in California and your wife is right here in North Carolina, tummy round as the earth, baby on the way. Now, in 1885, it would have taken the Pony Express two weeks to bring you the news. But with the birth of the telegraph, it would only take you a minute or two to find out if you were a mother or a father. . . ."

A few laughs, a few confused stares.

I smiled to myself as a note fell on my desk, tossed from somewhere across the room.

"Now," Mr. Wallace continued, "I warned you that today we would be doing a wee session of show-and-tell on modern communications. . . ."

I picked up the note, folded in fourths. Opened it and read over hastily scrawled words. An obscene love letter, something about licking me like an ice cream sundae. I looked over to the far end of the room, searching. Saw two or three girls looking over. Smiling slyly. A few winks and a tongue running over lips. I nodded politely and folded the note, noticed that Sara's desk was empty. Noticed Jeremy staring at me, catching my eye and mouthing *where is it*, with silent impatience.

"So . . ." Mr. Wallace was back at his seat. Arms behind his head, feet kicked up on the desk. "Is there anyone who would like to comment on the extinction of the Pony Express and those who stepped up to fill the space?"

There was a knock at the door.

I glanced up at the clock, saw a pair of hands at ten past nine.

Wallace shot up from his seat. Someone had just tripped up his timing and his face became one large scowl as he strode to the door. Opened it with a dramatic gesture in hopes of intimidating whoever had *dared* interrupt him in mid-thought. Wasn't prepared for what he saw, and Wallace traded in that mean look for one of outright confusion when confronted by Federal Express.

A delivery man by the name of Bobby. White pants and purple shirt. Dark skin, headphones around a neck tickled by slim dreadlocks. Package under one arm, clipboard in the other.

"Federal Express for Mr. Sebastian Montero?" he ventured.

I was already up and crossing the room before Wallace could react. Pen at the ready, I signed on the dotted line as Bobby bobbed his head to whatever tunes he'd been listening to earlier. Looked up from the form and smiled, said:

"Exactly ten past nine."

"I owe you one, Bobby."

"Think I still owe you two," he told me, handed over the package.

"Don't worry about it." I winked, slipped him a ten.

Bobby slapped me five in return and made his exit. I shut the door and turned to the rest of the class. "You see, everyone, Mr. Wallace is right. Pony Express, Federal Express . . . one word and one century make all the difference."

Pause as Mr. Wallace crossed his arms. Slight threat of a smile on his face, because he'd seen his share of smart-asses. Nodded, giving in to this brash interruption that had served his lecture so well. . . .

"Well done, *Mister* Sebastian Montero."

"Thank you."

"And I don't suppose you'd be willing to share what's in that package with the rest of us?"

I looked over at Jeremy, past the collective gaze of adoring high school girls, and saw his eyes dancing between me and the package in my hands. I kept my mouth shut as he let his lips spread slightly, corners of his mouth pointing north. Small traces of relief touching those features.

About time that kid learned how to smile, I thought.

Returned to my seat and let myself relax through to lunch.

11. I'm Safe

Big Niko delivered our slices to the table.

Pepperoni and mushroom for Jeremy, plain for me. A pair of perfect isosceles triangles, carefully measured amounts of sauce and cheese. Two sparkling Italian sodas. Service with a pat on the back, this was about as professional as pizza could get.

I gave him a nod. "Thanks, Niko."

"I do what I can," Niko said with a managerial flourish. Proudly stuck out his chest, unashamed of his B-cup man-breasts. Didn't even mind that his gut had them beat by a good couple of inches. He brushed a few crumbs off his maroon apron and asked if everything had turned out all right the previous day.

"Yes."

"Your friend Sara okay?"

"Didn't show up for school today."

"Anything wrong?"

"Probably taking the day off. Thanks for the car."

"It certainly put a run in Olaf's panty hose." Niko laughed through his lip-bristles. "He's working tonight, by the way. Said you should stop by, he wants to talk to you."

I nodded. Glanced around the fifteen or so red-checkered tables. Nothing there other than the lunchtime rush, a few kids enjoying off-campus gossip before getting back to the classroom grind.

Looked back at Niko. "All right, thanks for the mention."

"You got something going on with Olaf?"

"Not after tonight," I said. "Tell him I'll be here."

Niko looked down at the package in my arms.

"Is that it?"

"The very same."

Niko knocked on the table with sausage-link fingers. Winked and stole away to check on the kitchen. I watched him go back behind the counter as Jeremy shoved his pizza and Coke aside.

"Open it."

I snapped back to the moment and brandished the package. Tore off one of the ends and pulled out a few bound documents. Found a smaller envelope and opened it. Jeremy watched, edge of his seat. All those years waiting, and I kept myself at arm's distance of being able to relate. . . .

"Your father," I told him, slapping down the picture of a man round about his late forties. Face betraying a nose that looked as though it had taken its fair share of right jabs. Thin lips, eyebrows arching over eyes that had somehow grown younger with wisdom. "Meet Dromio Johansson. . . ."

Jeremy stared down at the picture. Chest swelling,

shoulders rising against his blue sport coat. I watched him take it in, face to face for the first time, and muffled my heart-strings as I produced another photograph.

"Dromio's wife, Nancy Johansson. Maiden name Bartholomew."

Jeremy didn't pay attention. Kept staring, lost in his father's eyes. It bothered me, and I kept on, pulled out another photograph.

"His daughter, Matilda . . ." I paused, hoping to get some kind of reaction. "No distinguishing marks or scars."

Jeremy didn't laugh, and I pulled out the last photograph. "Your father's closest friend and manager of his restaurant, Chaucer Braswell."

It wasn't working, and I snapped my fingers next to his ear.

His eyes shot up, once again with me.

I tossed down a stack of papers, full report on all of them.

Decided to preempt Jeremy's gratitude. "I told you I would."

"How did Big Niko get you all this?"

"He owed me."

"Does he really owe you that big?"

"He got Little Niko to get it for me."

"There's a Little Niko?"

"Big Niko's brother, over in Wilmington." I took a bite of my slice, had a drink of soda. "Though Little Niko actually got the information from a contact in the fire department."

Jeremy squinted. "The fire department is that powerful?"

"Sure." I forgot my own slice and lit a cigarette. "Fire department controls the weather, you know."

"Very funny."

"What difference does it make?" I asked, tapped some ash from a smoldering tip. "I want you to meet your father, it's important to me, there's the information. How about some applause for your friend and guardian angel?"

Jeremy glanced back down to Dromio's picture. Look of rehearsed worry coming back.

"He looks a bit rough around the edges. . . ." His fingertips played over the surface of the photograph. "A serious customer, you know? Am I going to be able to make *any* kind of an impression on a guy like this?"

I shrugged. "Don't know. That's what the switch is for, to find out with the least amount of risk possible. Gives us a pretty solid exit strategy, too, should Dromio Johansson turn out to be dirty water."

Jeremy didn't meet my eyes. "What if I want him to like me?"

"Jeremy, listen to me—"

"I hate listening to you."

"You're going to have to put that kind of crap on hold if you want to rise to the occasion."

"Don't give me this rise to the occasion bullshit as though you're somehow immune to what other people think about you," Jeremy snapped.

Smoke gathered between us. Pizza and soda left for Dumpster rats and alley cats.

"There something you want to say?" I asked.

Jeremy put on the voice of a thousand others. *"Did you hear about Bastian? I heard he's screwing the principal's wife. You think he gets special treatment for no good reason? Not what I heard,*

*I heard he's got other "connections." Probably wanted by the police,
you ever see him stay in one place for more than ten minutes? Well, I
hear he's got over twenty-five grand saved up from deals he's made.
That's just money saved up for college. No way, it's deals. Deals, like
drugs? I don't know, deals. . . ."*

Jeremy dropped the grapevine and let his breath play
catch-up.

I stared at him, playing it cool.

Jeremy looked out the window again. Down to his slice of
pepperoni and mushroom. Back out the window, then over to
me. "As for me, I don't know what to think about you. You're
the only friend I've got, but sometimes I'm not really sure
what that means."

And Jeremy might have had a point. About all of it, but I
wasn't about to let his words affect me. I let the facts seep on
through and hung the analysis out to dry, where it belonged.
Friend or no, Jeremy had trespassed, and I made sure he
knew I was staring right at him, *into* him if that's what it took.

"Let me tell you something, Jeremy . . ." A database of
words played around, and in an instant, a specific combination jumped out. Smooth, flawless: "Someone surrounded by
as many rumors as me is set for life. With that many stories
going around, nobody's going to know what's true and what's
a lie. Smoke and mirrors."

Jeremy wasn't impressed, but best friends hardly ever
are. "So what happens when the truth does come out?"

I gave my eyebrows a twitch. "When it does, if it does,
it'll just be another rumor. Another myth. So don't bother me
with *truth*. You just keep in mind that lies and deceit are what

kept you from your father, and now they're what's bringing you back to him."

The noise around us had mellowed. Easy listening now audible through speakers hung high on plaster walls. Soft jazz and elevator music.

"Are you ready to do this, Jeremy?"

Jeremy stared at me.

"Yes or no, there's still time to abort," I told him. "Yes or no?"

Jeremy looked as though he was about to respond. Mouth open, words somewhere between his heart and throat. A few balance-beam moments passed as activity slowed around the restaurant, but eventually, and very slowly, Jeremy picked Dromio's photograph up off the table. Slipped it into his coat and let a small amount of resolve sneak into his eyes as he nodded in the affirmative.

I returned the nod. I took the opportunity to cap things off, set the record straight.

"Nobody knows the first thing about me, Jeremy," I told him. Kept it steady, cigarette almost a memory now. "And that's why I'm safe."

"Bastian!"

The call came from across the restaurant, and I turned to see Hamilton. One of many who occasionally came round for a little help. Long hair and paint-splattered overalls accompanying him to our table. Eighteen-year-old with residence in a thirty-year-old body, looking down through round, wire-framed spectacles. Bouncing lightly from foot to foot, agitated movements as he spoke.

"Bastian, am I glad to see you. . . ."

Jeremy had gone back to looking out the window. Thoughts caught in a nearby traffic jam, eyes focusing on the days to come. Wondering to himself, though everything was starting to feel out loud. Secretive emotions coming to the surface with the approaching spring. Then summer, and after that, it was anyone's guess.

But in the meantime, school was still in session, and all of us were under the same gun.

"Well, Hamilton." I put out my cigarette and stood up from the table. "You're going to be even happier in a minute. What's up?"

12. A Very Big Secret

Mr. Wallace's British Lit class met at one in the afternoon.

Myself, I was out of school by five-till.

Pulling up in front of Jeremy's house by one-fifteen, ready to see what his mother wanted to talk to me about.

I parked in front of the redbrick house, right on the outskirts of Duke campus.

Turned off the engine and headed up the walkway. . . .

Jeremy's assumed father was the illustrious Peter King, a journalist from Chicago. He practically ran the *Durham Observer.* Between that and Brenda King's menswear store, the two had done very well for themselves. Good thing, too. Peter had been the one to set my mother up at the paper. Brenda and Mom had clicked almost immediately. A friendship between me and Jeremy had naturally followed, and I suppose this was how I ended up standing on their front porch, preparing for a heart-to-heart with Brenda King.

She answered the door with a surprised smile, blond hair and wide eyes shining through the screen door. "Sebastian! What are you doing out of school?"

"Mr. Wallace owed me a favor," I told her.

Brenda ushered me in and closed the door. "Where's Jeremy?"

"Mr. Wallace didn't owe him squat."

"How did he seem today?"

I pretended to be puzzled. "Fine. Same as any other day."

We stood at the entrance to their beautifully decorated living room. Brenda toyed with her fingers, didn't say anything. For all that she had managed to achieve, Brenda was never quite able to pull off the role of a successful American woman. Uncomfortable with the story of her life, it often felt as though she was expecting surrounding scenery to collapse, reveal the false fronts of an elaborate stage production. Same as it was that day. Tugging at her black dress slacks, looking off into a corner as family photos and her husband's Pulitzer Prize observed from a distance.

The smell of fresh coffee from somewhere in the house.

"You wanted to talk to me?" I asked.

"Come into the kitchen."

Spotless marble countertops greeted us. I leaned against one, watched Brenda root around in a few cabinets. Saw her find a couple of coffee cups and stride right past the coffee maker. Terse motions as she sat down at the kitchen table. Back straight, feet close together. Hands still holding on to that pair of confused java mugs.

I decided to make the first move. "Is something wrong with Jeremy?"

Brenda looked up as though suddenly awake. All at once

lucid as she plunged ahead. "A couple of weeks ago I told Jeremy that Peter King is not his actual father."

I let the information sink in. Nodded a few times. "Yeah, he told me."

"I thought it was time."

I walked over and pulled up a chair. Sat down opposite her.

"I don't know why I thought it was time," Brenda continued. "I swore to myself I'd never tell him. Can't commit to a secret like that then backpedal, and with every year that passed, this voice kept telling me just that. But by the time he turned eighteen, I just couldn't believe the reassuring voice anymore. And when he got accepted to Berkeley last month, I felt that it was my last chance before . . ." She gave a determined little nod. "So I just went ahead."

She looked at me then. Maybe searching for some kind of approval. Approval from me, of all people. Before I could put my best foot forward, she was moving on: "This is a . . . very big secret. Very big secret, Sebastian, the only other person I've ever told is your mother."

I wasn't prepared for it. "My mother?"

"My best friend."

"I don't really know what to say."

"Sebastian . . . this man, Jeremy's father, was a dark horse. He was all charm, and nothing else. But when you're a twenty-year-old college dropout, there *isn't* much else. And it turns out there wasn't much of anything after he got me pregnant. Left me two hundred dollars for an abortion, that's it. . . ." She paused, looked down at her hands. Her usually choppy voice was turning seismic. "And I was with Peter at the time. In Chicago, on and off with Peter. I told him the baby was his and we got married. And I know how that sounds, but I didn't want an abortion and I didn't want to be a single mother. I didn't think I could do it, and Peter was my only way out. . . ." She looked back up at me. "So we moved here, and eventually I met Anita. And her son, Sebastian. A mother and son, also from Chicago, and I saw what I might have been, and saw myself. And I had to tell someone. . . ."

Silence. I could almost hear how clean their kitchen was.

I smacked my lips. "How long ago was this?"

"Sixteen years ago. Give or take."

"Well, until I heard it from Jeremy, I had no idea about any of this, so . . . looks like you trusted the right person."

"Sebastian . . ." Brenda's eyes turned spherical and pleading. "Peter can't know. I don't expect Jeremy to keep it from him his whole life, that wouldn't be fair, but . . . I can't tell Peter yet, and until I do, he can't know."

"Know what?"

"That's very sweet, Sebastian, but—"

"You ever try to find him?" I asked, curious to see if Jeremy had left anything out.

Brenda sighed. . . . "A few years after Jeremy was born, I was up in Chicago on family business. By myself, and I thought it might be my only safe chance. So I hired a private detective. He came back to me around a month later with the news that Dromio Johansson had disappeared. . . . Some said killed over a gambling debt. Others said he went on down to Mexico, Canada, overseas. Too many rumors and stories, no real way to tell. No real surprise, either, just a sick kind of relief." Brenda was done avoiding my eyes, and added, "Good riddance to bad rubbish."

I nodded. "I won't tell."

Brenda let out a tired, one-syllable laugh. "Thank you."

"Can I get you a cup of coffee?"

"Yes, please."

I took her mug, stood, and went to join the coffeepot. Afternoon light cut through the steam while Brenda remained silent at the kitchen table. I poured carefully, filled her up a good three-fourths. Grabbed the sugar bowl and was by her side as she suddenly decided to ask:

"You don't think Jeremy's going to try and find him, do you?"

"Why would he do that?" I asked, downing Brenda's coffee in one go, scalding my throat.

"I don't know."

"Let me get you another cup of coffee."

I was back by the machine in a few short strides.

"He's just been acting so strange," Brenda called out. "He wasn't interested in any details about his father. Here I was, expecting to be bombarded with questions, but . . . not one. As though he had some other—"

"You said this man . . . Dromio Johansson, right?"

"Yes."

"You said Dromio Johansson's dead, right?"

"Disappeared, and only allegedly."

"*Disappeared* seemed to satisfy you just fine at the time. A *private detective* couldn't find Dromio Johansson well over *ten years* ago, how's Jeremy going to even consider looking for him now?"

"I know how it sounds. . . ."

I was back at the table with Brenda's coffee. She accepted it and took a sip before falling back on previous doubts. "Are you sure he didn't say anything about trying to find him?"

I looked down at her. Saw that worried look Jeremy had been talking about. The non-negotiable fears of a concerned mother. I sighed and sat down across from her. Put on my most serious expression and looked right into her waiting eyes.

"Truth is, Brenda . . ."

She leaned forward, hooked. Line and sinker.

I sighed again. "Truth is, after Jeremy told me, I tracked down his real father through the fire department and discovered that Dromio Johansson has resurrected on the coast of North Carolina. He owns his own restaurant, has his own family, and after establishing contact with him, I planned this trip to Wilmington so we could spend our vacation in the presence of the dead man who almost ruined your life."

Brenda's face turned to absolute bewilderment, and I pressed on. "Furthermore, when we get there, Jeremy and I are going to switch identities. He's going to pretend to be me, and I'm going to pretend to be him. I mean, Dromio Johansson was a real scumbag back when he was alive, right? With my plan, however, Jeremy won't have to risk any personal commitment. He can watch from a distance, get information as me he couldn't possibly get as himself. And should the guy turn out to be everything you described him as, I can take the helm and break off all contact with him so Jeremy won't have to."

There's nothing in this world less credible than the truth,

and Brenda just stared at me. Incredulous, trying to figure out what was going on. I took the opportunity to push things past reality and into the outer limits of absurdity.

"But none of this is as disturbing as the government conspiracy," I told her. Casual as can be. "Because Dromio Johansson's disappearance wasn't just a coincidence. That very year, there were three UFOs spotted over Chicago, fifteen abductions, along with several reports of increased sales of banana-nut wafers and the *Wall Street Journal*. And if you count the amount of letters in Dromio Johansson's name, they equal not only the amount of abductions, but also roughly the amount of minutes it takes for an alien with the body of a pterodactyl and the head of Lou Diamond Phillips to read a copy of the *Wall Street Journal* while eating a banana-nut wafer—"

"Sebastian."

I stopped. Looked up from my coffee, which I had been staring into with an increasingly maniacal look. Saw Brenda's face slowly give away to a smile.

"I get it," she said, smile widening into a grin.

I let my own smile make a sly appearance. "Do you?"

"Yes, Sebastian, I get it. . . ." She shook her head, relenting. "And you're right. You're absolutely right, it is . . . ridiculous for me to worry about this. I just—"

"It's only been a couple of weeks since you told him."

"I know."

"Of course he's acting strange."

"I know."

The weight abandoned Brenda's shoulders. Made way for relief as she brought coffee up to relaxed lips. Wiped her slate clean with a rush of air that must have been trapped in her lungs for years. "Thanks, Sebastian."

"Don't mention it."

"You're a good friend."

"I have my moments."

"Is there anything I can do for you?"

"When's the next Sunday Styles section coming out in the *Observer*?"

"Two weeks. Thinking of writing another column?"

I nodded. "Bit of a twist on the usual Young Diner's Review. I figure I'd give Peter something on a real upscale kind of place. Prom's coming up soon, thought it would be a good thing for the kids. I could even plug your menswear store."

"You got a date yet?"

"For the prom?"

"Yeah."

I drank my coffee. "Haven't really thought about it."

"Hey."

"Yeah?"

Brenda put down her mug. "I asked if there was anything *I* could do for you."

Well, that settled Brenda.

Hardly a moment to think about what had just happened, what I was getting myself into. One more problem laid to rest, and it was time to move on to the next. I had things to take care of and Brenda was willing to open a few doors for me.

So I went ahead and walked on through.

"I have a friend named Cesar, and he's got to look his best tonight. . . ."

13. Interlude II

Way I heard it from Dromio was this. . . .

Chaucer was behind the bar of the Blue Paradise. Red silk shirt and a black tie, black pants. Dark skin glowing under aqua-colored fluorescent lights, facial scars from an acne-riddled youth dotting his cheeks and lengthy jawline. Large hands sending a stream of grenadine into a pint glass of ice and Diet Sprite. Quiet night at the Paradise. Clock on the wall at ten past eight, and most of the tables were empty. A few waiters gone home early, laughter trickling in from behind the kitchen door. Even the jukebox could only bother to hum the likes of Fats Waller, B. B. King, and Brenda Lee.

Chaucer unsheathed a straw, dropped it in the drink. Set it down in front of Police Chief Hunt, who took a monstrous gulp. Wiped his sunburned brow, sweating despite another cool night in Wilmington. Scratched himself behind satellite-dish ears and took another swallow through chapped lips while Chaucer awaited further questions.

"So Dromio just up and left her?" Hunt's accent had a bit

of a Georgian feel to it, despite insisting that he'd never been to Georgia in his life. "That doesn't sound like Dromio."

Chaucer nodded. "Dromio left her pregnant and alone. . . ." He looked down the bar, where Dromio was comforting Lacey Dunston, a local woman in her mid-sixties. "Least, that's what he told me when I tracked him down, all the way from Chicago. This was a few years after his kid was born, and I found him in a coffee shop here in Wilmington. Minute I ordered my espresso, he got up from his table, came over to mine. Sat down with me and said, *So, Brenda finally decided to find me.*"

"Now, *that* sounds like Dromio."

Chaucer nodded again. Brown elliptical eyes remembering . . . "He knew right away. Only thing he didn't know was that Brenda had become Mrs. King and had decided to keep the baby, now a young boy by the name of Jeremy."

"What did you report to Mrs. King?"

"Dromio wanted Brenda King to move on with her life. Said it would be for the best, so I went back and told Mrs. King that Dromio had disappeared. Vanished, killed by gangsters, ran off to Canada, Mexico, can't remember which anymore. All of them, now that I think about it. Enough conflicting stories to make it seem the trail began and ended in Chicago."

"Why didn't you just have him killed?"

Chaucer shrugged. "Dromio thought *killed* was too much."

Hunt traced his finger over the bar. Regarded the collage of blue shells embedded beneath the glass surface before asking, "You lied to her about the man she asked you to find?"

Chaucer pulled out a rocks glass and filled it with ice. Deep voice always searching for philosophical asylum . . .

"You know, Hunt. I must have caught more people cheating on their spouses than a paparazzo on amphetamines. Not a fun thing to report back to a married woman, married man, married anybody. And eventually I just started approaching the cheaters myself. Told them I'd be willing to bury all evidence against them in exchange for recommitment to their spouses. If they really loved them, they'd usually just confess themselves anyway."

Chief Hunt's eyes grew wide under thinning eyebrows. "That's crazy, Chaucer."

"Possibly."

"You didn't feel bad about lying to Mrs. King?"

"Dromio tells you exactly what you want to hear, and he told me it was for the best. You know how he is."

"Jesus . . ." Hunt leaned back in his seat. Belly protruding as he lit a Virginia Slim and tossed the pack on the bar. "You must have been one terrible private detective."

"Oh, I was a great private dick," Chaucer said, pouring a hit of scotch. "I just wasn't a very good asshole. And Dromio knew it, too. Saw right through the hard-boiled exterior and figured this drifter was ready to settle down. Offered me the position of manager, and the rest . . ."

"History," Hunt concluded, and joined Chaucer in a silent drink.

Chaucer quickly took care of his and poured another.

The jukebox switched gears, mumbled one from Billie Holiday.

Hunt extinguished his half-smoked cigarette and lit another: "So what's the point, Chaucer? Why did Dromio call me here tonight?"

"I called you here tonight."

"There's a difference?"

"Something's come up," Chaucer said. Walked down to the other end of the bar and whispered something in Dromio's ear. Walked back up to Hunt and pulled out a yellow Post-it note from his pocket. "Wilson called me from the Hilton an hour ago. Said that Jeremy's friend, Sebastian, is gonna be receiving his messages there."

"These boys are staying with Dromio, but getting their messages at the Hilton?" Hunt wiped his brow again. "I don't get it."

"Neither do we." Dromio stepped into the conversation as though he'd been there from the start. Light blue shirt with an invasion of pink flamingos, cigarette in his right hand. Eyebrows arched at a greater angle than usual, problem-solving. "Furthermore, Wilson told me this was arranged by Little Niko."

"The pizza guy?"

"You know any other Little Nikos?"

"Now I'm definitely confused."

Dromio shrugged, took a drag. "Might be nothing, but it could be there's more here than meets the eye."

"What are you saying?" Hunt straightened up, suddenly back on the job. "You think he might not be your son?"

Dromio shook his head. "You should see the telegram he sent. All the detail, things he knew about that nobody knows. It's as though I'd written a letter to myself and pushed all the right buttons. No anger, no bitterness. Just a call to adventure. Like father, like son."

"No anger?"

"None . . ." And Dromio's eyes narrowed. Looked across the empty expanse of his legitimate business venture. Searching for something. Seeing people who weren't there, seated at tables, socializing over drinks, telling each other a thousand pretty lies over full-course meals. "No anger, no bitterness. That part, actually, does set off a few alarm bells."

Hunt clearly wasn't sure what Dromio meant by that, but knew what was expected of him. "I'll keep an eye out. Don't you worry."

"Thanks, Hunt."

Dromio, Chaucer, and Hunt all contemplated their drinks.

"Quiet tonight," Hunt managed.

"Calm before the storm," Dromio mused.

"You expecting a storm?"

"There's always a storm," Dromio told him, lost in thought. "It's calm we don't get enough of in this world. . . ."

Dromio wandered down the bar and began to close down for the night.

Chaucer and Hunt watched him. Seeing something new. Fast talk and swift words replaced with a wandering quality. Inner workings sapping his usual exuberance. Planning something as the tides crept slowly toward tomorrow. Overhead lights turned off. Glasses washed and returned to their respective homes. Locked doors shutting in the evening's conversation as the streets outside prepared to accompany them into the hours past last call. . . .

At least, that's the way I heard it from Dromio.

14. You Got Nothing

I picked Cesar up at seven, as promised.

Brenda King was waiting for us at her store, ready to repay me for our afternoon chat. She took a few measurements, shoulder, inseam, shoe size. Got Cesar dressed up in a nice CK suit, and he left looking like a cool million.

I drove him to the Mezzanine.

Checked in with the owner, Monsieur Mafollie, made sure everything was settled. A free meal for Cesar and Nicole in exchange for a dynamite review in the Young Diner's section of the *Durham Observer*. He offered to throw in a complimentary drink for me, but I had other things to take care of and politely declined.

It was round about ten past eight when I arrived at Big Niko's.

No rest for the workaday world, and the kitchen was a wildfire of commotion. Orders shouted back and forth, delivery boys checking their slips, flying pizza dough, and Big Niko in the middle of it all. A commanding, five-foot Napoleon under the whip of fluorescent tubes. He asked me a few questions about Wilmington and Little Niko. I asked him where Olaf was and he pointed me toward the back exit.

Cigarette break.

I found him leaning against the brick exterior of Big Niko's. Halfway through a Newport, menthol tendrils curling from his mouth like a nest of lazy snakes. White apron with stains of red. Black hair net keeping with the laws of sanitation.

I walked up to him with a solid stride and lit one of my own. Olaf regarded me with silent confidence, waiting for me to wilt. Cave in before the conversation could even start up.

I gave him nothing and let him take the first step.

"So?" he asked.

"So," I said, letting the humid night air enjoy the standoff. "I know this man by the name of Mr. Wallace."

"He got a first name?"

"Yeah, it's Mister. He's my English teacher. Independently wealthy, teaches high school for fun. He's from Glasgow. Born in Alloway, which is also the birthplace of Robert Burns."

"That's fascinating," Olaf told me. "Is Robert Burns going to get me my money?"

"Mr. Wallace is going out of town for a few days. He wants you to take care of his dogs."

"Wants me to what?"

"Mr. Wallace wants you to take care of his dogs," I repeated. The nearby Dumpster carried a trace of tomato paste and expired cheese. "He's going out of town for spring break and he's got ten dogs for you to take care of. An easy thirty bucks."

Olaf shook his head. "I told you I needed a good three hundred, fast."

"That's thirty bills per dog, Olaf. Ten dogs, thirty times ten. Three hundred. I can write it out for you if you like."

"You're not a bad talker for a little boy, you know that, Bastian?"

I held my ground, glad for the dark pool of shadow surrounding us. "You want this or not?"

"I never said I was willing to work for it." Olaf polished off his cigarette. Tossed it to the ground, crushed it underfoot. "Maybe I was selling myself short. Maybe I should ask for more. A lot more, at least enough to make sure that next time I get *money* instead of some after-school, paper-route, dog-walking bullshit—"

"You got nothing, Olaf," I informed him. "And the reason you got nothing is because there *is* nothing. A conversation overheard in a delivery car, that's it. I got you this gig with Wallace because, frankly, I can't be bothered with you making wild accusations. But go ahead. Go ahead and knock on Esther Shaw's door and tell her some sinister little story about her daughter getting an abortion. All anybody has to do is deny it. *You got nothing.* . . . Consider this your warning to back the hell off."

Olaf's lips curved into an amused smile. "Or you'll what?"

I didn't smile, expression always on script. "When it happens, you'll know."

Olaf took a moment or two before breaking out into a slow nod.

"Just messing with you, Bastian. . . ." Olaf took a step

back. Held up his hands, voice suddenly reasonable. "Enjoy your vacation, I hear Wilmington's real nice this time of year. . . ."

Something about the way he said it put me on edge, despite my clear victory. Something in the fading sound of passing cars. Surrounding trees taking on indefinable shapes for the occasion. A fleeting understanding that you were never too close to anywhere in Durham, North Carolina. Just us two out there. Locked in some kind of isolated battle that would make no effort to respect our current truce.

"Enjoy your three hundred," I told him.

My cigarette was nowhere near done, and I flicked it aside. Didn't watch it land. Turned my back on Olaf and walked back into Niko's kitchen. Past the hubbub and bustle, stainless steel shelves of secret ingredients. Didn't even stop to address Big Niko when he asked me how things had gone. His voice falling into the calamity of surrounding chaos. Walking with a purpose out the front door and to my car.

Trying to ignore the whispers telling me that all this was all far from over. . . .

15. I Don't Lie

I crouched in the bushes across the road and watched the two of them.

Watched my mother shake Esther Shaw's hand, the two of them silhouettes by the front porch light. Lips moving, not a word managing to cross the length of West Knox Street. A final goodbye, and Esther was in her BMW. Driving away as taillights became fireflies in the dark and faded.

I stood and crossed over as my mother made her way to the front door.

"Mom—"

My mother whipped around, hand to her chest. "Jesus Christ!"

"What was she doing here?"

"Bastian, you scared the hell out of me."

"What the hell was Sara Shaw's mother doing here?"

My mother breathed in, out a few more times. Breath slowing beneath her white undershirt. Hand falling back to her side as it smacked against her thigh. She looked up and down the street, then back at me: "Let's talk inside."

I followed her in.

She sat at the kitchen table, lit a cigarette. Offered me one. I shook my head. Decided to keep standing, on the defensive.

My mother contemplated her ashtray, then looked up. "She doesn't know."

"You're sure Esther Shaw knows nothing about the abortion?"

"Of course I'm sure. She came here to talk to you. For advice, just like everyone else."

"Advice about what?"

My mother stood up, went to the fridge. "You know, Mrs. Shaw isn't at all the way Sara made her out to be. She seems to be a loving, supportive parent."

"Who happens to picket abortion clinics and Planned Parenthood in her spare time."

My mother closed the refrigerator door, bottle of Coke in hand. "That's right. She's a woman of her convictions, and her beliefs defy ours. But her actions don't. She doesn't kill obstetricians, vandalize private property, or hurt anyone, for that matter. She makes brownies, not pipe bombs, Bastian. And it's her privilege, her absolute right, to take issue with whatever she likes and make her voice known. This is *not* about what Brenda Shaw does or does not believe in."

We stood facing each other for a moment. I looked down, looked back at my mother. Her hair was up, revealing a steady pulse in her neck. Blood rush living in the fast lane, and I stuck my hands into empty pockets. Shifted my weight from one foot to the other, felt worn and tired floorboards creak. Said nothing as she walked over to the counter, took down a glass, and made herself a rum and Coke.

I shuffled over and hoisted myself onto the counter. Sat myself down on what little room there was and watched her mix the drink with her finger.

"Mom?"

"Bastian, I think Sara made a big mistake not going to her mother. . . ." My mom focused on her drink, clearly going through thoughts a long time in the making. "I think things would have turned out all right between those two. Instead, I'm lying to a woman whose name *I* forged so her daughter could get an abortion, which I don't think she should have gotten in the first place."

"Having that baby would have ruined Sara's life."

"Eighteen years ago, I was Sara Shaw." She was looking at me now, eyes trapped somewhere in the past. "I was pregnant, alone, and if I had chosen to abort, you wouldn't be here right now. And I didn't have a man to stand by me. . . ."

She walked over to the table, sat down with her drink.

I was left staring into the space she had just occupied. Looking at a sink of unwashed dishes, right through it. Thoughts shifting gear, because it was the second time in one day I was having this conversation. And before I knew it, the words had forced themselves out:

"You always told me it wasn't his fault."

"What wasn't whose fault?"

I kept staring at the kitchen sink. "My father. You always told me it wasn't his fault you had to raise me on your own."

My mother's puzzled expression rang loud and clear in her tone. "He never knew about you."

I hopped down from my perch. Leaned my shoulder against the entrance to the kitchen and watched my mother smoke and drink. She cocked her head to the side, a loose lock of hair tickling her shoulder.

"Do you think that it was . . ." I searched. "Unfair not to tell him?"

"Bastian, he was just like you." She took a drink, had a smoke. Tilted her head back, watching smoke stream toward the ceiling. "He'd see someone in trouble and just had to come to their rescue. A Blue Hawk, through and through . . ."

I frowned. "Blue Hawk?"

My mother was in her own world, didn't hear me. . . . "I didn't want anybody to marry me out of pity. I didn't need him. Just wanted him, and those are two very different things. Felt it in my heart, and I was right. So I never told him I was pregnant, and when it ended between us, I was at one and a half months. . . . Bad timing, that's all it was."

I nodded, the entire house becoming an outlandishly sad cocoon for the two of us. "I would have liked to have met him."

"I know," she told me, graceful voice and all. "I know, and I'm sorry he's not alive to meet you."

"He might not be dead."

"He *is*."

"You could have kept a photo, something . . ."

"You've never been interested before."

"It's not like we haven't talked about him once or twice."

"Not like this."

"What was his name?"

"Excuse me?"

"You've never told me his name," I said. "Not unless his name was 'Your Father,' in which case his parents must have been total jerks."

Her face turned skeptical. "If I never told you it's because I never really knew his name."

My turn to be unconvinced. "You want to tell me how that's possible?"

"His name was Chester A. Arthur."

"My father was the twenty-first president of the United States?"

"Chester A. Arthur, that's what he told me his name was." She was smiling now, and it could only be because it was all true. "When I left him, he wasn't around. Out on business, and I was going through his things to see if I could scrape up any money to get me out of Chicago—"

"Mom!"

"It was a long time ago, baby." She gave a dismissive wave. "At any rate, I open up one of his bags, and what do I find but a surplus of fake IDs. Each one with his picture, and each one with a different name. . . . So if you like, we can call him Chester A. Arthur from now on. Do you want to call him Chester A.—"

"Father's just fine," I decided.

Another silence. I thought about all those IDs, all those pictures.

"Do I look like him?"

My mother cocked her head again. Looked at me with one foot on the chair, arm resting on her knee, drink resting in her hand. She sighed. "Not really. If there's one way you remind me of him, it's . . . He was incredibly charismatic. Got arrested for shoplifting on four different occasions, charmed the judge into suspending the case each and every time."

"Four times?" I just had to smile. "That's nothing short of extraordinary."

"Well, the man had a real knack for lying. Always for the greater good, but . . . There were times when I don't think he could tell the difference between what was real and what was . . . smoke."

"Mom . . ." I shifted my weight off the wall. "You trying to tell me something?"

My mother smiled. Put her leg back on the floor, drink on the table. Cigarette in the ashtray, extinguished. She walked over and hugged me. Quick and strong, and we parted with a swift kiss. Eyes on each other as she shook her head.

"Just promise you'll never lie to me."

My smile felt stiff. "I promise."

I turned and walked away, my mother's voice stopping me at the threshold to the hallway.

"Promise me something else?"

I turned. "What?"

"Next time you have sex with Sara, use protection. You get her pregnant again, and I'm not stepping in to help you, Bastian."

The resemblance to my father turned out to be dead right, and my expression didn't change. Kept a steady course, refused to acknowledge the lies I had told my own mother. The manipulation of truth needed to give her a personal stake: *save Sara and you save me, Mom.* All of it shoved as far down into me as it could go, even as I watched her stand there with her arms crossed. Middle of the room, asking for reassurance of something that technically needed no reassurance whatsoever. Pangs of guilt swept aside by notions of a greater good as I nodded in her direction with a one-word answer I had no right to utter:

"Promise."

I turned my back on her and made my way down the dark hallway.

16. Maybe You Shouldn't Go

An already long-ass day was made even longer at around eleven-thirty.

I had just finished packing. Clothes, toiletries, cigarettes, all crammed into a mid-sized suitcase. A garment bag with a designer suit just in case the occasion might arise. A few framed pictures of myself with Jeremy's parents. Just in case the occasion might arise.

Going down a checklist at my desk, preparing to record a new message on my answering machine, when there was a knock at my bedroom window.

I let Sara Shaw in. A very distraught Sara Shaw who needed to see me in person. Wrinkled clothes, strands of red hair arguing over which direction to go, eyes so wide they appeared lidless. Sentences a mess. I managed a few calming whispers, sat her down on the bed. Held her hand with as much reassurance as I could and listened as she told me about the phone call.

"Who was it?" I asked.

Sara gave a spastic shrug. "Never heard the voice before."

"What does he know?"

"Everything," Sara told me, each word a passenger abandoning ship. "My abortion. Which clinic, what time. He even knew the name of the doctor who did it."

I took a silent breath, tried to figure it out. "When did he call?"

"This evening."

"What time?"

"Bastian—"

"It's important. What time did he call?"

"Seven. Maybe five past, I don't know exactly. . . ."

None of it stood to reason. At least, not as far as Olaf was concerned. Our meeting had been at ten past eight, and withholding that kind of information from me would have just been *bad business*. There didn't seem to be any reason for him to have called Sara before then.

This was the work of someone else. . . .

"Bastian?"

I kept it to myself. "What does he want?"

"When I asked, he hung up."

"All right, let's be cool about this."

"Be cool?" Sara bolted up and stalked across my room. Met a wall and turned to face me. "There's someone out there with some *very sensitive information*! I'm sorry, but I can't *be cool* about this!"

"Shhh . . ." I stood and walked over to her, put my arms on her shoulders. Eye to eye with Sara as I told her, "We don't have much of a choice right now. I'm as scared as you are. This is you, and me, and my mother here. And I won't let anything bad happen to any of us. Least of all you. . . ."

She sniffed. "People have always told me that Sebastian can do anything."

The intimacy of the moment didn't leave much room for pride. "Well, tongues will wag, Sara."

"I know, I didn't believe any of it." She coughed out a nervous laugh. "When I showed up here after getting pregnant, to ask for your help—"

"You were wearing a yellow sundress."

"Yeah, my nicest one." She sniffed again. "I wore it because even though I hoped to God the stories about you were true, I also heard that you would . . . want something in return, so I tried to look my best, I was just that desperate."

"Sara—"

"But you came through. Every step of the way, and you didn't take advantage. You really did save me. . . ." Sara stared up at me, sky-blue eyes, as the clock approached midnight. "And now I know. You aren't going to let anything happen to me, are you?"

"I promise. . . ." I brushed a strand of strawberry away from her forehead. "Next time he calls, whoever he is, you tell him to call me at the Hilton."

Sara put on a sad expression. Sad or thankful, I'm reluctant to say I didn't know what to make of that face. She placed her left hand on my chest. Her eyes had drawn closer, without warning.

"Don't go to Wilmington," she said. Gave me a light kiss on the lips. "Stay here." She kissed me again before I could even register the first. "Stay here so you can take care of me. . . ."

And I couldn't even say how it happened. All of a sudden,

our lips were locked together, almost interchangeable. Excited, confused, energized, unhappy, lost in a riptide of emotions, and before I knew it was happening, I was putting a stop to it.

Holding Sara at arm's length, the two of us breathing from our mouths.

Devouring the air between us.

Certain of what had just happened, not at all clear what it had meant. No posters on the wall, no celebrity faces to cast judgment or approval. Just empty space open to speculation. Single-bulb lamp at my desk casting shadows, our faces half hidden in the minutes before midnight.

What to think, what to feel.

"What's wrong?" she asked.

I wasn't sure what the answer was, but I knew just what I wanted to say.

"Who's the father?"

"Bastian—"

"I deserve to know."

"I'm sorry I kissed you. . . ."

I suddenly realized I was in my undershirt and boxers, half naked. Or, to take the optimist's point of view, half clothed. Either way, I turned to my closet and started looking for a pair of pants. Realized I had packed them all, and remained with my back turned to Sara.

"It's all right that you kissed me," I said, staring at a jean jacket I hadn't worn for well over five years.

"You should think about yourself more often," I heard her say.

"I'm going to Wilmington, Sara," I told her. Continued to

stare at various articles of clothing, shoe boxes filled with memorabilia I never bothered visiting. "Please don't take this the wrong way, but Jeremy needs me more than you do right now."

"You do care about me, though, don't you?"

"You know I do."

"One last hug?"

I held back the sigh I felt.

Choked on it like a polite sneeze.

Turned back to her and gave her a reassuring smile.

Sara took one step forward, wrapped me with her farewell embrace. Held on and laid her head on my shoulder. Hair tickling my nose as I glanced over to my answering machine. Put my arms around her, not too tight, though. Never too close. Keeping it simple as I listened to her breath push against me.

Desperate wishes of an exit sign dancing in my mind.

PART THREE

SATURDAY

17. This Is Sebastian

Interstate 85 saw us safely on our way.

Pedal pressed down, windows witness to trees, farmland, demanding billboards, cows and horses, lonely strip clubs, road-kill, fast-food beacons, scraps left over from car accidents, rumble strips, and interstate signs, all brought into stark relief under the Carolina sun. Clear skies and seventy-five-degree weather accompanying us as we sped toward our destination.

Silent ride. Broken tape deck, and nothing good on the radio.

Tires doing seventy beneath our feet.

Windows open, breeze whipping around inside the car.

Each one of us staring straight ahead toward what was waiting. Sunglasses donned, quietly preparing. Watching the signs as Wilmington went from a 135-mile distance to 90, to 40, to 5. The air changing quality with approach. Traces of salt filtering through our nostrils, scattered sand appearing along the shoulder of the road. Indigenous plant life sprouting around us, tangled previews of palm trees and dune grass.

Slowing down to forty-five miles per hour as tourist traps

began popping up. Bike rentals, seafood shacks, real estate agencies, and jungle-themed miniature golf courses. Past UNC Wilmington, speed limit cracking down even further. Eyesores replaced by residential neighborhoods, the tall and statuesque houses of a time long gone now presiding over scenery.

Quarter to one in the afternoon, and we had arrived.

Fifteen minutes till our first meeting with Dromio Johansson.

Historic Wilmington seemed to make the sun shine a little more brightly. Small businesses, restaurants, drugstores that still sold cola out of contoured glass bottles. Red-bricked streets happily living in a cleaner, more ideal time. Populated sidewalks that never seemed to clog. Lively without the overwhelming clamor of Chicago. Calm atmosphere a far cry from the nearly forgotten streets of downtown Durham.

We parked near the Hilton.

Jeremy was worried about being late, so I put off checking for messages. We walked along the wooden docks by the Cape Fear River. Steady flow of water over a hundred yards wide, perfectly in tune with the surrounding atmosphere. Privately owned boats moored and relaxed alongside the retired battleship *North Carolina*.

Shorts and sunglasses abounding.

Jeremy and I stopped across from the courthouse and looked out over the river. Leaned against the railing, and I breathed deep. Took in the fresh air coming across the water while small waves lapped against the concrete foundation.

"We made it," I said, smiling.

Jeremy actually smiled, too, though his fingers were

mashing against each other. Thick sailor's knot of knuckles and nails. Legs trembling, and I could hear his breath moving faster than the seconds. Front teeth working on his lower lip. No way for me to immunize myself against emotion like that, and I began to feel it, too. Fought against it, aware of what my job was and ready to do it. . . .

"You all right?" I asked.

Jeremy looked at me. Even his sunglasses appeared nervous. "I'm scared."

"You're going to be fine," I assured him. "Both of us, you'll see."

He nodded. "So this is the place. We're meeting him here?"

"That's right."

Jeremy nodded again. Looked back out over the water.

A dog walked up to us. Sniffed around our legs and went on his way.

A mounted police officer passed by. Horse's hooves clomping to a waltzy rhythm.

"How did things go with Cesar last night?" Jeremy asked, making conversation.

"Haven't heard back from him, but everything was set up to a tee."

"Good, good . . ." Jeremy was hardly paying attention, but he kept on. "I ran into Paul Inverso the other day."

"Paul Inverso?"

"He was looking for you. Wanted you to call him."

"Was he sitting on the edge of a roof?"

"No."

"Then it can probably wait, right?" I patted Jeremy on the back.

Jeremy seemed to have made a career out of nodding, and he kept right at it. We both looked over the water, before turning away and scanning the streets.

"Damn it, Baz, it's a quarter past one," Jeremy said, the better half of his excitement fading. "Where is he?"

"So your old man isn't as punctual as you," I told him. "Relax, he'll be here."

Jeremy was in the midst of nod number fifty-three when I glanced across the street. Commotion on the bleached courthouse steps catching my attention. I took a few steps forward, narrowed my eyes. Took a few more steps.

Jeremy's voice called out from behind. "Baz, where are you going?"

"Wait here," I told him. Strode across the street, not entirely sure what I was about to do. On autopilot. Focused on a twenty-some-year-old woman on the steps. Dark hair, round eyes, all decked out in a professional dress suit. High heels. Pale cheeks flushed as she tried to make her way past a group of guys, each one a near carbon copy of the other. Seemed like college kids, khaki shorts, preppie shirts. Faded white hats. Tall and thick. Some more muscular than others, but every last one of them outweighed me by at least forty pounds. Sunburned faces covered by wide grins, surrounding this young woman. Voices all a mix, one in particular standing out as I made my way up the steps. Their ringleader, I guessed. Only one with dark hair, sculpted body. Seemed to be the one in charge, his accent a thicker shade of South than the others, saying,

"Come on, we're all good guys. We're just saying *what's up?*"

"And I'm saying I'm not interested," the young woman told them. Walked on down as they followed suit, a group of mercenary secret service agents.

"Oh, come on, you don't have to be like that," the ringleader sweet-talked.

"This is your last chance," she warned. "Get out of my way."

A series of sarcastic *ohhh*s arose, and another one of them added, "Yeah? Or you'll what . . . ?"

"When it happens," I spoke up, "you'll know."

That shut everyone up.

Real quick, and the gang turned in unison. All standing on higher steps, towering above me. Angry eyes. Unhappy with being challenged. I'd seen it a thousand times from a thousand others.

I glanced from face to face, topped it off with a closer look at the young woman. Caught better sight of her features, and liked what I saw. Button nose. Impossibly large eyes that must have taken a page or two from Saturday morning cartoons. Slender neck, and buoyant lips that didn't quite close all the way. Might have let myself stare for a while longer, just enjoying the details of crimson cheeks, lustrous hair, and long eyelashes, but it would all have to wait, as I asked, "Everything all right?"

Before she could answer, the ringleader stepped down to my level. Didn't help me much, he was still a good five inches my superior. Bending down slightly, in my face, and I could tell this was the start of something other than beautiful.

"Ain't no problem here," he told me. "You got a problem?"

"No," I answered. "Looks like I've got . . ." I looked around. "One, two, three, four, five problems, actually. Though I'm having a bit of trouble telling them apart. You all shop at the same store?"

"You looking to start something, faggot?"

"Now we're getting creative."

"Who the hell is this guy?" one of them asked the ringleader.

"Who the hell are you?" the ringleader echoed.

"I was about to ask you the same thing, Trevor," I said.

"My name's not Trevor. It's Bradley."

"That's funny, you look like a Trevor to me. . . ." I turned to the young woman. "Doesn't he look like a Trevor to you?"

"You both look like a couple of idiots," she replied.

And there was a fairly stunned silence from both of us. I was hardly through processing her gratitude when yet another voice cut through our gathering.

"Any problem here, Miss Michaels?"

I turned and saw an officer dressed in a typical light blue uniform. Round guy with thinning eyebrows and a robust stomach. Thumbs tucked into a gun belt on the verge of a nervous breakdown. Bowlegs that dead-ended in the most infinitesimal pair of shoes I'd ever seen on a grown man.

Official badge and a name tag reading OFFICER HUNT.

Most of the college kids were already dispersing as the young woman cast her assurances: "No problem, Officer Hunt. I was just leaving. So was everyone else."

She shoved herself between me and Bradley. Heels

clacking against the concrete steps, taking her along the side-walk with a frustrated swish of the hips.

Officer Hunt didn't budge.

Couldn't help but feel he was sizing me up especially.

"You ain't going to get away with this," Bradley said, face once again close to mine.

I didn't stand down. "I think I already have, Trevor."

He turned away, went to join the rest of his gang.

I did the same. Opposite direction, and caught sight of the young woman halfway down the block. I doubled my footsteps and called out for her to *wait a moment.*

She turned and crossed her arms.

I stopped in front of her.

Almost backed away when confronted with seething eyes. No hint of warmth or affection, just waiting out of some kind of habitual politeness.

"I don't believe we were properly introduced," I managed.

"How long are you in town?" she asked.

I shrugged. "About a week."

"Excellent. . . ." She shouldered her black leather bag. "For one horrifying second I thought you might have moved here."

I was left with my mouth hanging open as she turned her back. Continued on her way, leaving me alone in the middle of the sidewalk. Brain regrouping as I turned away from those legs and made my way back to the docks.

Jeremy was standing on the sidewalk with a confused look that mirrored exactly what I was feeling.

"What was that all about?" he asked.

"I'm not sure."

"Then let's forget about it and get back to what matters, shall we?"

"Yeah . . ." I looked back one last time, but she had already gone. "Sure."

I shook it off and turned back to Jeremy.

The two of us crossed the street, heading for the meeting place.

And a few steps from that place, the two of us slowed.

Stopped.

Saw a man standing there. Out of nowhere, as though he had materialized by magic. Hawaiian shirt radiating shades of pink. Face furrowed with concentration as he began to walk toward us. White shorts and sneakers. No socks.

Dromio Johansson was standing in front of us now.

The three of us forming a triangle, all silent.

I caught Jeremy in my periphery. Frozen in place.

The mounted police officer's horse clopped by again.

"Jeremy?" Dromio finally asked.

The moment had arrived and all of Wilmington seemed to be watching.

I briefly thought back to my conversation with Brenda King. Assuring her in good faith that she had nothing to worry about.

But Durham was a good hundred and forty miles behind us, and I stepped forward.

Took off my sunglasses. "Dromio?"

Dromio hesitated.

For a fleeting second it looked as though emotion was about to overcome him.

Control came back, though, and he took his own step forward.

Right up to where I stood, and he embraced me. A fierce bear hug, and I wrapped my arms around him. Feeling all the weight of eighteen years in that single, simple action.

We parted, and he ruffled my hair. Welcoming smile, eyes open and ready.

"Jeremy."

"Dromio . . ." I turned. Gestured to Jeremy, who remained immobile. Watching us side by side, his father's arm around my shoulders. He forced a smile to his face, jump-started his posture. Turned cool, almost relaxed, and I don't believe I had ever been more proud of him.

"This is Sebastian," I told Dromio. "My best friend. . . . And I never could've made it here without him."

18. The Blue Paradise

Dromio Johansson had a way about him.

I could sense something different in this man. Nothing in particular, what he said or did. As the three of us walked he asked us a few preliminaries. Our trip, were we tired, hungry. A few statements. Pointing out a small number of places, suggestions for future activities, gentle hints at the upcoming days.

Like I said, nothing in particular.

Nothing I could put my finger on, either. The way he talked, walked. Paying close attention to everything said, passing moments outside our conversation, even checking the skies on occasion, looking for something I could only guess at. Comfortable in his skin, but respectful of this outlandish moment in all our lives. Graceful but cautious. Confidence without daring. Allowing us to set the pace of our footsteps. Standing to my right in order to properly address both me and Jeremy, directly to my left. Something in his eyes of an X-ray nature. Seeping past our skin without actually piercing it. As though, by simply talking to him, given him access to our innermost thoughts. . . .

But there was a definite edge to him.

Something of a past in his face, something that wasn't yet immunized.

Something that told me to keep my guard up.

Something that absorbed my attention to the point where I had failed to notice how Jeremy was taking all this. . . .

"Men," Dromio announced, stopping all at once with a sweep of his arm. "This is my restaurant . . . the Blue Paradise."

Jeremy and I looked up at the aqua-blue sign hanging over the large double doors. BLUE PARADISE painted in large, sweeping letters. Set against the backdrop of a large dolphin carved out of wood. A decent-sized crowd of people were gathered outside. Mostly tourists. Leafing through menus and pointing with overzealous delight.

"What do you think?" Dromio asked.

"Impressive, Dromio. . . ." I took a moment to let Jeremy tack on his comments. He didn't and I went right on ahead. "Looks like the most popular spot in Wilmington."

"It ought to be at twenty-five cents a plate."

"Did you just say—"

"Twenty-five cents a plate, that's right." Dromio gave me a slap on the back and motioned with his head. "Come on in, men. I'll show you the system."

We followed him through the doors, into the bloodstream of the Blue Paradise.

A very appropriate feel. Two large dining rooms soaked in

blue. The space itself was cavernous,
ck of perspective or decor, Dromio had
n eccentric intimacy. The roar of conver-
a backseat to each table's personal dia-
*uno tickling the ivories for the comings and
goings of black-tie servers. Even the bustle seemed casual
and relaxed.

Dromio led us past a few tables. Between various handshakes from local patrons and staff members, he laid it all
down:

"The Blue Paradise operates on the premise that everyone is entitled to a good meal, and recognizes the fact that not
everyone can afford it. Fact is, that although all men are cre-
ated equal, not everyone is paid that way. So I've decided to
level the field."

Dromio walked through his restaurant with sure and
steady strides.

"Everybody who comes here never has to pay more than
twenty-five cents a plate. Except for the drinks of course. You
want a G and T, white Russian, or a sex on the beach, you
gotta cough up the green. 'Cause any man can get drunk, but
real men pay for their drinks."

Dromio led us over to a secluded table for five.

Motioned for us to sit down.

In doing so, Jeremy bumped against the table. Knocked
over a few glasses.

Could hardly choke out an apology. Just sat, helpless.

"Don't worry about it, Sebastian," Dromio told him,
stood the glasses back up.

\I decided to step in with distraction. "I don't get it, Dromio. What's the catch?"

"Catch?" Dromio sat himself down, smiled reassuringly at Jeremy.

"There has to be a catch. There's no other way you could possibly hope to make bank."

"Well, it has often been said that no good deed goes unpunished," he mused. "But would you believe I've actually ended up making more than just about any joint around here?"

"You charge twenty-five cents a plate."

"Twenty-five cents *suggested price*," Dromio clarified. "Let me show you what I mean."

Dromio signaled to a passing waiter. Asked him if he had the book for table 25. The waiter pulled it out, handed it to Dromio. Dromio gave him an affectionate pat, sent the waiter on his way. Took out a pair of armless black-framed reading glasses and held them up to his eyes.

"All right . . . ," he murmured before addressing us. "See this? Party of three was given a suggested total of seventy-five cents, not including drinks. The actual price would have been round about seventy dollars, give or take. But they've paid that *and* decided to tack on an extra twenty-five dollars above bank." Dromio put on a comically befuddled look. "Why do you suppose that is?"

Jeremy and I both looked at each other. Shrugged.

"Because the average Joe doesn't want to look poor. Rich people want to look richer. And neither realize that they're actually subsidizing other customers."

"But . . ." Jeremy spoke up for the first time, confusion triumphing over shyness. "But don't people take advantage of you all the time?"

"Most everybody's got a conscience, Sebastian. . . ." Dromio pointed over to the bar. "See that man sitting on the bar stool closest to us?"

I swiveled my neck around. Shocked to see a gargantuan, fleshy, pink man seated at the bar. Three full courses in front of him. Shoveling food down his gullet in a desperate attempt to torture his clothes.

"That man," Dromio told us, "that *lunar base* over there would come in here two, three times a week, eat himself sick, and never pay more than a quarter. Every single time, for *months*. And every single time, we'd smile and welcome him back. Till one day he comes in here, writes me a check for *two grand*, and from that day forward, the guy doubles the projected amount for each and every bill. Every single time. And just about every single person is going to do the same thing. Everyone pays for more than food is worth at a restaurant. The Blue Paradise works because I let people choose exactly how much we're going to take them for."

From behind us came a soft, female voice: "Jeremy?"

Jeremy and I both turned in our seats, stood up.

I immediately recognized Dromio's wife from the pictures Little Niko had sent. Nancy Johansson. Raven hair significantly longer now, a pair of nostalgically youthful braids falling past her shoulders. Same wide smile, though. Same eyes, exuberant and friendly, though bags were starting to make their presence known beneath. Dressed in a white surf-shop shirt and tight blue jeans. Left arm around the shoulder of Matilda, whose face reflected very little of the photograph I'd seen. Sixteen, straight black hair cut short. Smile of braces replaced with uncertain lips and moody eyes.

"My wife, Nancy," Dromio announced, rising. "And, of course, my daughter, Matilda."

I extended my hand. "It's a pleasure to meet you, Mrs. Johansson."

She ignored my hand and drew me into a colossal hug. "I'm so glad you found us, Jeremy." She pulled back. "And please, call me Nancy."

"Nancy." I gestured toward Jeremy. "This is my best friend, Sebastian."

Nancy did, in turn, accept Jeremy's hand. He returned the gesture with a meek shake and barely perceptible greeting.

"I hope you'll both feel completely at home here." Nancy turned to her daughter. . . . "Matilda?"

Matilda didn't budge. Just stared up at me, eyes searching for strength within their frames. Motions and murmurs of the restaurant steering clear of the tension surrounding us. She shifted her gaze to Jeremy, then back to me. When she spoke, her voice sounded every bit the way I expected.

"You don't look at all like my father."

Before she could receive any sort of admonishment, I shot back with, "You don't look like my father, either. Maybe we have different mothers."

"My dad says I don't have to like you."

"I'm sure that with time, you'll come to realize that's very good advice."

Matilda frowned.

"Good," Dromio spoke up, and I could hear a slight smile. "Well. I'm glad you two have so much in common. . . . Let's eat."

Matilda held my eyes for just a moment longer before sitting down as far away from me as possible. Nancy took her place next to Dromio. I sat back down and scooted in. Only Jeremy remained standing. Watching the four of us as we opened our menus. Playing with his hands, face unable to find an expression to fit the occasion. Breathing pure exclusion as he slowly sank into his chair.

Unfolded his napkin and politely laid it in his lap.

19. Stand Up and Be Counted

Jeremy was leaking into a urinal, gently banging his head against the wall.

The blue plaster rattled a bit, drawing the attention of a customer washing his hands. He turned to me with a puzzled look. I shrugged, as though to indicate I'd never seen Jeremy in my life. He shrugged in return. Dried his hands and left us alone with seafaring decorations and automated faucets.

"All right, relax, Jeremy," I said. "Don't fall apart on me. This is working like a charm—"

"It's not working like anything." Jeremy's voice was low and defeated.

"He doesn't suspect a thing."

"I don't mean that."

"Jeremy, stop doing that with your head."

Jeremy zipped up, flushed the toilet, and trudged over to the sinks. Washed his hands, working out his tension with soap and water. "I'm beginning to feel bad about this." Jeremy dried his hands with a paper towel. "He's being so friendly and open with us—"

"We don't know that, though." I took Jeremy by the shoulders, gently. Made him face me. "The man is cut from a different cloth than us, or anyone we know. From the old school. The way he walks, talks. The way he controls a room, this man didn't get to where he is today by *being friendly*. You know that, right?"

Jeremy gave a frightened little nod.

"Don't forget. . . . This is the man who abandoned your mother. I'm the one looking out for you now. And I don't intend on handing you over to him until I find out if he's on the level."

Jeremy walked over to the trash. Tossed his paper towel and missed. Thought about it for a minute, then turned to me. "How are you going to earn his trust unless you really impress him? Not to even speak of Matilda. She hates me."

"She hates *me*."

"She hates the you that is me."

"Well, all that's about to change. In the meantime, though . . ." I hesitated. Not sure how to bring it up.

"In the meantime, what?" Jeremy asked.

"This quiet act of yours, it's . . . well, starting to attract a little attention."

Jeremy stared, speechless.

"You have to *talk*, Jeremy—"

"I *am* talking," Jeremy hissed.

"*You* are nervous," I told him, gliding between landmines. "I'll tell you what, so is he. But if *you* want to gain his trust you have to show him that *you* are strong. Like him. Adaptable. Tough. No challenge too big. Someone puts their hand on you, they pull back a bloody stump. Show him that you can hang with the boys, that's *all* I'm saying. Stand up and be counted, *Sebastian.*"

Jeremy sighed. Cracked his knuckles and threw back his shoulders. "All right, Jeremy."

"All right."

"I'm sorry."

"Let's get back to the table."

We made our way back across the restaurant, weaving in and out between tables and busboys. I let Jeremy take the lead as I spotted a table set for two. Man in a white polo shirt sitting by himself. Blue sweater tied around his neck. Early forties, gray streaks appearing in otherwise brown hair. As I passed by, I saw him switch his glass of wine with the one across from him. Lean back and cross his arms, casually.

I kept walking.

A few feet past his table, I stopped.

Turned around and saw an attractive woman join him. Early twenties, with a newborn smile. Saw her say a few words, reach for her glass of red.

I strode back to the table just as she was about to drink.

"Let me guess," I said, prompting her to stop. She put down the drink as I pressed on. "First date. You just met him, right?"

"Yes," the woman said, confused. "I just met Henry, but—"

"I'm sorry," Henry interrupted. "You know this guy, Susan?"

"No," Susan told him.

"You know, Henry." I drew closer to him. "I've been thinking about joining a fraternity. But I'm new in town, so I really would love to know just where a guy can score some roofies around here."

I darted forward, got my hand into his breast pocket, and came out with a small baggie of pills. All in the blink of an eye, and Henry was up on his feet. Chair falling back on the floor, ordering me to give them back. Half the restaurant losing interest in their lunch, and Dromio was already by my side.

"Is there a problem?" he asked, all business.

"Roofies," I told Dromio. "Our good friend Henry popped one into Susan's drink."

Henry bristled. "I did no such—"

"What are roofies?" Susan asked, suddenly concerned.

"Rohypnol. Illegal possession for anyone who isn't a certified doctor. Undetectable in liquid, you'd never know you're drinking it. Half an hour from now you start to feel tired. Then dizzy. Somewhere in the middle of your main course, Henry will tell you you're drunk. Offer to escort you home." Jeremy and Matilda walked up and joined us. "It'll be several hours before you finally wake up. But by then, it'll be too late . . . and you won't remember how it happened."

I turned to Henry. "You can leave, now, quietly. Or you can wait for the police, and we'll all go down to the station while they analyze those pills. But I've got a pretty good idea which option you're going to go with."

Henry was silent. Fuming, clenching his fists together. Trapped.

Dromio, Jeremy, and Matilda all stood by me. Watching.

Restaurant at a standstill.

"You don't know who you're dealing with," Henry warned me, voice low.

"Neither do you," I told him, unwavering. "My name is Jeremy Johansson, and this is my father's restaurant. Get out."

Henry held his ground for a moment.

Glanced around from face to face, no way out.

Turned and walked away.

"That's right!" Jeremy called out all of a sudden, making me jump. "You keep walking! Show your face around here again, and I'll BREAK BOTH YOUR LEGS! LEFT AND RIGHT, YOU TWISTED OLD FREAK!"

"All right," Dromio said, putting an arm round both of us. Keeping cool as he squeezed our shoulders. "All right, that'll do, men. That'll do just fine. . . . Good work, the both of you."

"Should have kicked his ass," Jeremy muttered.

"Don't worry about it, Sebastian," Dromio told him. "Go on and sit down."

Jeremy went back to the table.

Dromio turned to me. I honestly wasn't prepared for the smile on his face. Wide and warm, full of undeniable approval. Reaching out to rub the top of my head. It was the closest contact with fatherly pride I had ever experienced. Hard not to feel it in my stomach. . . .

"Not too shabby," Dromio told me. "Not too shabby at all, Jeremy."

"Thank you."

"That was quite a risk you took there."

"Didn't have much time to think about it."

"Well, good thinking." Dromio looked over at Susan. Still disoriented, gathering her things from the table. He looked back at me, expectant. "So what do we do now?"

Without hesitation, I walked over to Susan's table.

Picked up her coat and helped her with it.

She smiled slightly, and I told her not to worry about it.

Took out fifty cents from my pocket and placed it on the table.

Let her know that the meal was on us.

I turned to look back at Dromio.

Saw him wink and motion for me to join the rest of the family.

20. Interlude III

Way I heard it from Dromio was this. . . .

The top was down, inviting sixty miles per hour's worth of wind to blast through the convertible. Dromio's hair going wild, sunglasses battling against the afternoon sun. Checking the rearview every now and then. Keeping tabs on me as I followed his car to Wrightsville Beach. Glancing over at Jeremy whenever he could. Riding shotgun, eyes on the passing scenery. Squinting against speed. Not saying anything, words replaced with a cool scowl.

Dromio let the radio do its thing for a few minutes.

An oldies station that was starting to make Dromio feel just that way.

"Hotel California" started playing, and he grimaced.

Snapped it off, and sighed.

"When did 'Hotel California' become an oldie?" he asked, shaking his head. "Hell, when did 'Hotel California' become anything?"

"Yeah," Jeremy agreed, still looking across the blur of knotted trees. "The Eagles suck."

A few more minutes of windswept silence.

"So, Sebastian," Dromio began. Corrected himself. "You prefer anything else? Baz, Bastian, what do they call you?"

"They call me whatever they like, I'm not picky on names."

"Okay, then . . ." Dromio gave it another go. "Sebastian. How's my son doing?"

Jeremy glanced at him quickly, then back away. "What do you mean?"

"He's not what I expected."

"What did you expect?"

Dromio shrugged, flipped his turn signal. "You know, I used to be quite the card player. I don't know if Jeremy told you that or not. I'm sure he must have learned a good thing or two about me from . . . Brenda. And one of the earliest lessons I learned was that if you're playing poker with a group of strangers, people you've never met, the first *unbelievably good* hand that comes along, say four of a kind or a low straight flush . . . When you get that hand in a game full of strangers, you dump it. Don't play it, just fold and see what happens."

Jeremy hid his interest by pretending to be engrossed with the glove compartment. "So why do you fold with four of a kind?"

"Because it's too good to be true. In a game with strangers, you're never certain if someone's fed you an amazing hand just to have you lose all your money to a phenomenal hand."

"So what did you expect Jeremy to be like?"

"I didn't expect him to be so . . . ideal, is what I mean." Dromio checked the rearview again. "There's so much of me in him. The way he acts, carries himself. It's almost as though I'd raised him myself."

"But you didn't," Jeremy said, looking directly at Dromio for the first time.

"I know." Dromio returned the look for as long as he could. "And I thought he would be more angry. A bit more uncomfortable . . . introspective."

"You never wanted to find him. All these years?"

"I got older and learned to let go. Doesn't mean I didn't want to."

"I'm sure he'd like to hear that."

"Want to know something strange?"

"Shoot."

Dromio slowed down as the first bridge to Wrightsville appeared in the distance. "I feel closer to you than I do to my own son. I know it sounds crazy, but I can't really bring myself to ask him anything . . . personal."

Jeremy watched the bridge approach and shrugged. "What do you want to know?"

"Is his father good to him? I mean his other father."

"Peter King's a good guy. . . ." Jeremy circled around his words with slow steps. "A journalist. Pulitzer Prize winner, that sort of thing."

"They get along well?"

"Standard father and son, I wouldn't know what else to tell you."

Dromio nodded, absorbed information. "And his mother? She say anything about me?"

"She thinks you're dead. Good as dead, anyway. Far as I can tell, that's all right with her."

"Does Jeremy resent me?"

Jeremy snuck a peek into the passenger-side mirror. Saw my car following, glanced away. "At this point, I'm not really sure what Jeremy's feeling."

"Stands to reason."

"Anything else?"

"He got a girlfriend?"

"Nope," Jeremy replied quickly. "Let's turn the radio back on."

"Good idea. . . ." Dromio hit the dial, and music flew up into the open air.

The convertible cruised onto the bridge. Rose at an angle, flying upward over a small river of sea water. Small boats cutting through the sun's reflection, making waves. Fishermen and vacationers floating along an otherwise tranquil surface.

Dromio patted Jeremy on the back. "Thanks, Sebastian."

High over the water, Jeremy looked out over the stretch of islands. Gave a passive nod of the head and let his words get lost in the roar of the passing wind. . . .

At least, that's the way I heard it from Dromio.

21. Top of the World

Jeremy and I were officially in.

By the time I pulled into the driveway, I had lost all reservations about my plan. The rest of lunch had gone without a hitch. Dromio telling anecdotes, Nancy poking gentle fun at his controlled boasting. Even Matilda had bloomed slightly, metallic smile coming out of the shadows on more than one occasion. Their questions had remained tentative, and I had no problems keeping up with my role as Jeremy. Jeremy's few inconsistencies went unnoticed, and he mostly remained neutral. Let the family focus on me, and I hardly noticed as he blended in with the tablecloth.

Hard to believe it was already four-thirty when I got out of my car.

Took in Dromio's beach house, all three stories towering over me. By far the largest house on the shores of Wrightsville, deserving of stained-glass windows and its own congregation. Ocean sounds from beyond the dunes. Waves crashing, and I could have sworn it sounded like applause.

We got our bags out of the trunk. Walked up outdoor stairs to the second floor.

Sand scraped beneath our sneakers, grinding against the wood.

"Welcome to our house," Dromio announced as he opened the door.

He led us into an expansive living room. Finished wooden floors home to a pair of expensive white couches with matching easy chairs, all surrounding a large shag rug. A massive entertainment system took up one corner of the room while the opposite wall had been converted into a fully stocked bar. Dark oak shining, lined with polished brass bars and beautifully carved stools. Remaining space filled with old basketball trophies, family photos, signs, and decorations, all of which seemed to be collectibles. Sunlight poured in through a wall of sliding doors, beyond which lay an enormous veranda.

Jeremy and I slowly walked into the space, dumbfounded with awe.

Couldn't even bring ourselves to drop our bags.

"Not a bad piece of work, right?" Dromio smiled from the adjoining kitchen, cracking open a beer.

We nodded.

Dromio glanced at his watch. "Put your bags down and get settled, men. I'll be back in a jiff, just got to make a phone call."

He left us alone in the room.

The instant Dromio was gone, I felt a smack against my shoulder.

"Are you an insane person?" Jeremy hissed at me.

"Ow." I rubbed my arm. "If I am, I guess I learned from the best, Jeremy."

"What was that scene back there, at the Blue Paradise? The guy with the pills, Henry, you could've gotten us killed!"

"James wasn't going to kill anyone."

"Who's James?"

"The guy with the pills."

"Henry."

"James," I corrected. "Those were actors back there. From Jenny Inverso's acting workshop. I met them through her. They owed me a favor, and this was me calling them into action. We set the whole thing up in Durham."

Jeremy's eyes widened. "You *are* an insane person."

"The woman's name is Sloan."

"I don't care!" Jeremy's voice cracked under the strain of whispering. "Is there any reason you didn't let *me* in on it?"

"Because your father was watching, and you're not very good at this."

Some of the fight went out of Jeremy. He looked down at the ground. Shoved his hands in his pockets and gave his bags a light kick. Looked back up, eyes on the fence between pained and relieved.

"I suppose they do like you, now," he mumbled.

"They like both of us."

Jeremy looked back down. "Could you just . . . tone it down a little?"

I leaned over a bit to get a better look at his profile. "What do you mean?"

"Just not so over the top, all right? A little less superman, you know?"

"We want them to *like* me, Jeremy."

"Yeah, not adopt you."

He tapped his foot against the wooden floor. . . .

"Jeremy, what—"

The doorbell rang, end of the round.

Dromio's voice came from another room in the house: "Jeremy, could you get that?"

The two of us started toward the door.

Bumped into each other.

Jeremy gestured toward the entrance. "Jeremy, right."

I took my cue and opened the door, completely unprepared for what I saw.

Standing before me were a pair of identical twins, dressed in matching designer suits. Middle-aged, but built of strong stuff. Wide shoulders, a double-vision set of scowling mouths. Cold eyes under matching black hats, traces of gray in their vaulted eyebrows. Rings on their fingers drawing attention to large hands clasped in front of them. Ready to strike, it seemed.

Something out of a movie where things end very badly.

I gave myself a mental pinch and determined that I wasn't dreaming.

"Can I help you?" I asked.

"You can tell us if Dromio Johansson is in," said the one on the left.

"Who's looking for him?"

"Be glad that's none of your business," the one on the right deadpanned.

"Just tell us if he's in," Lefty added.

I suddenly felt very eighteen years old. Searching for words, but only coming up with one-syllable nouns from my first-grade spelling list.

Fish. Chair. Duck.

Snout.

"Just what do you two think you're doing here?"

Before I could even realize those words hadn't come from my own mouth, the twins brushed past me and into the living room. Dromio had returned and was standing in the middle of the floor. Face set, ready. Unflinching as the two approached him.

Jeremy stepped back, out of their way.

The oxygen seemed to drain out of the room.

"Close the door," Dromio told me. "It's all right."

Killed over a gambling debt.

I did as I was told as Dromio and the twins faced off.

"We got tired of waiting for you to stop by," Lefty said.

"Never got the invitation," Dromio shot back, joke lost in his own humorless face.

"You think this is funny?" Righty asked.

"*This,*" Dromio told them, "is my house. Let's not do this in front of the kids."

Out of Righty's coat came a silver-plated gun. Not pointed at anyone yet, just resting by his side.

I went cold. Muscles bunching as Jeremy took another step back, barely audible gasp of air caught in his lungs. Both our eyes going to the glint in Righty's hand as Lefty pulled out his own piece and actually pointed it between Dromio's eyes.

"They're not going anywhere," Lefty informed him. "And don't forget whose house this really is. Don't leave us hanging, and don't even *think* of trying to talk yourself out of this one."

"Don't think at all," Righty jumped in. "You just give us what's ours."

"There's nothing here for you." Dromio's voice didn't change. Unwavering features staring straight through the barrel's front and rear sights. "You don't have a leg to stand on and you know it."

"We'll ask you again," Righty insisted, leveling his own pistol at Dromio. "And consider this very close to your last warning."

"You're not getting shit," Dromio told them.

"No?"

"Nothing."

"Guess what happens after we take care of you. . . . Last chance."

Jeremy's eyes widened.

And somewhere in the back of my mind, I thought about my mother. . . .

"Go ahead and shoot," Dromio told them.

And although gunshots rang and echoed in my head for the rest of the day, all that reality had to offer at that moment were two dry clicks.

Jeremy frozen in his tracks, hands clutched around his stomach.

Jaw unhinged, attracting flies.

My own mind lost without a map. Struggling to understand why Dromio was still standing, even as a pleased smile spread across his face. Conquered his cheeks, nothing but lips from ear to ear.

"Had these been actual gangsters," Dromio announced, "I'd be dead by now."

The twins burst out laughing.

I couldn't even begin to relax as Dromio joined in. Exchanged handshakes, all three now very different people from two minutes ago. Twins now jovial and inviting. Dromio back to a state of general ease.

I was the first to break paralysis. Not quite ready to cave in to mirth, my heart still telling me that I had almost died right there. Burial at sea.

Jeremy followed suit, and the two of us did our best to smile.

"Hey, Dromio." Lefty wiped a tear from his eye, fingers still grasping the small silver pistol. "Where'd you get the midgets?"

"Not very good bodyguards," Righty giggled, putting his gun away.

Dromio gestured in my direction. "This is my son, Jeremy. And this is Sebastian. Wouldn't mess with him if I were you, though. Tough as nails, can't get a word out of that kid."

"Dromio . . ." I managed to find my voice somewhere in all of that. "I can see that *you all* are laughing, but I don't believe I've heard this one."

"These are the O'Neill brothers." Dromio put an arm around each one. "They own a savings and loan business. I get together with them every Saturday to discuss needy cases. They're nuts about gangster culture, in case you couldn't tell. You should see their home. Looks like Capone's personal Garden of Eden."

"You dirty rat." Lefty grinned, wandering over to the kitchen counter.

"Top of the world, Ma," Dromio replied.

"You do this every Saturday?" I asked.

Dromio laughed. "Nah, just thought you'd get a little kick out of it."

"Are those real guns?" Jeremy managed.

"Couple of twenty-twos," Righty informed us. "Unloaded, don't worry."

"No such thing as an unloaded gun," Jeremy said.

"There is when it's not loaded," Lefty reasoned.

"Or when it's in my bedroom safe," Dromio added. "Seriously, I apologize if we scared you. The two of you handled yourselves so well back at the Paradise. I just figured this kind of thing would be right up your alley. Nothing wrong with a little theater, right?"

Dromio winked at me, and I gave him a smile.

As though I had been in it all along.

"All right." Lefty wiped the slate clean. "Who's in trouble this week?"

"Lacey Dunston." Dromio sat himself down at the kitchen counter with the O'Neill brothers. Guns gone, everything back to what passed for normal in that house. "Don't foreclose on her house next week. She needs an extra month, and I know she's good for it."

Righty looked skeptical. "She hasn't paid us in over six months."

"Got it covered," Dromio assured them. "Chaucer is

about to set her up in the paint shop Mrs. Ladd left to my foundation."

"Mrs. Ladd left you the paint shop?"

"I got her granddaughter into UNC Wilmington."

Lefty shook his head. "Why don't they just go ahead and make you an official chair?"

"I think you have to be an employee to get a chair." Dromio lit a cigarette. "Negotiating a teachers strike doesn't quite get you there."

I shifted my sights among the three of them.

There was something very familiar about all this. . . .

"Point is," Dromio wrapped it all up, "Lacey Dunston is a good woman with a lifetime's worth of bad luck. I'll sign for her, if that's what it takes."

"No worries." Righty smiled. "After all you've done for us."

"No worries there, either," Dromio assured them. Made a gun with his thumb and index, shot off a silent round at both of them. "Paperwork's in my study, go ahead and pick it up."

The O'Neill brothers left the room.

Dromio looked over at us and held up a pair of apologetic hands.

I was still trying to keep track of the names, favors. Who owed who what, the web expanding outward in my head. I tried to cut through it. Take it all in stride, though I felt the day slipping out of my grasp as the afternoon grew old.

"You work for those guys?" I heard Jeremy ask.

"Work with them," Dromio told us, walking toward a phone on the wall. "Things can get a little hectic around here. Again, I apologize. Just let me check my messages."

It dimly occurred to me that only three minutes or so had passed since first setting foot inside Dromio's house. I could see Jeremy toying with the same notion. The two of us checking each other for imaginary bullet holes, feet coming unglued as we began to feel out our new surroundings. Framed photographs calling us over. Decorations and furniture inspected as the beep of an answering machine cut through the silence, followed by a recorded message:

"Mr. Johansson, this is Henderson at the aquarium. Everyone here really appreciates your help with the loggerhead benefit. If you could just swing by tomorrow, we can nail out the details. Thanks again, we owe you one."

Another beep as Jeremy and I turned to listen. . . .

"Dromio, it's Kelsey. I know you're very busy, but if you could give me a call later on. Donnie's all taken care of. I just want to make sure that everything went through with the check you gave us. For the records, you know. . . . Oh, and for the record . . . thanks. Thanks again, Dromio. For everything."

By the end of the message, Jeremy and I had made our way over to Dromio's side.

Unyielding sense of déjà vu as we listened to the last one.

"Dromio, I need you to come over here right away. I don't know what happened, but John's having . . . one of his moments, I don't know. Maybe he stopped taking his medication. . . . I don't know, please. He's locked himself in the bathroom and won't come out, says he'll only speak to you. Please hurry. . . . But don't kill yourself getting over here."

Beep.

Dromio sighed, scribbled something on a notepad.

"That last message sounded serious," I volunteered.

"Nothing that can't be fixed," Dromio told us as the O'Neill brothers returned. Each holding matching folders. Dromio caught their attention and motioned to the door. "I'll walk you guys out, we can talk about the rest tonight. Something I got to take care of."

The O'Neill brothers nodded as all three headed for the exit.

"Nice meeting you two," Lefty told us.

"Hey, Jeremy!" Righty called out as they made their way out. "You're one lucky son of a gun with the father you got. You know that?"

I nodded, on impulse. "I do now."

"Sorry again about all this." Dromio threw on a windbreaker and stepped out the door. "You two make yourselves at home. Have a drink, get rested up. I'll be back in an hour."

The door closed with a windswept slam.

Jeremy and I were left to our own devices.

Standing shoulder to shoulder by the answering machine.

Sound of the ocean through glass doors, waves crashing one by one.

Dominos.

Jeremy turned to me. "Dromio . . ."

"Yes."

Both of us thinking the same thing, about the messages on Dromio's answering machine. Like reverse chameleons, as though our environment were adjusting to us.

The phone rang.

I turned, reflexively.

"Don't answer that," Jeremy told me, instinct bringing us to strangely familiar ground.

The phone rang four more times.

Dromio's voice on the machine: "Johansson residence. Leave a message."

Beep.

Then the voice of an elderly woman: "Dromio? This is Lacey Dunston. The O'Neills just called me. . . . Thank you so much. You really are the best. I'll see you at the party tonight."

Click on the other end.

The tape stopped.

Rewound, ready for playback.

It was ten till five on the coast of North Carolina.

Jeremy and I picked up our bags and began to explore. . . .

22. The Most Acceptable Hypocrisy

Our arrival had somehow become an event.

By ten in the evening, Dromio's house was filled to capacity. An impossible headcount spread out into every available space. Mingling in the living room, sitting by the bar, spilling onto the veranda, local residents from all walks of life drinking, dancing, socializing. Tables of food set up outside and in, bartenders called in from the Blue Paradise, oldies rock blasting through sixteen separate speakers.

Not one unfriendly face in the whole crowd.

Not one person who didn't have something to say about Dromio Johansson.

Jeremy and I had lost each other several times. Found each other again, only to be torn apart by reaching hands, inquiring minds. Questions raised, stories told, there was no longer any way to ensure that either one of us was doing his duty as the other. Free fall. Free rolling, but that's what the entire evening seemed to be about, and I just went ahead and let go. Had a few drinks, cigarettes. Not acting any different than usual, just feeling different. Same old me with a blood transfusion. New life. Getting to know the crowd as it grew in size and spirit. Hearing from every last individual that I truly was Dromio's son.

No question about it.

And in the midst of all of this, Jeremy and I caught up with each other once again.

Cornered by Chaucer, the Blue Paradise manager.

Introducing us to his Czech wife, Nikki.

Yet another story about Dromio, loud over the blaring music.

"So the costume party ends, right?" Chaucer paused to give his wife a mammoth kiss on the shoulder. . . . "And Dromio says, *Everybody take off your masks!* And I take mine off only to see that he's paired me with Nikki, who absolutely hated me!"

"More than anyone I'd ever met!" Nikki declared, wrapping her skinny arms around Chaucer and kissing him full on the lips.

Jeremy looked away, embarrassed.

Myself, I was entirely caught up.

Chaucer disengaged himself from his wife and had a drink. "You know what, Jeremy? You definitely got that Johansson gene in you!"

"You think so?" I asked.

"I can see it!" Chaucer put two fingers to his eyeballs and sent them pointing toward mine. "Plain as the nose on Dromio's face! What do you think, Sebastian?"

We all turned to Jeremy, who had been standing in sideline silence with an untouched bourbon in his hands. Not necessarily tuning out, though it did feel as though the entire party were swirling around him. Preoccupied eyes repelling all music and laughter. Untouched by anything other than the present conversation. Might as well have been standing in his own private study, entertaining guests as he raised his eyebrows.

"What do I think about what?" Jeremy asked tentatively.

"Jeremy and Dromio!" Chaucer reiterated. "Are they a perfect match for each other, or what?"

Jeremy turned and regarded me with mild detachment, a polite veil over eyes holding far deeper concerns. "I certainly never thought it was going to go *this* well for him!"

"I can only imagine how relieved you must be!" Nikki laughed. "Now you don't have to worry about holding Jeremy's hand anymore! He's doing fine on his own!"

"Yes, my work here is done!" Jeremy agreed, trying on a smile three sizes too big for his face.

I felt something brush against me. Turned and saw Matilda by my side, all dressed up in a black dress with thin straps. Her eyes peered up at me as she made a strange, surreptitious motion with her head.

I didn't get it, and moments later, Matilda was leading me through a thicket of bodies. I looked back and saw Jeremy trying to follow. Held in check by Chaucer and Nikki, who weren't through talking up their romance. The crowd closed in around us, and I lost sight of all three. Almost lost my balance as Matilda effortlessly slipped around every obstacle presented.

We made it out to the veranda and were greeted by a blast of fresh air. Crisp sea breeze churning conversations as Matilda scanned the crowd, eyes narrow behind her glasses.

"If you're looking for me, I'm right here," I told her.

She tapped me on the shoulder and pointed. "There she is. . . ."

I squinted.

Out toward the terrace edge, a young woman in a red strapless dress was stationed. Her back to the party. Long black curls sweeping against her shoulders. Champagne glass in her left hand, looking out to the ocean. A solitary lighthouse.

And then we were beside her.

"Jeremy," Matilda began. "I'd like you to meet my best friend, Christina."

Christina turned to face us.

Possibly preparing to smile, but every last trace of forthcoming courtesy disappeared as we locked eyes.

"Christina," Matilda continued, unaware, "this is—"

"We've met," Christina said, eyes making no secret of her displeasure.

I was having a bit of trouble believing it myself. "Best of my recollection, we weren't actually introduced."

"What?" Matilda found herself caught between the two of us. "When did this happen?"

"Courthouse steps, this morning," Christina told her.

"Courthouse steps, this morning," I echoed, never taking my eyes off hers.

"Dromio's little boy . . ." Christina shook her head. Already deciding how this conversation would conclude. "I should have known. Bit more skinny, maybe, but the bloated ego makes up for it."

I turned to Matilda. "Seriously, she's only treating me this nice because I'm your brother, right?"

"I'm treating you this way *despite* the fact that you're her brother," Christina told me. "Half-brother, actually."

"Which makes you a half-friend of mine," I threw back, energized for no apparent reason. "Though half of me is none too certain it wants to be, which makes you a quarter-friend."

"I could have handled those guys today on my own."

"I was just trying to help."

"Next time, don't."

"Hold it," Matilda intervened. Grabbed Christina and pulled her aside. Couple of feet away, and I saw them exchange words. Even out of earshot, the two of them seemed to relate on common ground. Even in the middle of a heated argument about Matilda's brother. Even as conflict wound down and Christina finally relented.

Matilda led her back by the arm.

A mother forcing her child to apologize for stolen candy.

"Matilda says I don't have to like you," Christina told me.

"There's a lot of that going around."

"I don't know what that means. . . ." Christina received an elbow to the ribs from Matilda. "But I suppose it wouldn't hurt to be polite."

"Well . . ." I flashed a smile. "You know, Ambrose Bierce defined *politeness* as—"

"*The most acceptable hypocrisy,*" Christina volunteered. "Yes, I know that. Do you know how he defined the word *quotation*?"

I blinked. Swallowed. *"The act of repeating erroneously the words of another. . . ."*

"So it's going to take a lot more than this to impress me." Christina faked a smile and added, "Good to have you with us, Jeremy."

"EVERYONE, CAN I HAVE YOUR ATTENTION, PLEASE?"

The music cut off. All eyes on Dromio, standing on a raised platform with a microphone in his hand. Crowd gathering, even those inside pressing against each other to get a better look.

"Jeremy, Sebastian . . ." Dromio looked out into his audience. "Let me get the two of you up here."

I tried to get a last word in with Christina, but she was already walking away. No other choice than to make my way through the throng of followers and onto the stage. Jeremy joined up, stood on the other side of Dromio.

"Jeremy, Sebastian . . . ," Dromio began. Addressing us as he played to the rest, words that were probably heard several miles down the shore. . . . "These people are my friends, my family. I've shared everything with them all these years. And now, I want to share you as well. Each person here has said to me, at some hard moment in their lives, *God will thank you, Dromio, for what you are doing.* And I always told them that I didn't need any thanks."

A few murmurs from the onlookers, sounds of a congregation.

"But now, I want you all to know that someone has heard you all. Somewhere, someone has sent me a son I never thought I'd see. And not one son, but two. . . ." Dromio put an arm around me. "Welcome to my family, Jeremy." Dromio took his other arm, drew Jeremy close. "Welcome, Sebastian."

Applause.

And that applause rose, turned into a roar that put the ocean to shame. Elated faces and ecstatic voices, all welcoming me to their shores. Welcoming both of us as the music kicked in again. Everyone dancing now, crowd rippling with rhythm and energetic fervor.

From my elevated place, I saw Christina impassively survey the spectacle, then turn and walk down the stairs.

I jumped down from the platform and followed.

23. Dromio, Part Two

I caught up with her on the beach.

Christina was walking barefoot in the sand.

Heels hanging from her left hand.

"Hey!" I trotted up to her, and she turned around.

Crossed her arms. This was now twice in one day.

A nearly full moon shone down on her. Skin glowing a supernatural blue, floodlights from Dromio's house barely glancing off her red dress. Acerbic lips visible under the soft glimmer of her impatient eyes.

"So . . . ," she said.

I waited for more.

Got nothing but the wind in my face.

She wrapped her arms around her body.

"You want my jacket?" I asked.

"You're not wearing a jacket."

"You want my tie?"

"No."

"My jacket's back at Dromio's."

"You going to get it for me?" she asked. "Or is the idea

that I should go back to the party? With you? Loosen up, maybe join the Dromio fan club?"

"Why not?" I said, trying to interpret whatever language she was speaking. "Admission's free and you get a nifty little newsletter in the mail every month."

"I was just going out for a walk. By myself."

"You want company?"

Christina looked genuinely offended. "Excuse me?"

"That was a joke."

"You know how I could tell?"

"How?"

"Because, so far, not a single joke you've made has been funny."

From nearby came a scratchy voice, "Jeremy Johansson?"

I turned and saw a man walking toward me. The lights from Dromio's house streamed from behind him, couldn't make out a face or features. Body one long shadow. Envelope jutting out of his right hand.

"I'm Bill Wilson," he said, and even face to face, there wasn't much to make out. "Manager of the Hilton. I've got a couple of messages for your friend, Sebastian. He told me it would be best to give them to you. . . ."

I took the messages.

Turned back to Christina, saw a look of confusion on her face.

"Bastian's dyslexic," I told her, off the top of my head. "Don't tell anyone." I turned back to Wilson. "Thanks for taking our messages."

"Yeah, just stop by the Hilton anytime you want to check up."

"I certainly will."

"Look forward to it." Wilson gave a wave and walked back to the house.

I opened the first envelope and held the note up in the air. Against the light, trying my best to make out the message. Gave it a quick scan. . . .

Not what I wanted to see, and I kept it to myself.

Must have shown up on my face, and Christina asked, "Bad news?"

"Nothing." I carefully folded the note in fourths. "Just Sara."

"Is she your girlfriend?"

"I don't have one of those. Sara's just someone I'm trying to help out. That's all."

"Jesus Christ." Christina looked up to the sky, gave a humorless laugh. "Dromio, Part Two. Unbelievable . . ."

And without another word, she turned her back to me and walked away.

I watched her leave. Legs taking her down the beach. Body dissolving into the night, leaving barely discernible tracks in the sand. I looked out to the ocean. High tide approaching, silver waves celebrating collapse. I chewed on my lip, absently rubbed Sara's message with my thumb.

Opened the second message, a quick note from Paul Inverso, reading, *Investigations have turned up surprising results. Must talk in person or over the phone.*

I shook my head, trying my best to admire Paul's genuine interest in helping me. Misguided as it was.

"I think Sara's beaten you to the punch, my friend," I mumbled. Crumpled the note and shoved it into my back pocket. Looked back down the beach to see if Christina had reemerged from the shadows. Too soon, all I got for my wishes were the sounds of Dromio's party tugging at my sleeves.

Pure jubilation coaxing me into leaving my problems for tomorrow.

PART FOUR

SUNDAY

24. Good Morning

I woke up to the crying sounds of seagulls.

Stirred, soft roar of the ocean joining in. I shifted, clean sheets wrapped around me. Pillows adjusting their shape to fit my movements. Opened my eyes to sunlight streaming through the windows. Yellow and orange spotlights gathering round my bed. Warm walls greeting me, silent house asking if I had slept well.

"Yes, I did," I murmured.

Stretched and sat up, throwing my legs over the edge of the bed.

Walked to the window and opened it.

Took in a panoramic view of the empty beach, spanning north and south.

Breathed in, shoulders rising with ease.

All problems on hold, wondering about this new world I had stepped into. All of Saturday's events floating along with whisper-thin clouds. Unable to identify what I was feeling. Becoming, maybe. Some part of me left behind in Durham. Making way for Dromio, Nancy, and Matilda.

Christina.

Watching the transition of a new day as the sun grew brighter.

"Good morning," I told the waking world.

Smiled and closed the window.

25. No Such Luck

I was standing in the empty kitchen, phone to my ear. Barefoot on shiny, wooden floors. Undershirt and boxer shorts disheveled from the efforts of sleep. Taking the opportunity for a private call, house still wrapped in its comfortable little coma. Microwave clock letting me know it was 8:15 a.m.

Turning to 8:16 as Sara picked up on the other end.

Panicked voice getting straight to the point, and once again Olaf was back in my life.

"Olaf?" I tried to keep my voice low. "He's the one?"

"You know this guy?"

"I was expecting someone with some kind of connection," I explained, not really answering her question. Not wanting to admit that my previous instincts had been wide of the mark, losing both of us valuable time. "Someone from the clinic, someone with access. Olaf's a pizza guy, he doesn't even know the combination to the safe."

"Well, he's got connections with *somebody*." Sara sounded angry. Scared, desperate, wasn't sure which one. The phone lines didn't specify. "He knows the time, the details, he even knows the doctor who attended me—"

"He knew all that the last time he called—"

"He knows about your mother's forgery, Bastian."

The air rushed out of me. Complete vacuum, took just about every rational thought I had along with it. A kick to the stomach would have been better. "What proof could he possibly have?"

"I don't *know*," she wailed. "But if he goes to the cops, they'll be more than happy to get whatever evidence *they* need."

"Did you tell him anything to make him think he was right about the forgery?"

"I denied it up and down, didn't make a difference. He's threatening to send your mother to jail."

"Then he's going right there with her."

"My guess is he's already been there," Sara told me. "And he's got a lot less to lose than you . . . and your mother."

"You his agent all of a sudden?"

"Damn it, Bastian!" Her cry shot into my ear, and I moved the phone a good foot from my head. "You know this guy so well, *you* tell me if he's bluffing!"

I sighed. Brought the phone back to my ear. "No. He's not bluffing."

"What are we going to do, Bastian?"

I took a breath, wondered if it was possible to go soft in the span of just one day.

Collected myself, remembered who I was.

"We're going to fix this," I told Sara. "I've dealt with this guy before, he's small-time. Whatever he wants, I'll take care of it. And this time, I'll make sure it's the last little favor he gets from me."

Sara's voice lapsed into a fearful kind of relief. "Yeah?"

"Yeah." I reassured her, back in control. "You got a way to contact him?"

"Yes."

"You tell Olaf I'll call him this evening at Big Niko's."

"You sure you know what you're doing?"

"I always know what I'm doing."

The sound of footsteps caught my attention.

Shuffling, early morning footsteps coming closer.

"I have to go." Whispering now, fast words. "I'll call you tomorrow."

A touch of melancholy as Sara told me, "Love you."

There wasn't much else to say other than, "Love you, too. Bye."

I hung up, as a voice from the doorway greeted me with: "You're up early."

I wasn't sure I'd heard right, and I turned.

Christina was standing at the threshold.

I blinked. "You're up . . . here."

She walked into the kitchen. Dressed in white boxers and a matching T-shirt. White ankle-high socks sweeping the floor. "Was that Sara on the phone?"

"Huh?" I still wasn't sure what was going on.

"Your non-girlfriend, Sara. Was that her?"

"Yeah."

"Interesting . . ." Christina took down a glass from one of the cabinets. Went to the fridge, rooted around inside. Bending at the waist. She came out with a carton of orange juice and caught me staring. Raised an eyebrow. "You always call your girls at eight in the morning?"

"I don't have *girls*," I informed her. "I just happened to be awake. Thought I'd get up with the sun, prepare breakfast for my loved ones . . . and you."

"Mm . . ." Christina poured her orange juice. Took three large swallows. Watched me over the rim of the glass.

"I had this idea," I began. "This crazy notion that after last night we probably wouldn't be seeing each other again."

"No such luck." Christina put down her glass, refilled it. "Matilda invited me to spend the week here. Help her cope with her new brother, but it looks like she's going to be holding *my* hand through this whole fiasco."

"How is it that you're best friends with Matilda?"

She stopped the glass short of her lips. Set it back down and crossed her arms. "What do you mean?"

"How old are you?"

"Twenty-one."

"What do you do?"

"I just graduated with a double major in political science and public policy."

"Is that all?"

"And a minor in Latin American studies, what's your point?"

"Matilda's sixteen years old and has a major in nothing. She has a driver's license."

Christina bristled. "Who's *your* best friend?"

I almost found myself saying *Jeremy* before catching myself. "Sebastian."

"He's a quiet, respectful person, with a clear understanding of how to relate to people without treating them like acquisitions." Christina's voice was on the rise. "*You* are overconfident, egotistical, and self-involved to the point of being blind. How is it that *he's* best friends with *you*?"

"I think I see where you're going with this."

"Matilda happens to be a genius. Certified. Could fit everything she's learned in high school on the tip of one synapse. She's brilliant, despite the fact that it doesn't show up on her *driver's license*."

"Brilliant enough to earn a special place in *your* heart? How unbelievably *charitable* of you."

"Charitable!?" Christina wasn't even pretending to keep quiet anymore. "You want to talk about a twisted sense of propriety, take a good look at your dad. Helping people with one hand, slipping them into his pocket with the other—"

"I personally saw him save a woman from losing her house yesterday!"

"And might I add that *you* don't seem to have a problem admitting to your own intelligence and good looks—"

The argument came to a halt as Christina realized what she had just said.

Good looks . . .

I couldn't think of anything to say, either. Just watched her try to rewind, stop, tape over that last comment. Cheeks flushed, breath lifting her up, down. Her hair was pulled up, and a few curls had fallen free. Dancing in her face, tickling her eyelashes.

No easy task for me to hold back my smile. . . .

"Ah, spring!" Dromio announced as he entered the kitchen, wrapped in a ruby-red bathrobe and rubbing his eyes. "When a young man's fancy wakes up the whole damn rest of the house."

All at once the boxing ring was gone, replaced again by the kitchen.

Christina gave Dromio a polite nod. Returned the orange juice to the fridge and left the way she'd come in.

"I see you met Christina," Dromio said, opening the fridge and pulling out two egg cartons.

"Yeah, last night."

Dromio laughed. "Yes, it looks to be a very interesting week at *casa Dromio*." He took some more items out of the fridge. Green peppers, cheese, onions, Tabasco, mushrooms, sausage, caviar, baby shrimp, tomatoes. It was as though Dromio had just decided to take inventory. "Let me tell you a little something my old basketball coach told me. . . ."

I sat myself on a nearby counter, a little amused. "You played basketball?"

"Scholarship got me through my first and only two years in college."

"Were you any good?"

"Every player makes a difference, but it's the coach that makes those players dance."

"So what'd your coach tell you?"

"He said, *Dromio . . . getting along with a woman is a lot like putting up a really good fistfight.*"

"How's that?"

"*It doesn't matter if you're able,*" he said, closing the refrigerator door. "*It only matters if you're willing. . . .*"

Dromio left those words hanging as he set about chopping the green pepper. Rhythmic knock of his knife against the counter. Began to hum, and I found myself mesmerized by the simple expediency of his actions. Remembering yesterday. Moments when every last event seemed to dance on the tips of his fingers.

As though Dromio's will was the world. . . .

"Hey, Sebastian." Dromio motioned with the knife. "Come on over and help me chop this onion, will you?"

I jumped down from the counter.

Realized a moment later that Jeremy had just walked in. Same early morning state as everyone else. Shuffling over to Dromio's side, taking the knife without a word. I watched as Dromio instructed him to dice, not slice. Jeremy diligently set about his business, and it felt as though a change were coming over him as well.

A swifter and more refined control over his actions.

Not that there was any real efficiency to his movements, but still . . . I could see little of the typical self-consciousness that kept his arms, legs, and fingers from properly functioning. Simple inexperience accounting for his oversized chunks of tomato, and when Dromio silently took the knife out of his hands, showed him the proper grip and execution, Jeremy just went with it. No sheepish look, or murmured apologies as he took back the knife and tried again.

Actually getting it right this time.

Clearing his throat to speak, a more direct approach to his words as he asked, "Why are we chopping vegetables at eight-thirty in the morning?"

"Omelets à la carte," Dromio proudly responded. "World's greatest creation, the omelet."

"I've never really been a fan."

"Doesn't surprise me."

"Why's that?"

I remained standing against the counter. Watched Jeremy take the conversation in stride.

"See, you talk tough, Sebastian," Dromio explained. "But tough ain't nothing if you're timid. Way you make your eggs is the way you make your life."

"Scrambled?"

"Well, sure." Dromio gave a little laugh. "Sunny side up is for blind optimists. What I'm talking about is the daring quality of ingredients." He made a broad sweeping motion, again with the knife. "You put all you've got into it, everything you see before you. And, boom, life is an adventure."

"What if your life ends up a mess?"

"That's why you got your friends and family to help clean up." Dromio put an arm around Jeremy and looked over at me. "Am I right, Jeremy?"

I looked at the two together, father and son.

Almost surprised to remember who I really was.

Gut check.

Jeremy looked at me, waiting for my line. . . .

"Absolutely," I managed. "Though in my opinion nothing says clean like a good shower."

And so I quietly excused myself.

There were things to think about. Nothing to be done but wait for events to play themselves out. Wait for my chance to talk to Olaf. Wait to see what Dromio was all about. Wait to see when and whether this masquerade would come to a close. Wait and see if Jeremy would pull through this without blowing all of us out of the water.

playing it cool

Though Jeremy seemed to have things more or less under control.

I walked into the bathroom and turned on the shower.

Steam collected, clouding the mirrors.

A water-colored portrait of myself stared back.

Jeremy and Dromio. Chaucer's words from the party came back to me through the thick cloud. *Are they a perfect match for each other, or what?*

"Yes," I replied, keeping my voice low. "Yes, I suppose they are. . . ."

I locked the door. Took off my clothes and left them in a crumpled heap on the floor. Stepped into the shower and slid the polymer door shut. Thought about waking up that morning, standing on the balcony and sensing that the day held something new for me. Could only imagine the same thing had happened to Jeremy, could see it in his conversation with Dromio that morning. Scales tipping in an undetermined direction, and I made the decision to let it go for the time being.

Let Jeremy and Dromio be.

I closed my eyes and turned the heat as far up as I could stand it.

26. Blue Hawks

Calling Sara while the rest of the house slept was one thing.

Calling my mother during waking hours was a whole other headache.

It didn't occur to me till after breakfast. Omelets laid to rest, dishes cleaned. Christina keeping a discreet distance from all conversation. Nancy announcing she was going for a walk on the beach, Dromio tending to his answering machine. Matilda sticking to me like glue, and I had to wait for her to slip off to the bathroom before announcing that I was going for a walk myself.

I left through the living room door and took to the streets.

Walked toward the center of the island, where locals staked their claim on bars, surf shops, and small restaurants. Up to the Wrightsville pier, all patched up after its violent clash with Hurricane Fran in 1996. Public-access beach littered with families. Young girls in two-piece bathing suits. Teenagers riding their bikes, throwing territorial glances in my direction. Noontime sun not caring that summer was still months away.

A bit of sweat breaking out under my black pants, white shirt, and lightweight blue jacket.

I walked up the ramp to the pier. Wooden planks sturdy beneath my shoes.

Opened the door to the indoor bar and arcade. Yellow, incandescent lights illuminating the smoky space, crammed with video games, pinball machines, and beat-up pool tables. A few ancient stragglers hanging around. Hands clutching cans of Miller Lite, weather-beaten faces stretched well past their prime. Watery eyes staring into familiar corners, up into the inviting glow of muted TV screens. A few looks my way. Then nothing, even suspicion taking up too much energy in that isolated, little shoe box.

No pay phone in sight.

I wandered over to the bar.

Splotchy signs above me spelling out one-fifty for a hot dog.

Two-fifty for a hamburger.

Beer and spirits displayed along a makeshift shelf.

The bartender put out his cigarette and wandered over. Asked if I needed any bait.

Before I could answer, I looked to my left and saw Nancy Johansson perched on a stool. Plastic cup of orange juice in front of her. Looking up from her drink, never guessing that I would be there, staring back. Eyes locked, and both of us must have been sharing the same expression. Guilty amazement, instantly replaced with surprised smiles.

"Jeremy!" She held up her hand in a modified wave.

I walked over. "Hey, Nancy."

"What brings you here?"

"Do you want any bait?" the bartender asked again.

"I'm fine."

"I just came in to get out of the sun," Nancy told me.

"How was your walk?"

"It was hot. Aren't you hot?"

I looked down at my skin. "I was born with a tan."

"Yeah, you really got this Italian/Mediterranean thing going on."

I nodded awkwardly.

Nancy didn't add anything else.

I realized it was my turn to explain. "I was just trying to rustle up a copy of the *New York Times*."

"I don't think you'll find one in this place."

"You come here a lot?"

Nancy finished off her drink. "Not really. Every now and then, whenever I go out walking and it gets too hot."

"Need another vodka and orange?" the bartender asked her.

"No," she said abruptly. "Just an orange juice, please. . . ."

Bartender set a small can in front of her and took a dollar off the counter. Nancy opened it without a word, poured its contents into the plastic cup. She stirred the ice with her straw. Followed the spiral flow with her eyes. Ring finger gently tapping the bar.

I thought about sitting.

Glanced around instead. Saw a couple of kids pumping quarters into a video game, plastic guns in their hands. Waiting for their cue before locking and loading. Blasting away at foreign assailants. Delighted cries as cyberbullets flew and quarters flowed.

"Hey, Nancy?"

"Yes, Jeremy?"

"Is everything all right?"

"Yes." She smiled, a soothing kind of melancholy blooming. "I'm glad you're here, Jeremy. I don't know if you're enjoying yourself—"

"I am."

"But I do know that this is very good for Dromio." She gazed over the bar. "There's a lot . . . involved with being a part of Dromio's life. And a lot of that comes from what used to be his life. Bad people, bad places. Places like this . . ." She paused. Thought, then continued. "Well, that's not fair, I suppose. This place isn't all that bad. But the spirit, the feeling that comes with these four walls."

"If these walls could talk," I offered, keeping with caution.

"Exactly . . ." She took another sip, gave a slight smile. "I once took a trip back to Chicago with Dromio. We were driving around, seeing the sights. And we ended up in his old neighborhood. Not where he was brought up, but where he lived after losing his basketball scholarship with the Blue Hawks. . . ."

I frowned. "Blue Hawks?"

Nancy was in her own world, didn't hear me. "The place had undergone a bit of a restoration. Some neighborhoods get lucky, I guess. Nothing spectacular, you understand, just enough to distance it from Dromio's mean streets. . . ."

I pulled out a cigarette and lit up.

"And then he told me to stop the car. . . ." Smoke traveled across Nancy's eyes, but she didn't seem to notice. "He

pointed over to a bar where he used to drink, shoot pool.
This little dive called the Almond. Didn't look like it had
changed that much. The sign outside still had this 1970s
look to it. Gaudy neon, I'm sure you've seen it in the
movies. Short little building, all these new constructions
grown up around it. I was checking out some of the stragglers outside, when Dromio started to cry. I mean really let
it run, Niagara Falls." The smoke finally got to her and she
coughed, straightened up in her seat. "I'm sorry if this
makes you uncomfortable."

I started, forgetting for a moment who I was pretending
to be. "Not at all. It's okay."

"I just remember this very clearly. He was crying and crying, and trying to tell me what it was like back then. I mean
he's always had a small part of him that looks back fondly. But
only as someone who made it out of there. Sitting in that car,
all he could do was tell me that he never wanted to go back. *I
don't ever want to go back*, he kept saying. *I don't ever want to be
that again.* Took him a long time to get himself together, and
we left. After that, I don't believe we ever talked about it
again. . . ."

Nancy looked at me then, something I couldn't quite
place. "And that's how I know he won't ever come in
here. . . ."

My cigarette had all but died between my fingers.

I didn't move to put it out.

Nancy finished her drink. Stood up and left a tip.

She gave me a pat on the shoulder. "I think this is going
to be very good for both of us."

I didn't know what she was referring to. Her and me,

Dromio and her, me and Dromio. A web of connections starting to grow in my mind, jump-started by our conversation.

"Is this just you and me?" she asked.

I suddenly remembered that neither of us was supposed to be there.

"This is us," I agreed. "You know if there's a phone booth around here?"

She smiled. "Far wall, over by the pinball machines."

"Stupid place for a pay phone."

"See you back at the house, Jeremy."

Nancy walked out the door. Blinding sunlight poured in, violent shafts of pure white. I shielded my eyes, and the door closed behind her. Just me and the fishermen, now. Video games joined together in an electronic symphony.

I lit another cigarette, went over to the phone.

My mother was home, enjoying her Sunday morning. "How's Wilmington?" she asked between mouthfuls of a late breakfast.

"Not so bad," I told her. "Once it gets used to you. Any calls?"

"You got a call from Paul Inverso, says it's urgent."

"Any from a guy named Olaf?"

"No Olaf. You want a list?"

"Don't worry about it," I said, took a drag. "They'll take care of themselves."

"Who are you and what have you done with my son?" She laughed, another mouthful somewhere in there. "I was secretly hoping a vacation would get you to relax a little, I just never thought it would actually *happen*."

"First time for everything."

"All right, what's wrong?" she asked. I could almost see her putting fork and knife down, crossing her arms. "You don't sound like yourself."

"Haven't been feeling much like myself, actually."

"And nothing's wrong?"

Well, I suppose *wrong* wasn't really the right word. *Curious*, perhaps.

"The other night," I told her. "Remember? When we were talking about my father?"

"Oh." I heard a radio in the background switch off. "Yeah, honey, what about it?"

"You told me he was a *Blue Hawk, through and through.*"

"Yeah, I guess I might have."

"Is that some kind of expression I don't know about?"

"It was an expression he always used. Something to do with a basketball team he used to play on."

"He played basketball?"

"Well, that's what he told me." Her voice became dismissive, casual. "Didn't strike me as much of a basketball player, so I just assumed . . . you know, him and his lies. . . . Something going on with you?"

I looked around. Something was certainly going on, but I wasn't ready to stipulate whether it was happening to me or the world I had always lived in. All the right conditions for losing one's cool, and I wasn't going to go down that road. Not with everything else that was happening. Proceed with caution, and I brought myself in for a smooth landing. "Fifteen across in the *New York Times* crossword mentioned something about a Blue Hawk, that's all."

"How many letters?"

"Three."

"So I guess the word *basketball* doesn't fit."

"Neither does *father.*"

"But *dad* does."

"Starts with an *x*."

I heard her laugh. "All right, I'm thoroughly useless. Anything else, Bastian?"

"Nope."

"Talk soon?"

"Count on it."

We said our goodbyes and I hung up.

Took a few steps into the center of the arcade.

Looked back at the phone.

Looked away.

The two eight-year-olds were done blowing shit up. Possibly out of quarters. Standing near the bar, guns put to rest in their holsters. Now working on a pair of ice cream cones, chocolate and strawberry.

Same delighted smile on both their faces.

I stood there for a while longer.

Took off my jacket, threw it over one shoulder.

Let Jeremy and Dromio be had lasted no more than an hour.

I stepped out into anxious daylight and headed back to Dromio's.

27. Betta Fish

Dromio had business to take care of, and it turned into a field trip for the whole family.

We tucked ourselves into Nancy's minivan and made tracks for Fort Fisher.

Christina sat next to me, pressed as close to the window as she could.

We arrived at the North Carolina Aquarium at around two in the afternoon.

Tumbled out of the car. Walked up a wooden ramp leading to the circular concrete building. A large grotto extending beneath us, the aquarium's lower level. Watery beds for dozing alligators, last of the prehistoric predators enjoying the sun. Dreaming of swamps and stealthy hunts.

Henderson greeted us at the entrance. Head of the aquarium, head and shoulders above all of us. He looked like a placid Boris Karloff. Frankenstein's monster free of disfiguring scars, all dressed up in slacks and a corduroy jacket. Shook hands with Dromio and escorted us into the aquarium, the unique smell of aquatic life filling every square foot.

"You should really be proud of your old man," Henderson told me. "This is going to do a lot for the loggerhead turtles. By holding our auction at the Blue Paradise and catering it for free—"

"Twenty-five-cent gratuity charge," Dromio reminded Henderson with a sly smile.

"We got guys with metal detectors combing the beach." Henderson slapped him on the back, laughing with gruff affection.

I caught Christina grimacing.

The rest of the family spread out to various wings of the aquarium. I stuck by Dromio, followed Henderson to his office. He opened the door and ushered Dromio in. As I began to follow, Dromio put out his arm, barring the entrance.

"Nothing going on behind these doors other than business as usual," he told me. "Besides . . . you want to discuss turtles, or you want a chance alone with Christina?"

I looked around to make sure everyone else was a safe distance away.

"What are you talking about?" I asked.

"Don't play innocent with me," Dromio smiled, hand on the doorknob. "Go talk to her. Take her to see the sharks being fed, she might learn a thing or two about compassion."

Dromio closed the door on me before I could argue.

Newly formed questions left unanswered for the time being.

I grudgingly took his advice and tracked Christina down.

Found her in an enclosed corridor. A single row of fish tanks like filmstrip on either wall. Blue tubes of light bathing the hallway, bubbly sounds of self-cleaning water. A faint, electric hum that seemed to come from everywhere.

Christina was standing in front of a tank inhabited by a single, diminutive betta fish.

I slid up beside her. Watched the pink and puffy loner do laps in its aquatic chamber.

"Betta fish," I told her.

"Interesting," she said flatly. "The plaque under the tank says Betta splendens."

"Otherwise known as betta fish," I continued. "Also known as Siamese fighting fish. Don't let their size fool you. They're known for attacking and killing other fish. Regardless of age, race, or creed. Put two of them in the same tank, and they'll go at each other's throats. Won't stop until one of them is dead."

"I can sense the point you're trying to make about us two." Christina quickly moved down to the next display.

A group of moping angelfish greeted her.

"What do you have against saving loggerhead turtles?" I asked.

"Nothing," she said, staring hard at the striped triangular creatures floating between pieces of coral. "I saw *Turtle Diary* twice."

"What's that?"

"A movie from the mid eighties," she told me, snide edge to her voice. "You're probably too young to remember it."

"Has Matilda seen it?"

"Are we going to have this discussion again?"

"So you only have a problem with *Dromio* saving loggerhead turtles. . . ."

She began to walk down the corridor.

I trotted after her. "You don't want to talk about Dromio?"

"No."

"Should I change the subject?"

"Changing location would be a big start."

"You think the betta fish represent us?"

"You certainly seem to think so."

"And you seem to think that you're somehow different from Dromio."

Christina stopped walking, faced me.

"I don't go around parading myself like Dromio."

"Dromio parades?"

"It's all he does."

"Guess I must have missed all the elephants."

"Don't try to be funny, you're no different than he is." She drew closer, lowered her voice. "It doesn't matter what I do, what matters is that when I do it, I keep it to myself."

"And what exactly do you do?"

"It's none of your business."

"But you're going to tell me anyway, aren't you . . . ?"

Christina looked abashed. Insulted even. Mouth open, standing at less than half a foot away. Scented soap and cherry lip gloss toying with my thoughts, eyes searching for some response other than the one she finally gave:

"I clerk for a civil rights lawyer in Wilmington," she informed me, words coming out at a fast and reckless clip. "Which means I spend most of my time dealing with any number of cases that slip through the cracks of the legal justice system. I volunteer part time for the AFOP and the

NCLC. I'm also a member of Greenpeace and Amnesty International, but seeing as how my day job doesn't pay enough, the best contribution *I* can make is writing letters and personally soliciting our congressmen and lawmakers in the hopes that, just maybe, they'll find the time to tackle issues that, basically, appeal to absolutely *none* of their constituents—"

Christina stopped.

Just a little too late.

"Don't mean to rain on your parade," I said. "But the really interesting thing about the betta fish is that when it sees its own reflection, it will instantly attack. Smash its head up against the mirror. Over and over until it's effectively killed itself." I paused, first time seeing Christina actually listen to me. "Back there, I was actually trying to make a point about you and Dromio. Not us. . . ."

Christina's eyes softened, though not in any way that made me feel better.

"Well," she managed, voice level and reined in. "I'm going to go see the sharks being fed. . . ."

She turned away and walked down the corridor.

I listened to her footsteps recede around a corner.

Remained standing by myself. In the company of glassy-eyed swimmers and a single, solitary betta fish.

28. We Don't Listen to Desperation

The main room was a gigantic, round, two-story cylinder.
Solid concrete walls.

From my elevated vantage point, I saw Matilda and Jeremy standing in front of the aquarium's proud centerpiece. A twenty-thousand-gallon water tank, splitting the room in two. Reinforced glass walls home to a gang of stealthy sharks. Sleek bodies torpedoing back and forth, cold black eyes and teeth that sent all thoughts of betta fish scurrying for cover.

I made my way along the wall, following the winding ramp down to the main floor. Walked between a few Sunday afternoon families, smaller displays of starfish, moray eels, and meandering stingrays. Light shone down through the glass ceiling. Crisscross patterns of sunshine decorating my path.

Christina saw me approaching.
Said something to Matilda and yanked her away.
I walked up to the shark tank, looking after them.

"Why do women always go to the bathroom together?" Jeremy asked.

"To talk about us."

"You mean, you and me?"

"Yes, Jeremy," I said, looking up at a passing shark. "Every woman who has ever gone to the bathroom with another woman has done it to talk, specifically, about you and me."

"You know what I mean."

"If they haven't figured us by now, how are they going to unless we tell them?"

Jeremy sighed. Once again, something different about him. No frustration or panic, just a breath of air that hinted at deeper thoughts. Calm self-analysis as he stared into the shark tank. Pondering. Finding a small sentiment in his mind that I suspect had been fast approaching since that morning.

"Maybe we should just tell him."

I froze.

Nowhere near the surface, but inside.

A shrill kind of voice insisting that Jeremy needed to be taken down a peg or two.

"That's just desperation," I told him. "We don't listen to desperation, Jeremy."

"It's not desperation," Jeremy insisted, looking around. "Honestly, what's the point of doing this anymore?"

"He's a Blue Hawk."

"A what?"

"It's an expression," I explained, thinking quick. "It means he's a little on the shady side."

"Look, I've spent a little bit of time with him now—"

"Yes, a *little bit* of time."

"Yes, *a little bit of time*," Jeremy repeated, eyes strong against mine. "Not as much as you have, I'm *very* aware of that—"

"I haven't spent *nearly* enough time with him," I flung back. My brain hiccuped and I added, "Not nearly enough time to figure him out."

"If you haven't figured him by now, how are you going to unless he lets us?"

"Because there is more to this than just you and him."

"Yes." Jeremy's stare hardened. Wasn't going anywhere. "There's you."

"There is me," I concurred, searching for a way to paddle upstream. "But you don't really seem to think I'm a proper gauge for the situation, so how about Christina? She's got any number of problems with Dromio—"

"You haven't agreed with a single word she's said, Baz—"

"And there's Nancy—"

I stopped.

Not fast enough, and Jeremy jumped in. "What about Nancy . . . ?"

A maelstrom of activity exploded in my head. Decisions battling for the floor. Remembering Nancy's quiet descent into her drink, Dromio's past, the implicit pact of trust when she looked at me through the smoky air of the arcade and asked me,

Is this just you and me?

I shoved it all aside with a desperate executive decision.

"I went for a walk this morning, remember?" I began talking fast, whispering. "I went to the pier and walked into the bar. Nancy was there, and she was drinking. . . ."

A small shadow of doubt was crossing Jeremy's face.

Exactly what I wanted.

"Drinking what?" he asked.

"She was having a screwdriver," I told him. "She was having a drink at noon, okay? And I asked her what was wrong . . . and the subject of Dromio came up—"

"Bastian—"

"I know you want to abandon the switch, but—"

"No, *Baz.*" Jeremy grabbed onto my head with both hands. Twisted me toward the shark tank. "*Look.*"

And there was the shark tank.

Light blue water glowing with afternoon sunlight.

And through the looking glass . . .

I pressed my face close. Squinted past the underwater prowlers and caught sight of a young couple. A girl with wavy blond hair and a wide, fluoride smile. Hand in hand with an earnest seventeen-year-old. First-generation Mexican American, eyes still remembering where he came from. Genuine hope displayed in a smile of well-intentioned teeth.

"Is that . . . ?" I squinted a bit more.

"Nicole and Cesar?" Jeremy croaked.

"Oh, God."

I grabbed Jeremy and jerked him down below the glass. On our asses, both our backs pressed against the concrete base of the tank. Got a few strange looks from passing people and I tried to act casual. Smiled with misplaced charm as Jeremy dug into my shirt, nails getting ahold of some skin beneath.

"It's Nicole and Cesar!" he whispered furiously.

"I guess Cesar owes me a big one."

"Start by asking him not to talk to us!" Jeremy hissed. "Matilda and Christina are gonna be back any second!"

I looked to my right. Looked left and saw an exit leading outside.

Double doors looking to be around fifty feet away.

A hanging sign reading: KOI DECK UNDER CONSTRUCTION.

I nudged Jeremy and pointed. "There's our ticket."

Jeremy shook his head. "That's where the alligators live."

One last look to my left, and I saw Cesar and Nicole rounding the shark tank.

Arm in arm.

No time to appreciate the trouble my work had gotten us into.

I grabbed Jeremy's arm, yanked him to his feet. Walked away with swift steps toward the exit. Trying to act nonchalant, despite the fact that we were almost running. Jeremy muttering prayers under his breath as we spanned the distance in less than three seconds. Both of us slamming against the doors, stumbling out into the humid collection of winding water. Out onto a half-finished walkway. Hardly enough time to notice the majority of wooden fences had been torn down. Ten-foot gaps in safety. Nothing separating us from the alligator pits. . . .

Heard Jeremy swear, stop in his tracks.

I had no such opportunity, and ran smack into him with a solid bump.

Saw him totter on the edge of the koi deck.

One foot in the air, flailing like an unmanned fire hose.

One arm reaching out for me.

Grabbing on to my shirt.

More skin gone, but that hardly seemed to matter as we tipped over.

No difference in which one of us was Jeremy and which one of us was Bastian.

Both of us preparing for a five-foot drop into alligator-infested waters.

29. Shortly After We Didn't Die

Jeremy and I burst into Henderson's office.

Dromio and Henderson shot up from the desk. Stared at us for a moment as water freely dripped from our clothes. Off our hair, into our eyes, down our faces. Rude squishing sounds from our sneakers as we took a few more steps, Jeremy's arm around my shoulder.

"What in God's name happened to you boys?" Henderson sputtered.

"The koi deck is under construction," I replied.

"I know." Henderson reached into a nearby closet and came out with a couple of towels. "There's a sign outside that says that."

"Yeah, sorry about that. . . . The words *koi deck* had us confused."

"Could be worse, son. The only alligators out there right now are decorative plastic ones."

"Yes, I noticed that shortly after we didn't die."

"Sebastian . . ." Dromio walked over to us, concern replacing confusion. "Are you all right?"

"My ankle hurts a little," Jeremy said, toughening his voice as we sat him down. "No big deal, I've been through worse. Much worse."

Dromio asked Henderson to round up the rest of the family, then went out to the car to get us a change of clothes.

Jeremy and I were left alone. Bodies now comprised ninety-nine percent water. Towels damp and overextended, unable to do any more. Small, aquatic figurines making fun of us from various corners of the room as the water continued to drip onto the floor and form puddles.

"How's your ankle?" I asked.

"Same as it was when Dromio asked."

I let the bitterness slide. "Stands to reason."

Jeremy leaned back. Looked up at the ceiling and wiped his face. "We still have things to discuss."

"Not now."

Dromio came back with a bundle of clothes. Dumped them on the desk and sorted them out. Not a word, systematically putting together two separate outfits. He gathered one of them under his arm, pointed to Jeremy.

"All right, Bastian, you first. . . ."

Jeremy stood and limped over to the bathroom.

"Hold it," Dromio said, meeting him at the door. "We don't know what's wrong with you. You're going to need help with your pants."

"I'm fine."

"Your ankle isn't."

"I'm *fine*."

"*Now*, Bastian."

"All right." Jeremy hobbled through the door. "Screw it, let's go."

Dromio closed the door behind them.

I looked around. Not wanting to sit on or spoil anything else.

To Jeremy's credit, I didn't hear a single cry of pain from behind the bathroom door.

Nancy, Christina, and Matilda came into the office. Each one voicing their concerns. Matilda coming up to me and laying an arm on my shoulder. Hand against my face. Even Christina caved in to the situation, though her concerns were mainly limited to Jeremy and his ankle.

Henderson came in with two pairs of sandals boosted from the gift shop.

Further explanations and discussions as Dromio came out of the bathroom with Jeremy.

"Just a mild sprain," he announced. "We keep him off it, he should be fine.".

"You sure?" Henderson asked.

"Basketball, y'all." Dromio smiled. "Seen this a few times. Trust me, he's fine."

"Told you I was," Jeremy grumbled, struggling not to wince as he leaned against the desk.

"All right," Dromio said, clapping his hands together. "Field trip's over. We're getting Sebastian home. I've got some business to take care of at the Blue Paradise, so we'll drop me off there first—"

"Can I come with you?" I jumped in, automatically.

Jeremy shot me a look.

Dromio hesitated. "You sure you don't want to go back to the house and dry off?"

"I can do that here," I said, picking up my pile of clothes.

"Well," Dromio said. "Sure. Learn the tricks of the trade, certainly couldn't hurt."

Jeremy seemed to think otherwise, but he kept it to himself.

I went into the bathroom, stripped down, and toweled off. Tumbled into a pair of jeans that could have doubled as a parachute. Slipped an irregular-sized T-shirt over my head, followed by a large red sweater. Straitjacket sleeves that hung down low, and I rolled them up with considerable effort. Slipped on the gift shop sandals, and those seemed to fit just fine.

Picked up my clothes and caught my likeness in the mirror.

Stopped short.

The ridiculous size of my new clothes outbid by two words, stitched into the sweater, legible despite the tricks that reflections play on us all:

BLUE HAWKS

30. Perfect Spanish

The sun was planning its retirement as we pulled up to the Blue Paradise. Easing into dinnertime, and there wasn't much of a crowd outside. Dromio got out of the car. Christina and I clambered out of the back, let Matilda slide out. Matilda took the wheel and drove off with the rest of our group. Dromio went inside and left me standing on the street.

Left me standing next to Christina.

"You're still here," I told her.

"It's not because I like you."

"Good to know," I replied. "Because you haven't really made that clear at this juncture."

"I've got work to do and my ride's picking me up here."

"Okay."

"So you don't have to stand next to me anymore."

"I know."

I stood outside for a while longer. Sky turning orange and pink as twilight crept in among the buildings of historic Wilmington. Slight chill in the air. Nightlife making its gradual appearance. Both of us looking around as though expecting something to happen. Neither one of us willing to comment on it.

A green Volvo pulled up across the street, turned off its engine.

"*There* he is." Christina sounded relieved.

A blond-haired, well-built man in his late twenties stepped out of the car. Dressed in a suit and tie, wire-framed glasses, and Converse sneakers. He locked up the car and made his way over. Overly efficient smile as he approached.

"Boyfriend?" I asked.

"Used to be," Christina replied, waving.

"Any reason you still hang out with him?"

"He's an assistant Spanish professor at UNCW, and I need him for my work." She cut off our conversation as her ex stepped onto the sidewalk and gave her a large hug.

Large, long hug.

I watched, waited, and finally they split apart.

The man instantly turned to me. Looked down from his six-three vantage with a clear sense of his own superiority. Perfect teeth eating away at every feature in his face. A lifetime of books and seminars giving him clear dominion over me. . . .

"Anton . . ." Christina linked her arm with his. "This is Jeremy."

Anton shook my hand. Grip so firm, it bordered on assault. Pumped my arm with that same one-note grin plastered on his face. Even before he opened his mouth, I knew there would be an overbearing, territorial lilt to his voice.

"Christina's told me a lot of awful things about you." He laughed.

Kidding on the square, Anton meant every word.

"Interesting," I deadpanned, then switched to Spanish. *"I don't think she's mentioned you once."*

Anton wasn't expecting the comeback or the language. That smile froze on his face, and he dropped my hand. Tried his own hand at the romance language. *"Well, we go way back."*

"Way back to when she broke up with you, or even further?"

"Hey!" Anton switched back to English. "I broke up with *her*!"

"What!?" Christina had been watching the whole exchange, confused right up until she decided to get indignant. "*I* broke up with *you*, Anton!"

"Let's not talk about this now, Christina."

"You brought it up!"

"*He* brought it up!" Anton pointed at me.

Christina looked between the two of us, debating who to be more angry at. Turns out it was a draw and she just rolled her eyes. "Screw it, I don't care. Let's just go, Anton."

Shouldered her bag and walked across the street.

Anton chased after her, and the two continued to squabble as they got into his car. I watched them drive off, trying to make out Christina through the back window. Squinting to catch one last glimpse. Not finding any real comfort in whatever victory I had just achieved.

Standing alone outside the Blue Paradise, twilight in full bloom around me. Temperature sinking into a cool kind of depression. About to give the outside a rest when a hand fell on my shoulder, spun me around, and brought me face to face with Bradley.

Affectionately known to me as "Trevor."

His gang of walking polo shirts congregated behind him. Wide, confident grins. I was starting to get sick of seeing those. Tired of broad shoulders. Done with imitation tough guys, I had more pressing things to attend to.

"I told my boys we'd find you here," Bradley said, the only one with any spark of fire in his eyes. "You didn't tell us you were Johansson's kid."

"My apologies," I said flatly. "Christina never introduced us."

"So it's Christina now?"

"It's always been Christina. Could be that she was simply more interested in telling me."

"You want to start with me, Johansson?" Bradley got in my face. "You want to come to *my* town and take away what's rightfully mine?"

"What's *yours*? What the *hell* are you talking about, Trevor?"

Bradley shot out a large hand, fingers wrapped all the way around my arm. Jerking me closer to him. Nose to nose, his breath a warm gust of cinnamon gum. "My name ain't Trevor, it's Bradley, and you be sure and *tell* the goddamn surgeon it was Bradley who turned your smart-ass, little face inside out!"

"Hey!"

Bradley turned to the Blue Paradise entrance.

I followed suit and saw Chaucer standing there. Arms at his sides, fists at the ready. Knees bent slightly. Face of a killer outshining his purple silk shirt and dark red blazer. Hard stare closing the distance between him and the Bradley gang, each one already folding like cheap chairs.

"Let him go and get out of here."

Bradley's grip tightened, cutting off circulation.

"You hear what I just said, you overstuffed teddy bears?" Chaucer's voice made it clear he was done playing around. "I got the police chief inside, and you can finish your midterm papers from jail, if that's what you really want."

Once again, the gang began to move on.

Past Bradley, who held on to me just long enough to say, "You can't hide behind your daddy's friends forever, Johansson. . . ."

He tossed me aside with a mere flick of the wrist. I stumbled back as he made his way down the block. An almost visible cloud of steam rising from his body.

"You all right?" Chaucer asked, brushing me off as though I had actually fallen.

"Is Hunt really inside?"

"Off duty. He was just an afterthought, though. Had those little boys outnumbered with the color of my skin."

"Guess some things never change."

"Perception is my weapon." Chaucer smiled. "Your father's waiting inside."

I took one last moment to look down the street.

But Bradley had already vanished into the early shadows of night. Unfathomable rage still lingering. Floating around me, a sense that there was more to this than a simple, overblown dispute.

Coming into town and taking what was rightfully his. . . .

I shrugged it off and went in to see what my father and his friends were up to.

31. Dad

The Blue Paradise didn't serve dinner on Sunday nights. Slow time for business, especially during the off-season. Dromio called it *downtime*. End of the week. A night for people to have a drink, sit a spell, and reflect. Enjoy conversation without the hubbub and bustle of a crowded restaurant. Let the evening go wherever it was headed.

Relaxed moments singing along with the jukebox.

Not a lot of customers just yet, and Dromio let me stand behind the bar, serve up a few drinks.

Schooling me in the art of the pour, measures, and mixtures.

"Now, just a dash of curaçao," Dromio instructed as I gave a half-second tilt to the bottle. "That blue stuff spreads through a drink like porn stars on the page, so be sparing. And now stir. . . ."

I popped a straw in, gave it a whirl. "So rum, vodka, gin, tequila, triple sec, and blue curaçao."

"The Blue Paradise special."

"Isn't this just an electric lemonade?"

"With one small difference," Dromio told me, dropping a cherry in the pint glass. "We don't call it that."

I laughed and presented the drink to Chief Hunt.

He thanked me and went to tip his hat before remembering he was off duty.

"So what's the verdict?" Dromio asked him.

Chief Hunt took a sip. Smacked his lips together and raised the glass up over his head. "A perfect Blue Paradise if I've ever had one. Like father, like son, right here in this drink."

"Congratulations, Jeremy." Dromio gave me a slap on the back. "You done good."

"Thanks, Dad."

A sudden silence fell over us.

Chief Hunt looked up from the blue skies of his drink.

Vision split between Dromio and me.

The jukebox changed its song, and a strange look crossed Dromio's face.

"That's the first time you've called me Dad."

It was true. Previous choices to steer clear of the *d-word* now abandoned. Forgotten in a single moment of what felt like absolute purity. Slipped out somehow, and I tried to stay away from who I really was. Keep it simple, distant. Trying out the moment like a new skin. Letting it grow on me because it had simply felt *right*.

Because it was actually the first time in my entire life I had ever said those words.

"Thanks, Dad."

Chief Hunt surreptitiously slid on down the bar.

Dromio put a hand on my shoulder. . . . "Want a drink?"

"Isn't that illegal?"

"Sure." Dromio pulled out a rocks glass. "So is you serving drinks. Hunt's willing to look the other way, so I say *why not?*"

I nodded. "Why not?"

Dromio pulled out another rocks glass. Went down the bar and poured us a couple of drinks. He came back, handed me mine. I held it up to the light. Ice and a translucent, light brown liquid.

"Scotch," Dromio told me.

Held up his drink for a toast.

Kept it simple, just the chime of glass.

I took a tentative sip of my drink. A sweet sensation slid over my tongue and down my throat. Ice-cold drink somehow warming my stomach. Aftertaste spreading in my mouth. Tasting the scent of new, wooden floors. First time drinking scotch, it was turning into quite a day for me.

"How'd things go with Christina?" Dromio asked.

"We don't see eye to eye on a few things."

"Like what?"

"Everything. . . ." I took another sip. "Including you."

"Mm."

"Yeah, she's not wild about you."

"Not everybody is going to like you in this world," Dromio told me, pulling out a pack of cigarettes. "You have to expect that. Respect that, even."

"Just about everyone seems to like you." I accepted a cigarette, a light. "Christina seems to be the only one who doesn't."

"Christina's a good kid." Dromio nodded to himself. "She does a lot of good for a lot of people."

"So do you."

Dromio lit his cigarette. Chased the smoke away with a silent exhale, looked out over his kingdom with watchful eyes. Taking time with his thoughts, absently stirring his drink with an index finger.

"How long have you been doing this?" I asked. "Helping people."

"Since before I left your mother," Dromio replied, plain English. "I doubt she told you anything about this side of me, but I don't blame her. I helped people, sure, but I don't know if I meant it. What my motives were. Wasn't until after I left her that I really started being myself on purpose."

I sensed there was no tiptoeing in this conversation. Decided to free up some questions that had been wandering my mind. "Was she the only one?"

"What do you mean?"

"A lot of broken hearts in Chicago?"

"Yes." Dromio showed no remorse, no pride. Just the facts. "Guilty as charged."

"So what changed after my mother?"

"When you're young, you tend to act . . . irresponsible at times. But leaving it at that would be a cop-out."

"How so?"

"There's only one thing that makes you kids mindless perverts. There's only one thing that makes you substance abusers. There's only one thing that makes you reckless. There's only one thing that makes you violent. There's only one thing that makes you a pack of shameless liars. But the only thing, the one difference between us and you . . ." Dromio took a drag, a drink of his scotch. "The one important difference is that when adults do those things, we don't call it that."

It was as though Dromio were confessing on behalf of the whole adult world. "A Blue Paradise?"

He nodded. "A Blue Paradise. . . . You see, Jeremy, age stopped being about biology a long time ago. Especially here in America. It's no longer enough to just get old. Most adults just age, they never really stop being young, childish. Growing up is something you have to choose. It can happen at any point in your life, but it usually takes something very big to get the ball rolling. . . ."

Dromio looked down into his drink. Brought it up to his lips, paused. Followed through with the motion, took a swallow. "I never really thought about it until now, but . . . when I abandoned your mother, that was it. The big event, that was the moment I decided to grow up."

For the first time, I noticed that Dromio wasn't very tall. Maybe five-eight, possibly a half-inch shorter. I took a drink, staring at him over the rim of my glass. Wondering how he managed to hide that. Make himself large enough to fill an entire room with just one look. One footstep, one well-placed word. Something I wanted to understand. Be a part of.

My second skin tightened around me.

Random shapes in my mind searching for a complete picture. . . .

"You really played basketball?" I asked.

"Feel like taking a walk down Dromio Lane?" He smiled, snubbed his stogie in the ashtray.

"I hear it's a pretty tough neighborhood," I admitted,

lighting another cigarette. "But I also hear it's worth it just to say you made it through."

Dromio's smile turned to laughter. "You're some piece of work, kid. . . . Yeah, I played ball. Got to know the bench real well, but a team is still a team."

"Nancy tells me you guys had a real sense of camaraderie. *Blue Hawk, through and through.*"

"Indeed." Dromio mimed shooting a foul shot. He followed the imaginary trajectory with his eyes. "Swish."

"Were your teammates as wild as you?"

"Wilder," he told me, suddenly serious. "The only problem with the Blue Hawks was the ridiculously high turnover rate. Always getting into trouble, always getting suspended. There are probably more ex–Blue Hawks flying around Chicago than any other college team."

I scrawled a few notes across the back of my mind. "That many Blue Hawks, it's a wonder one of them didn't get to my mother first."

"Yeah, it got real bad for a lot of guys. By the time I was kicked out of college, they were thinking of reforming the entire scholarship system. But as I said, that was after I got the ax—" Dromio paused. Made room for more memories before shaking his head. "Fortunately, nothing like that's going to happen to anybody in this family. There's a good old-fashioned trust fund waiting for Matilda. And now that you've come back to claim your place, one for you, too."

"Does the name Chester A. Arthur mean anything to you?" I asked abruptly.

Dromio took a moment. Concentrated and zeroed in after

about a full thirty seconds: "Twenty-first president of the United States, right?"

"Dromio, I—"

"Excuse me a second. . . ."

Dromio traveled down the bar, over to a waiting customer. I watched him chat it up. Smile and let the Johansson charm flow like wine. Trying to see if I could spot something. Some other sign, anything that might explain the coincidences and contradictions doing battle in my mind. . . .

"Penny for your brain," Dromio said, unexpectedly by my side again.

I realized my thoughts had wandered off. As they came rushing back, I noticed they had brought reinforcements along with them.

"Permission to speak freely?" I asked.

"I believe we already were."

"I was just thinking that this week is going to end at some point."

Dromio nodded, used to such musings at his age. "Way the calendar works."

"Truth is . . ." I paused. Slowly beginning to think I truly had a right to all these hopes. "Come the end of the week, I'd rather stay here. With you and Nancy. And Matilda."

Dromio's eyes betrayed a mix of concern and clandestine thoughts. "But you have to go back. You know that, right?"

"There's really nothing waiting for me back home."

"You can't mean that."

"I do."

"Don't family count for nothing?"

"Yes, my mother and I get along swimmingly." My brain

screamed a sudden reminder, forced me to add, "And my father, too, we get along fine, but . . . everything else . . ."

I trailed off.

Dromio stared at me, and I was surprised at what I saw. A cast-iron look, intense and direct. Mind saying something, words staying put. He reached over and took my drink. Switched it with his. Took a sip of mine, then motioned to me.

"Drink."

I frowned, puzzled. I lifted, took a sip.

Grimaced.

Recognized a trace of what I had been drinking. Not a very big one, though. A far more bitter taste hijacked my senses, rose through my nostrils. Piercing, only a hint of my previous experience with scotch.

"That's Dewar's," Dromio told me. "Brand name, but far from the best. Matter of fact, there's a lot of bars use it as their house whiskey. Now this"—Dromio lifted what was once my drink—"is Johnnie Walker. Blue label. A bottle goes for well over a hundred dollars. Two-ounce pour of this goes for thirty dollars at the Blue Paradise. It's among one of the premier Scotch whiskeys on the planet."

He paused. Gave me a moment with my bottom-feeding drink.

"I get it," I said, wondering if this was what they meant by humility. "Be thankful for what you have."

Dromio shook his head. "Far more important: be thankful for what you have, no matter what you once had. 'Cause one eventually becomes the other, and there's times when all it takes is one week. . . ."

He polished off my drink. His lesson lowering my stature even further, but more than that . . .

The way he said it . . .

"Can you read palms?" I asked.

Dromio laughed. "Am I getting too heavy for you, Jeremy?" He laughed some more, though it did little to break the solemnity of the moment. "Don't let me bring you down, I don't know what's going to happen to you any more than a weatherman knows what tomorrow will bring—"

"I'm going to have to interrupt this for a second." Chaucer had slid up to us, smiling at me with an apologetic cadence to his words. He turned to Dromio, grew serious. "They're waiting. . . ."

"I don't know if tonight's a good night." Dromio threw a glance in my direction. "You think you can host it?"

"This man's come a long way," Chaucer said. "I can host, but he's come to do this with you."

"Think he'll understand?"

"I know he will. That's not really the issue, though."

I watched the two, in the tall weeds. No idea what was going on.

"So I should sit in a little," Dromio mused.

"At the very least." Chaucer had suddenly become a legal counselor. "Explain the situation, take an hour or two, and he'll go home happy. Besides, he's not the only one there, right? Plenty to be had. . . ."

Dromio nodded. He straightened his hair and turned to me. "Business, Jeremy. I know this is a little abrupt, but can you busy yourself awhile?"

I was still wandering the surface of another planet, but even so . . . "Sure."

Dromio nodded. Walked off with Chaucer without another word. I saw the two disappear through an unmarked door. Left me behind, commended to my own contentment.

"Hey, kid!"

I glanced over. The fat man from yesterday's lunch had just squeezed himself onto a pair of bar stools. Tightwad turned cash machine. "What do you recommend tonight?"

A quick look around showed me to be the only one behind the bar.

Chief Hunt had also vanished at some point, and I thought, *why not?*

I straightened myself out. Wandered over, trying my best to imitate Dromio's understated swagger. Picked up a rag and wiped the counter in front of him. Tossed a coaster onto the glass surface.

"I make a killer Blue Paradise," I offered, borrowing a quick flash of Dromio's smile.

"Never actually had one before. What's in it?"

I winked. "Nothing but pure originality."

"Well, okay!" The fat man smacked his meaty hands against the counter, chubby smile pleased with my reply. "Let's get this evening started right!"

Not a bad idea, and I turned my back to him.

Took down a collection of bottles.

Poured, poured, poured, poured, poured, and stirred.

Popped a cherry in there and blessed it with a name all its own.

32. Wrong Room

Almost eight in the evening, and the scene hadn't changed.

Most seats at the bar occupied, though not a single face from an hour ago. Chaucer had come back five minutes after disappearing with Dromio, took over for me. Calling out a few favors every now and again. Bottled imports, shots of bourbon or tequila, the occasional Blue Paradise. As my actions became automatic, I began to wonder. Nancy had called in earlier, spoken to Chaucer. I overheard him saying that Dromio would be back home around nine-thirty.

And it got me thinking.

About his conversation with Chaucer.

About what Dromio did with time spent away from his family, all the scouting I should have been doing on Jeremy's behalf.

In a little less than a day, these had slowly become my own concerns.

We ran out of blue curaçao after a while, and Chaucer asked me to get some from the stockroom.

"Through there . . ." He pointed to the unmarked door at the end of the bar. "Down the hallway, second door on the right."

I nodded and went ahead.

Into a long corridor with white walls. Cardboard boxes resting beneath pale, naked light bulbs. Blue Paradise sounds barely filtering in. Stale air. The motionless quality of a cool, dry place.

I walked down to the second door on the right. Trying to make as little noise as possible, library footsteps. Put my hand on the doorknob. Stopped short of turning and listened. . . . Dromio's voice. Dull and muffled as though speaking through a sweater. Silence. Another voice, also incomprehensible. A pause, followed by laughter and groans.

Coming from the second door on the left.

I walked over and put my ear against the solid metal.

More conversation, casual.

I looked back at the stockroom.

I muttered Chaucer's instructions under my breath. Changed them slightly. Repeating this revised version over and over until I was finally able to convince myself:

"Down the hallway, second door on the left . . ."

I pushed down on the handle and entered with every intention of looking thoroughly stunned.

Turns out, it wasn't that far of a stretch. . . .

Wasn't too hard to believe the card table. Green felt top in the middle of a room with cinder-block walls. Multicolored clay chips stacked and spread out. Blue-back Bicycle cards distributed. Wasn't too hard to believe Dromio seated there, shuffling a second deck. Wasn't hard to believe the O'Neill brothers seated across from each other, twin faces surprised at my sudden entrance. Wasn't even that hard to believe Chief Hunt. Long arm of the law, dressed in his civilian clothes. Cigar kicking around in a nearby ashtray.

A strange turn of events, no doubt.

But hardly surprising.

Hardly as surprising, no doubt, as being confronted by a wide-eyed Mr. Wallace. Same formal wear as he wore in the classroom. Same head of hair, raging wildfire contained by a lengthy ponytail. Same sharp blue eyes behind wire-framed glasses. Seated at the table, I could only assume he was wearing the same trademark combat boots on his size-twelve feet.

Same everything except for the fact that he was in Wilmington.

At the Blue Paradise.

In a little back room, seated at a card table, with Dromio and a cast of characters who all knew me as Jeremy Johansson.

Dromio didn't miss a beat. Ever the gracious host, he rose from his seat, smooth-called me. "Hey there."

My eyes darted to Wallace, then back to Dromio. "Sorry. I was looking for the stockroom." I started to back away. "I thought it was the second door on the left, guess I was wrong."

"No, don't worry about it." Dromio sounded pleased. Even cheerful as he put an arm around me and brought me over to the table. "Come on in, we're all friends here. You already know Hunt and the O'Neill brothers. . . ."

They gave me a lukewarm greeting, nods, and indefinite hand gestures.

"And over here we have Mr. Wallace. . . ."

Sweat broke out all over my body, heart caving into my chest.

"Mr. Wallace, this is Jeremy King. . . ."

Mr. Wallace finished taking a sip of his beer.

Eyes on mine.

Set the bottle down, rose out of his seat.

Held out his hand and smiled. "Jeremy King . . . fancy meeting you here."

I automatically shoved my hand out. Grabbed on to his, pumping furiously. "Not nearly as surprised as I am, Mr. Wallace."

And all faces around the table expressed just what I was feeling.

"You two know each other?" Dromio asked.

"Jeremy King is in my first-period American history class," Wallace said, reaching across the table and clapping me on the shoulder. "Also my fifth-period British lit class."

"Small world, this world," Hunt mused, blowing out cigar smoke.

"Getting smaller by the day," one of the twins agreed.

"If you see Sebastian," Wallace added, "tell him thanks for getting Olaf to look after the dogs."

I murmured a misplaced thank-you. Nothing more to add. Too much energy spent fighting through my confusion. Mouth shut as Mr. Wallace sat back down, going along for the ride. Gathering the cards and shuffling.

"So, you going to grab a chair?" Dromio asked me.

The room suddenly felt much smaller. "You mean play?"

"You know the rules to five-card draw?"

"Yes. . . ."

Dromio pulled up a chair and sat me down next to him. Pulled out a thick wad of money and thumbed through a couple hundred. Motioned for Hunt to count out some chips. Hunt slid a stack of red, blue, and yellow across the table as Dromio handed him a thousand in cash. Sat down next to me and finished shuffling the second deck.

"Yellow chips are twenty-five dollars," Dromio explained. "Blues are fifty, reds are hundred. Antes are twenty-five, and there's no limit on what you can bet. . . . Don't let these jerks boss you around, either. Stand tough, kiddo."

I nodded mechanically and tried to follow along as Dromio dealt. Sharp snaps of the wrist, pure elegance as each card slid to a halt in front of each gambler. Each gambler leaving their features behind. Eyes replaced with opaque windows. Lips set like I beams. Not a glimmer of emotion from any of the men at the table. Fear, hesitation, joy, and exuberance all gone and buried.

No way to tell who was holding what.

No way to tell why Mr. Wallace had kept it all to himself.

No way to tell who was who.

A table of unmoving statues, and to my left, Dromio spoke up:

"Your bet, Jeremy. . . ."

I checked my hand, and saw four jacks and a two staring up at me.

Laid my cards on the felt and told my face to shut up.

Reached for a stack of red chips and made my move. . . .

33. Bad Eyesight

It was almost ten when we got back to Dromio's.

The rest were in the living room playing Trivial Pursuit. Jeremy was stretched out, leg propped on a pillow. Meeting and greeting, checking up on the ankle, and during the flurry of activity, I stole away.

Had to try Big Niko's three or four times before getting Olaf on the phone. Kitchen going full steam on the other end. Could hardly make out his words over the kitchen's mighty roar, but it turned out to be a quick, seamless conversation.

He wanted to meet in person.

Tomorrow. Wrightsville Pier. Three in the afternoon.

Didn't give me any other hints, not a half foot of rope to hang on to.

I hung up the phone.

Sat on the edge of Matilda's bed and stared into space for a while. Unmoving in the company of several overflowing bookcases. Yellow walls covered with framed certificates, blue ribbons, and awards. Shelves proudly displaying trophies of scholastic excellence.

"Like father, like not-quite-son," I mumbled to myself.

Rubbed my eyes and flopped backward on the bed. Feet still planted on the off-white carpet. Stuffed animals surrounding me, offering their sympathies.

"Jeremy?"

I shot up, back to seated position.

Matilda was in the doorway, jeans and a red jacket. Oval glasses magnifying concern. "Are you all right?"

"I thought you were all going out to the beach."

"Yeah, Sebastian's foot is doing a lot better. . . ." She walked in and bent down under her desk. Rummaging around on all fours. Bare feet dusted with sand. "I just came back to get a few supplies."

"Sorry about being in your room." I coughed. "Dromio told me you have your own phone line."

"Yeah." She stood up, now holding a flashlight and a red metal box. "Didn't want anyone listening in on you and your girlfriend, I guess."

"I don't have a girlfriend."

"Christina said you have a girl named Sara."

I motioned toward the red box. "What do you have there?"

"A bit of an impromptu chemistry set. There's an unusual amount of phosphates in the sand tonight. Can't take a step without lighting up the beach. I thought I'd collect a few samples. If there's too much, it probably means we're getting runoff from the inlets somehow. Not good, because if phosphate levels go over nine point nine, then you end up with unfettered algae growth. That leads to low dissolved-oxygen levels, which chokes out other organisms, and . . ." Matilda's voice trailed off, and she looked down at her feet, ashamed. She clicked the flashlight on and off a few times, sighed.

"What's wrong?"

Matilda shook her head. "Sorry. I get a little carried away with . . . you know, with the heady stuff."

"Don't say that."

"I guess I'm really just a geek."

"Do you play the cowbell?"

"No."

"Then you've got nothing to worry about."

"God, who talks about phosphates?"

"I was enjoying it, really."

"That's nice of you to say."

"Facts aren't really nice or naughty."

"You think it's strange that Christina's my best friend."

"No . . ." I picked up a stuffed giraffe and turned it over in my hands. "From what I can gather, you're an insanely smart girl. And Christina's not only smart, but very selective. I'd be proud to have her as my sidekick."

Matilda gave a timid laugh. Mouth covered to hide metal wires.

Wandered over to the bed and sat next to me.

Hands pressed down beneath her thighs, knees together. One foot on the other.

"You like Christina, don't you?" she asked. No direct eye contact.

I made a so-so motion with my head. "I'll admit, she's a tall drink of water."

"What's that mean?"

"Nobody's ever actually explained it to me." I smiled.

Matilda didn't.

Rubbed her feet together, swallowed. "Do you think I'm a tall drink of water?"

I turned to her. Quarter profile staring any which way but mine. Finding something familiar in Matilda's search for acceptance. Emotions resting on her sleeve, all things beneath her skin stuck to the surface. Tense shoulders and shaky breaths.

"Matilda . . ." I put my hand on her shoulder.

She looked over, cautiously. Reluctant. Shimmering eyes magnified behind her glasses.

I took them off, folded them.

Smiled down at her.

Saw one of her eyes trying to adjust, cross slightly with the other.

"I have really bad eyes," she managed.

I shook my head. "Whereas I'd say you just have really bad eyesight."

Matilda bit her lower lip. Top bunk jutting out to keep her smile secret.

Laid her head sideways on my shoulder and drew close, arms around me.

I felt some tears soak into my shirt. Not a choke or sob from Matilda, and I managed to get one of my arms around her. Rubbed her back gently. Chin resting on her head, windswept hair rubbing against my neck. Trying not to let despair get the better of either one of us.

We stayed that way for a few minutes.

Trophies and stuffed animals keeping a modest distance.

Sound of a cartwheeling ocean outside the window.

Matilda sniffed loudly, breaking the spell. She pulled away and wiped her eyes, nose. Sniffed a few more times, eyes at red angles from each other. Flushed face wet with tears.

"Hey," I said.

She turned back to me with one last sniff.

"Have a giraffe," I offered, extending the stuffed animal.

Matilda let her lips curl up and laughed, braces and all. She took the giraffe from me and held it close. Rocking just a little bit, the timeless reassurance of all things soft and fuzzy. The giraffe remained as it was, nose nuzzling her cheek.

I unfolded her glasses and slipped them back on her face. Gave her a kiss on the cheek. "Go and get your phosphate on."

She laughed again. Picked up her flashlight and red metal box. Stood and walked to the door, pausing for a minute at the threshold. She turned, leaned against the frame and regarded me with an inquisitive squint.

I playfully mimicked her squint.

"It's nothing," she said, shaking her head. "I actually do think it's strange that Sebastian is your best friend."

"Why's that?"

She tilted her head to the side. Looked up to the ceiling, thinking. . . . "It just seems that you're much more his friend than he is yours."

I blinked, tried to let it slide. "Sebastian's just got a lot going on right now."

"I can tell." Matilda straightened herself. "I certainly wouldn't want to be around when he blows."

She smiled and went on her way. Galloping down the stairs, full recovery it seemed.

I stood and walked over to Matilda's window.

Looked out onto the beach. Moon still low on the horizon, an immense, brilliant nickel washing over the water. Shining down on the figures of Dromio, Nancy, and Jeremy. Shadows in the sand. Horsing around, Dromio's arm around Jeremy's long-lost shoulder. Attempting some kind of three-legged race, each one holding a crutch beneath their free arms. Nancy running along with them, shouting out words of encouragement. Lively cries and the sounds of mirth all headed my way.

Up through Matilda's window.

Thinking I heard Jeremy's own laughter, but only because it was the one sound I didn't recognize.

34. Interesting Night

The moon had worked its way up there.

Same beach, different lighting.

Later on in the evening hours, an entire house just as I had found it that morning.

Fast asleep.

Darkened windows looked down on the terrace from above. I leaned against the railing, arms crossed, staring out to the sand. Trying to see if I could somehow pick out which footprints were Dromio's. Looking for some kind of phosphorous glow. A sign, maybe. Voices rustling in the dune grass, the occasional flash of light from a seafaring boat. Rum and Coke by my side, cigarette in my other hand. Two vices joined by their creator, affectionately known as *Grandfather Thought*.

And I had to admit, the day's experiences had me talking to myself.

It was all there. My many encounters with Christina. The seesaw of what Dromio would tell me and what I actually wanted to hear. Matilda and her immobilizing intelligence.

Nancy sitting in a two-bit bar, drinking screwdrivers from a plastic cup. Mr. Wallace, a sudden accessory to my song-and-dance. Coincidence revolving around Blue Hawk anecdotes. Jeremy's sudden rebirth. Bradley's psychotic ranting. Olaf's trap already set, no clear way to get out of it. Sara and my mother stuck in the middle of it all.

My mental list blurring.

Notes caught in the rain, words running together now.

Nothing short of an illegible mess.

I was having trouble thinking back to anything before Paul's suicide threat. . . .

Paul, I thought, ocean tumbling along with my thoughts. *I should probably call him.*

The very thought swept aside by a screen door sliding open. Heels on the wooden terrace, and Christina was standing by my side.

"Back already?" I asked.

"It's almost midnight."

I nodded, took a drag of my cigarette. Caught a glimpse of her in my periphery. Hair down, curls bending to the wind's will. Looking straight ahead, eyes lost in a vanishing point over the ocean.

"How'd it go?" I asked.

"My ex is a jerk."

I nodded, took a sip of my drink. "Rough day at the office, sounds like."

"You have a good night?"

It was as close to a normal conversation as we had gotten. "Interesting night."

"You play in Dromio's poker game?" she asked, instantly

adding, "Don't act shocked or anything. It's nearly legendary around these parts. The only place a guy can enjoy an old-school five-card-draw game. The whole family knows about that poker game, everyone does. Dromio even knows that they know, but he acts like—"

"Yeah, all right." I couldn't muster up any kind of real retort. "Dromio is the Devil's chief of staff, yes. He doesn't even bother to level with his own family, I get it . . ."

I kept looking out over the water. Expected Christina to leave. Destiny didn't seem too interested in us as a pair.

"I'm sorry," Christina said.

"What are *you* sorry about?" I asked, instantly regretting my tone.

"I'm sorry I've been so hard on you."

I waited.

Christina kept it to herself for a bit. Standing straight, hands holding on to the railing. "More than that, though . . . I'm sorry I've been so hard on Dromio. I'm not going to lie about how I feel but . . . he *is* your father. I don't have any right burning down the house before you've moved in. You're his son, and I let that get away from me . . . and I'm sorry."

It was unexpected, but welcome. "Thank you."

"I suppose I just think of you as older than you are, sometimes."

I gave a half laugh, looked over at her. "Come again?"

"Shut up, I'm not repeating that."

I caught her smiling and gave into a definite laugh.

Stomach somersaulting, letting me know I was enjoying this.

Christina turned her back to the ocean. Propped her

elbows on the railing and leaned back. Pulled a bit of hair out of her eyes. "I suppose after dealing with Anton I can tolerate anything."

"Huh . . ." I hoisted myself onto the railing. Sat side by side with Christina. "All this nonsense about how you can't stand phonies, and it turns out you used to date one."

"I was young."

"When did you two start going out?"

"A year ago."

"Seriously, what did you see in that guy?"

Christina didn't answer right away.

"Oh . . ." It was appallingly obvious. "Yeah, well the guy's got quite a body."

"You have a body."

"I'm not going to think about whether or not that's a compliment."

"A little on edge, there?"

I shook my head. "Tired."

"What are you doing tomorrow?"

Her tone was far too recognizable. The ringing quality of someone in need of a favor, something that rekindled a feeling I desperately needed to come back, to feel *in control* again. Didn't want to let on, and I jumped off the railing, picked up my drink. Walked a few feet away and placed it on a small glass table. Sat down on a webbed lawn chair, and lit another cigarette. "What do you need?"

"You speak fluent Spanish."

"That I do."

"I need an interpreter."

"Hold up." I held up my hand. "Didn't you minor in Latin American studies?"

"Yes."

"And you never once took a single Spanish class?"

Christina bristled, crossed her arms. "Of course I did."

I crossed my own arms. Crossed my legs, ready to enjoy what I was about to hear.

"All right, fine!" Christina threw her arms in the air, walked over to me. "I couldn't conjugate verbs. And I also had a problem with where to put the little accent thing. Vocabulary was another small obstacle. And my accent was"—Christina sat down next to me—"well, German, somehow."

"Did you, in fact, learn anything at all?"

"I learned how to cheat off my neighbors."

"So you're not so lily-white after all."

"Are you going to help me or not?"

"Absolutely."

"Good." She reached out and took hold of my hand. "Thanks, Jeremy."

It felt good to have her next to me. Hip to hip. The flip side of Christina, an odd sensation in that near-midnight moment. Forgetting that I was eighteen and she was twenty-one. Side by side, face close to hers. Eyeing the path of her fingers as they brushed a few lost strands of hair from her face. Lips parted slightly. Holding her hand in mine, something worth feeling.

I inadvertently rubbed my thumb against her palm.

"I'm going to bed," she said abruptly. Stood up and

straightened her shirt. "You should, too. We've got work to do tomorrow."

Christina stalked off and slid the terrace door open.

Stepped through and closed it.

Not even a chance to say good night.

One hundred percent sure that, out on the beach, each and every sand crab was laughing at me.

"Shut up," I told them.

Put out my cigarette and abandoned my drink for the sake of much-needed rest.

PART FIVE

MONDAY

35. Stay on Your Toes

There were no dreams, and somewhere a hand was trying to shake me from sleep.

I groaned lightly, eyes still closed.

Last night coming back to me in layered recollections.

The smell of Ivory soap.

"Christina?" I managed to croak out.

"She's busy not liking you. . . ."

I opened my eyes and shot up.

Morning. Nine-fifteen, judging from the digital clock. Jeremy sitting next to me in bed, a pair of crutches in his lap. Fully clothed. Freshly showered, too. Damp hair a darker shade of blond. Lucid eyes, a smirking expression on his face that he could have only stolen from me.

Suddenly remembering what Matilda had said last night.

I certainly wouldn't want to be around when he blows.

I sat up straighter. "You told."

"Not yet."

"Then why the face?"

"I was born with it." Jeremy repositioned himself on the bed. "You didn't come out last night."

"Had some things to think about."

"Dromio?"

"Yeah, actually. . . ." I was once again fully operational, choosing my words. "Certain things have come to my attention. A picture is starting to develop, but I'm still not sure what it is."

"Find out anything at the Paradise last night?"

"Too much. . . ."

I did a little give-and-take. Recounted my conversation with Dromio. What he had learned from abandoning Brenda, certain details of his past. Took out a few details as well. Things that concerned me, my own investigations. Skipped down the page to the poker game.

Halfway through, Jeremy told me to go brush my teeth. . . .

We walked into the bathroom, and I told him about Mr. Wallace. Jeremy listened, leaning against the wall. Face replaying last night's every emotion. Confused as I still was. Unanswered questions happy to find another person to taunt.

"Why would Mr. Wallace not—"

"Believe me, Jeremy"—I spat a shot of white into the sink—"I've gone through every last question."

"How long is he staying in Wilmington?"

"Wallace said it all depended on how much money he made at the game."

"How did you do?"

I rinsed my mouth, spat one last time. "I lost it all."

"You lost a thousand dollars!?" Jeremy bounced from the

wall, crutches sent clattering on the floor. Stood on one leg for a few seconds, thought about it. "Who'd you lose to?"

"Mr. Wallace. All of it. One hand."

"So Wallace is going to be staying around here awhile."

"Stay on your toes."

"Thanks for the advice. I'll see you later."

"Where you going?"

"Dromio's taking us sailing."

"Any reason I wasn't invited?"

Christina popped into the room. Hair up, mascara and lipstick. Black-framed glasses I had never seen before perched on her nose. All traces of our last conversation buried under a well-fitting dress suit and flesh-colored stockings. Poised and prepared as she looked me up and down.

"You look like crap," she said.

"Thanks." I put my toothbrush away. "If just one person notices, then it's all been worth it."

I turned on the shower as Christina called out, "Get ready and let's go!"

"I'm sorry!" I called back over the shower. "I can't hear you!"

"We're going to be late!" she yelled. "Get moving!"

"What!?" I put my hand to my ear. "I'm sorry, there's water!"

"PRICK!" Christina yelled, storming out of the bedroom.

"Well." Jeremy pulled a sailor's hat from his back pocket and put it on his head, made as though to leave. "I can see things between you two have improved somewhat."

"Jeremy, wait. . . ." I tried to find another way of asking, but came up short. "Is there any reason I wasn't invited sailing?"

"Guess I just didn't get around to telling you."

Nothing funny about it. Serious as a heart attack.

"Yes," I told him. "I know. There's things I haven't told you about."

"I can tell."

"And I can tell that you're not going to keep this under your hat for much longer."

"You're right."

"There are some things I have to look into."

"Like what?"

"I can't tell you."

"Then I can't promise you anything."

Small sprinkles of water escaped over the shower curtain. Dropping on the tiles, walls, and counter. Scattered drops landing on Jeremy's sailor hat, eyes unmoving beneath the brim. Water beating down in a frantic drumbeat. Situation slipping, fuse already lit. Whatever luxuries were left in our friendship, time was no longer one of them.

The meter was running.

"So," Jeremy said. "What happens now?"

"Now I ask you to give me until tomorrow," I began, certain that things wouldn't hold much longer than that. "Let me do what I have to do. Whatever happens, come tomorrow evening, we come clean. See how all this ends."

"Why should I?"

There was no longer anything astonishing about the hostility in these conversations. "Because, like it or not, I got you down here. Without me, you wouldn't be standing in this bathroom, deciding whether or not to repay every last thing I've ever done for you."

"So now I'm just another name in your database of favors owed."

"Friendship doesn't seem to be doing all that much for me."

"Then today is my day with Dromio...." Jeremy bent down and picked up his crutches. Stuffed them under his arms. "We're going sailing now. Later on we're going to the Blue Paradise for dinner. And I don't want you anywhere near us. Figure out what you have to. Find out whatever you like, but do it on your own. That's the deal, you can take it or leave it."

Steam was rushing past us.

Out the door, escaping through the window.

Emancipation.

And Jeremy had me trapped. A tough-guy act that had somehow become very real to him. Second skin topped with a ridiculous hat that did nothing to soften the intensity. Making sure I knew he was staring right at me, *into* me if that's what it took. The upper hand, every last card stacked in his favor, checkmate. Sending me to the mat by an unseen left hook.

"If I see you again today," Jeremy concluded, "then I'll know your answer."

He pivoted. Got a good grip on his crutches and swung out of the bathroom.

Stopped.

"Stay on your toes," he advised.

Reached back and closed the door behind him.

36. Where It All Comes From

I threw on a white dress shirt, black pants, and a thin, like-colored tie.

Christina already had the engine to her chalk-white Volvo running.

We left Dromio's house at ten, though a good part of my mind was still back at the ranch. In the bathroom, dealing with Jeremy. Struggling to accept an entire day of exile. Any number of possibilities, a research scientist without a grant. Trying to map out some kind of counterstrategy. Figure out if there was anything I could do to gather just a bit more information to tip the scales one way or another.

Fifteen minutes into the ride, Christina reached over and smacked my shoulder.

"Hey!" She honked the horn as well, looking over at me. "You want to pay attention?"

"Huh?" I came to, realized I had missed a large part of the rundown.

"Jeremy, I'm going to need your full participation here. This isn't a class trip."

"Right." I tried to shelve my problems. Crumple my to-do list and focus. "Where are we going?"

"Okay . . ." Christina sighed. Rubbed the bridge of her nose beneath her glasses. "Let me start over again. We're dealing with migrant farmworkers. Mexican field labor. There's over a million of them in this country, spread out over all fifty states. They're the ones harvesting the fruits and vegetables found in supermarkets and restaurants, that's where it all comes from. It's not like they grow on trees, Jeremy."

"Actually, some fruits do," I corrected, putting on my sunglasses. "But I'll forgive the muddled cliché."

Christina clenched her jaw and continued. "We're talking about entire families working in fields under some of the harshest conditions. Men, women, children even. Breathing pesticides, living in unsanitary conditions. Just a couple of years ago, the U.S. Department of Health and Human Services found that migrant farmworkers have an estimated forty-nine-year life expectancy. You or I are lucky enough to be part of a national average that puts us at seventy-three. Infant mortality claims every thirty out of a thousand, twice that very same national average—"

"Christina—"

"And do you know what the wholesale price of a bushel of tomatoes is?"

"No, but you've made your point." I sighed, cracked the window open a bit. Saw signs of urban life slowly disappearing. "What are we going to do when we get there?"

"We're going to have a meeting with a group of these men and see if we can convince them to allow their wives to acquire driver's licenses."

"I still don't know what's going on."

"The key element of survival is family," Christina explained. "Everyone works, everyone stays together. A family unit, there's no other way to survive. To the men, a driver's license means more independence for the women. Hence, a threat to the family unit. Add to that the tradition of a patriarchal people, and certain conflicts arise."

"But that family-unit argument's not entirely without merit. What am I going to say to convince them otherwise?"

"Okay, first of all, migrant workers live in a state of constant displacement. The average family moves every three months. From Carolina, up to Illinois, to Washington State. Pickup trucks are like tools, indispensable, and so are drivers. Second, more drivers helps to delegate responsibilities. A good deal of these children go to school, and the nearest ones are sometimes over an hour away. Women who can drive won't destroy these families, they'll make them stronger. And third, *you* aren't going to say anything. You are *translating* exactly what I tell you to, as is said. No charm, no double-talk. And take off your sunglasses, they'll think it's disrespectful."

"As disrespectful as, say, wearing glasses you don't really need?"

Christina pushed her glasses up her nose and ignored the allegations.

"You know how Ambrose Bierce defines the word *immigrant*?" I asked.

"Jeremy—"

playing it cool

"An unenlightened person who thinks one country better than another."

"This is *not* the time," Christina flung at me. "This is not the time for cynical aphorisms, and it's certainly not the time for humor. This is important, and you'd better recognize it!"

Enough outrage in her words to make me want to eat mine. I couldn't even manage an apology as Christina composed herself. Checked her watch and turned off onto a smaller stretch of back road.

"We've got a lot to prepare," she said. "Listen up. . . ."

Two hours and another world later, we had arrived. Slowing the car down as we pulled close to a sweeping field, row after row of endless green speed bumps. The bent figures of distant workers dotted the landscape. Hardly a tree or spot of shade for miles, an overhead sun taking extra pains to make its gospel known. I squinted through my window. Saw tractors and pickups stationed up and down various inlet roads, unpaved and dusty. Christina pulled up to one of them. Came to a stop as a foreman with nearly pitch-black skin held up his hand, signaled for us to roll down our windows. Tipped his baseball cap upward and told us we had to park here. Something about a group of trucks headed for the packaging plant.

Christina nodded and parked alongside the road.

We got out and were immediately questioned by the foreman. Polite enough to stave off conflict, but clearly not prepared to allow unsolicited visitors. Christina proved to be all business. Produced several documents, phone numbers, written agreements. I got a few looks from the foreman and he asked us for our IDs. I felt the bottom fall out from beneath me, quickly said something about leaving my license at home. Christina shot me a fast and furious look, improvised with some kind of bureaucratic back talk. The foreman quickly grew tired with it and waved us through. Christina gave a polite thank-you. Took back her license, motioned for me to follow her, and we made our way down the uneven road. Down the endless path, leaving her air-conditioned vehicle behind.

Christina walked with steady strides on sensibly chosen shoes.

I continually lagged behind, unable to keep from looking around. Unable to count the amount of workers, phantom shadows swinging gardening tools, yanking at roots. Past a long conveyor belt, a massive assembly line of people on either side. Occasional children aiding the adults, five-year-olds dressed in jeans and bright-colored T-shirts. Standing on crates and toolboxes so that their small arms could reach passing vegetables. Pick out the ones unsuitable for market. Hardly eye level with the work they were doing.

My footsteps slowing some more.

Forgetting how to walk with the intention of arriving somewhere.

Searching for a fit, someplace in my head where this all might make sense.

I managed to regain momentum, catch up to Christina.

"Aren't there child-labor laws in this country?" I asked.

"They're voluntarily helping their family," Christina answered. "Learning a trade. There's a very good chance they'll still be doing this when they're older."

My footsteps slowed again.

A few open-air trucks rumbled by, filled to capacity with stacks of fresh produce.

By the time they had passed, we had made our way beyond the tended fields. Into a small clearing of sparse grass and protruding rocks. A few children ran around, playing hide-and-seek among a line of small, tightly bundled shacks. Low to the ground. Long strips of wood nailed in disorganized rows, noticeable gaps in the walls. Round roofs like turtle shells, covered by layers of light blue tarp.

Christina nudged me and nodded toward a pickup truck.

Underneath it was a little girl. Lying on a small blanket, taking advantage of the shade. Looking up at us with curious eyes.

I knelt down and asked what her name was.

She didn't answer.

Knowing I could get away with it, I introduced myself as Sebastian.

She held up a small toy chair. Crudely fashioned from twigs and strings.

I told her it was a very nice chair. Asked where her father was.

She pointed past me.

I looked over my shoulder and saw a few men leaving one of the shacks. Quiet and ready, eyes more stoic than any I had ever seen. I stood and straightened my tie. Overwhelmed by their numbers and days of endless labor etched in their faces and thick, callused hands.

"Jeremy," Christina whispered. "I need you on your best game."

I nodded. Forgot about Ambrose Bierce and got myself together.

"Ready when you are," I told her.

Christina nodded and led me over.

Nearby, the whirring sounds of machinery remained an intrusive presence as we introduced ourselves to everyone. Settled in for a long session of negotiations. Stuck to my role as translator, the go-between.

Word for word.

Not one sly maneuver or attempt at improvisation, because the day was growing hotter, and I knew this wasn't my show.

37. The Price of Fame

I didn't say very much on the car ride back. Concentrated on leaving experience behind with distance.

Three o'clock fast approaching.

Christina dropped me off around the corner. Drove off with a pleasant wave.

I didn't return it, just watched her car turn left onto Cape Crane Road. The time had come for my meeting with Olaf, and I headed over to the pier.

Up the wooden ramp toward the arcade. My hand on the rail, careful of splinters and loose nails. Taking it slow, casually rising above sea level. Preparing myself with each footfall. Playing the impending conversation in my mind, searching for an edge. Coming up empty each time. Imaginary exchange always ending the same way. No better than a condemned prisoner wondering what to wear for his execution.

Halfway up the ramp, I finally gave it a rest.

Put on a pair of sunglasses and slipped into character.

Slipped into the dingy arcade.

Strode through the smoke, drawing the barman's attention.

"Need any bait?" he called out.

I ignored him and walked out onto the pier.

Left foot, right foot, sturdy boards beneath each one. Past couples and bored teenagers. Locals, occasional outsiders. Lonely men, hand in hand with domestic six-packs. Lost in thought. Watching the waves rush in to meet the land, lose momentum, and return to the ocean. Closer and closer to the end, where fishermen stationed themselves for hours at a time. Lines cast, rods grounded. Sitting in beach chairs that were always too big or too small. Waiting around in rubber boots and windbreakers. Day after day, weeks on the calendar nothing more than mere formalities. . . .

Even with his back turned, it wasn't hard to spot Olaf.

Standing at the very end, facing the ocean.

Wind playing games with his hair.

I came up next to him, rested my arms on the railing.

Cloudy sky above and over the horizon, a spectrum of pure gray.

"Well, here you are," Olaf said. "Sara's little helper."

"You ready to tell me what this is all about?"

"You know, speaking of little helpers . . ." Olaf turned away from the ocean. Leaned back, put in a good stretch before continuing. "I ran into your friend at Big Niko's. That little twerp Paul Inverso. Says you should call him first chance you get."

"Not all that interested, Olaf."

"Maybe he wants to offer you a loan."

"How much money do you want?"

"Not one for small talk, are you?"

"Not today."

Olaf nodded. Reached into his jacket and pulled out a small, square tin. "Schimmelpenninck?"

"I don't know what that is."

Olaf opened the tin. I looked over and saw a row of ten small cigars, lined up like sardines.

"Don't smoke those," I told him.

"Me neither." Olaf took one out, clamped it between his teeth. Put the tin back in his jacket and struck a match. "I just figure now's the time to start."

"I don't have all day, Olaf."

Olaf lit the cigar. Puffed, tilted his head back, and added a bit more gray to the air around us.

"Twenty-five large," he said.

I tightened my stomach, didn't let it show. "Twenty-five thousand?"

"Twenty-five with three zeros, yeah."

"I don't have that kind of money, Olaf. Don't know where you think I'm going to get it."

"Try dipping into that savings account of yours."

I backed away from the railing, faced Olaf.

Looked around, not a single fisherman showing any interest.

"How do you know about that money?"

"People talk. . . ." Olaf puffed on his Schimmelpenninck. "Rumors. Whispers from the treetops, and you'd be amazed how easy it is to find out what's true and what's not. . . . Nobody's ever safe, Bastian."

"I've been saving that money for over five years."

"You should have thought about that before poking Sara."

"That wasn't me."

Olaf just laughed. "Yeah, then how come your mother forged the signatures on the permission forms? Maybe you can tell me. Or maybe she can when I go to her for the money you won't cough up."

"All right, you win." I took off my sunglasses. Not necessary anymore. Everything now exactly as I had envisioned it. No room to maneuver, caught between Sara and my mother. When the time came, I would have to pay the piper, but for the moment . . . one last play. "That's going to take some time."

"You've got till six in the evening tomorrow. We'll meet on the top floor of the parking deck across from the Hilton. Have my money in twenties, please. No fifties."

The store was closed, and Olaf was ready to go. He tossed his cigar off the pier, took a few steps past me, then turned. "Speaking of the Hilton, I understand you're in pretty tight with that crowd. Get me a room for tonight, and make it a suite. Proud to say, I'm feeling very lucky right now."

"You got a last name?"

"Stevenson," he told me, winking. "Six o'clock tomorrow, Sebastian."

About-face, and Olaf was walking back down the pier.

I waited twenty minutes before following.

Back through the arcade, same familiar bait conversation.

Out and down the ramp.

Still walking tall. Defeated, but keeping all things from

watching eyes. Even managed to fool Christina, waiting for me in the parking lot. Business suit abandoned for jeans and a black Amnesty International T-shirt. Hair back down and glasses gone.

"How'd the meeting go?" she asked.

"I thought you had paperwork to do back at the house," I replied, walking up to the car and lighting a cigarette.

Christina shook her head, held out her arms. "Just went back to get changed."

"I like what you've done with the place."

"How did your meeting go?"

"As planned."

"Dromio and the others aren't back from sailing yet." Christina opened the driver's door. "Want to wait for them back at the house?"

"Are we friends?" I asked her abruptly.

Christina looked confused, closed the door. Frowned over the edge of the hood. "What are you talking about?"

"I need a lift to the Hilton."

"Sure." Christina opened the door again. "You're acting weird, you know that?"

I nodded, opened the passenger door. Tossed my cigarette aside and slid into the seat.

"Don't forget to buckle up," Christina said.

I reached back and pulled on the strap. Got hold of the clasp and snapped it into place as the car started up.

Safety first.

38. Is There Anything I Can Do?

Christina and I walked through the revolving door and into the lobby.

Classical music drifting along the cavernous space. Chandeliers hanging down like giant earrings, a uniform glow spreading to all corners. Understated murmurs of conversation from hotel staff and customers as I crossed the dark red carpet to the front desk. Waited for service. Took some mints out of a glass jar. Offered one to Christina, who accepted with a quiet nod.

A twenty-some woman in a red uniform appeared behind the counter. Well-trained smile and close-cropped blond hair coming out of nowhere. "May I help you, sir?"

"Yes, you may." I smiled back. "I'd like a room for tonight."

"Very well, sir. . . ." She gave the computer a few keystrokes, looked up. Saw Christina and looked back down. "For two?"

"A suite, actually. But it's for a friend of mine."

"Well, we can do that. . . ." A few more jabs at the keyboard.

"I'll just need your credit card number to reserve it until he makes the payment."

"I'm actually going to be paying for it."

"And will you be paying with a credit card?"

"Cash."

I caught Christina's perplexed expression out of the corner of my eye.

"And what is your friend's name?" the blonde asked.

"Olaf Stevenson."

"Just for the one night?"

"Hopefully, yes."

"The total is four hundred twenty-five dollars."

I pulled a thick stack of twenties and hundreds from my pocket. Felt Christina's eyes pressing against the tender as I thumbed out three C-notes. Six twenties. Reached into my pants and found a five. Counted it all out once more before handing it over.

"Very good, sir. . . ." The blonde counted the money herself, then flashed her pearls again. "When your friend gets here, he can register at the front desk and pick up his key."

"Thank you so much." I smiled for one last question. "Where are your pay phones?"

"Across the lobby, by the bathrooms."

I pocketed the rest of my money and went back across the lobby.

Christina was next to me. Sidestepping in order to face me. Repeatedly losing her balance as she pummeled me with questions about the room, Olaf, the money.

"Seriously, where did you get it?"

"Dealing drugs."

"What?"

"Just kidding." I stopped in front of one of the pay phones. "I won it in Dromio's card game."

"But just this morning Sebastian told me you'd *lost*."

"Yeah, well, screw Sebastian," I said with a little more venom than planned. "I don't have to tell him everything. I lost it all on the first hand, crushed by four queens. Dromio bought in for me again, then I made it all back and then some. Learned a valuable lesson about the company of strangers, a happy ending for Jeremy Johansson, now"—I picked up the phone and started dialing—"could I please have a moment here?"

Christina blinked, held back further questions. "Sure."

She stood next to me for a moment longer. Blinked again and went into the ladies' room. The door swung closed behind her, and in a matter of seconds, my mother was on the line.

"Yeah, I'm real busy, Bastian." Statement illustrated by what sounded like absolute chaos in the background. "Two deadlines and a meeting with senior staff, what can I do for you?"

I got right to the point. "That last check you were going to deposit for my college fund?"

"Yeah, I'm sorry, I still haven't had a chance—"

"It's all right," I said, hurrying things along. "Don't do it."

"What, why?"

"I can't get into it right now."

"All of a sudden, you just don't want me to deposit the check?"

"That's right."

"Bastian, *what* is going on in Wilmington?"

"There is *nothing* going on."

"Are you in trouble?"

Funny question, it turned out.

I looked away from the phone and saw Cesar walking toward me. Toward the bathrooms, directly next to me. No sign of recognition in his eyes. Not just yet, but seconds away from opening his arms and calling out my name across the well-dressed lobby.

"Everything's fine, Mom," I said quickly. "Gotta go, bye."

I hung up and started for the men's room.

Realized that wouldn't do and changed directions.

Ran into the ladies' room instead. Slammed the door behind me and leaned against it, just as a nearby stall opened and Christina stepped out. Eyes widening as she jumped back, screamed. Hand over her mouth for just a moment before crying out, "What the *hell* are you doing in here?"

I glanced around, prayed it was just the two of us. "That is an excellent question."

"I know!"

"And there is an excellent answer."

Christina crossed her arms, tapped her foot.

"Be sure and remember to wash your hands," I advised her.

"Get out."

"Right."

I reached behind and pulled on the handle. Bowed like a servant retiring for the evening and backed out. Let the door close and cautiously turned. Took three steps into the lobby, froze on the fourth. Ten yards away was Cesar's better half, blond hair in her eyes as she walked toward the bathrooms, searching through her purse.

I whirled around, retracted my previous steps.

Realized there was no sanctuary to be found in the ladies' room.

Pivoted, crossed my fingers, and crashed into the men's room door. Shoulder-first, right arm covering half my face. Enough visibility to see Cesar at the sinks. Facing away from me, rinsing his hands. A long row of stalls on the opposite walls and I charged. Ran into the first one I could and slammed the door behind me. Sat on the toilet seat with bated breath. Heard the water turn off, then nothing.

Waited.

From beneath the stalls, I saw a pair of sneakers walk up to my door.

Cesar's concerned voice asking, *Everything all right in there?*

I shot out my hand and locked the door, and mumbled something.

"Sir?"

Silently cursing all who were good of heart, I began to whimper. Fake a few choked sobs. Lowered my voice and put an arm over my mouth. "I'm fine."

"Are you sure, sir?"

"Fine." I switched to a grief-stricken Georgian accent. "I'm fine, please. Don't worry."

I thought that might be the end of it, but: "Is there anything I can do?"

playing it cool

"No," I sobbed, trying to scare him off. "I . . . I just caught my wife goin' upstairs with another man."

"Oh . . ." Awkward silence. Feet turning away. Then turning back. "I'm sorry about your wife."

Goddamnit. "It's all right, son. You just go on ahead, I'll be fine."

"I have a friend back home, Sebastian, and he always says—"

"Screw yer friend!" I screamed out, kicking at the door. Saw Cesar's feet jump back and pressed it further. "Screw yer friend, Sebastian don't know nothin'! YER FRIEND'S FULL OF SHIT!"

"All right, sorry, man. . . ." Cesar began to back away as I continued to sob. Just loud enough to get him out. Just soft enough to hear the door open and close.

I instantly dropped the act and leaned back against the wall. Rubbed my face. Kicked my feet out and waited. Let out a long, winding breath and looked up at the ceiling. Closed my eyes. Felt the stall walls closing in as I grudgingly admitted there was nothing to be done. Asking my mother not to deposit my last check had been nothing short of delusion. A sorry imitation of taking control. Olaf would get his twenty-five thousand tomorrow, and I would be cleaned out.

And strangely enough, there was a sad kind of relief there.

To come out the other end of this with me as the only casualty . . . my mother and Sara in the clear. Olaf out of my hair. A lot of explaining to be done, but at least it would be over. A good notion to get used to. Jeremy would be shedding

235

my name in a little over twenty-four hours. It would have been nice to have had my questions about Dromio answered before losing all my money to Olaf. Have my own financial safety net to fall back on, but for the time being . . .

Push come to shove, I had still done what I'd come here to do.

I heard the bathroom door open.

The sound of high heels approaching and a knock on the door.

Opened my eyes.

Wasn't ready to smile about any of this, but there was one potential salvation in the middle of all this madness.

"Christina?" I called out.

"Jeremy?"

"What are you doing in here?"

"Putting the scales of the universe in balance," she replied. "Are you all right?"

I got up from the seat and opened the door.

Christina greeted me with a worried look. "I didn't know where you had gone."

"People do their best thinking in bathrooms." I went over to the sink. Washed my hands slowly. Deliberately. Thirty seconds of soap and hot water, like they teach you in kindergarten. Christina walked up next to me, and I turned off the water.

Looked at her.

Noticed for the first time that she had a small birthmark on her lower neck.

"You want to have dinner with me?" I asked.

Christina wasn't expecting it. "I thought we were having dinner at the Blue Paradise."

"You hate that place, anyway."

"Yeah, but . . . what about Dromio?"

I smiled, best I could, knowing it would have to wait for tomorrow. "I know where he lives."

"Are you sure everything's all right?"

"It'd be a lot better if you had dinner with me," I told her. Serious as I had ever been. "For real, it'd be a hell of a lot better."

"All right."

"What?"

She reached up next to me and pulled down a paper towel. "I said, all right . . . let's go out tonight."

The door opened and Christina spun around.

A bizarre, hollow kind of vacuum in the air as Mr. Wallace walked through the door. Took one look at us and continued on his way. Not a hint of surprise or recognition. Just made for a stall, walked in, and closed the door behind him.

All of it just fine by me.

I took the towel out of Christina's hand, still clutched to her chest. Dried my hands and headed for the door. Held it open for her and made a sweeping motion with my other arm. She followed her cue, stepping through and asking me where I wanted to go.

"Anyplace dark," I told her, and the two of us crossed the expansive lobby. Feet gliding over the carpet. Doormen wishing us well through the revolving doors. Out onto the streets of Wilmington, walking east, away from the sunset.

39. Honest Boy

Christina took me to a reasonably upscale bar and grill.

The host seated us at a cozy booth near the bar. Electric lanterns accompanying each table, giving everything a warm, intimate feeling. Quiet atmosphere, televisions on mute. I was almost able to ignore the walls covered in fishnets, plastic porpoises, and other eyesores.

Relax and enjoy my last dinner as Jeremy.

Not a lot of business, and the waiter was by our table instantly. "Hey, Christina."

Christina looked up from the menu, warm smile. "Hey, Tom."

"How was your weekend?"

"Two days long, just like the last one."

"A lot of that going around. What'll you have to drink?"

"Corona, Tom."

My turn came next, and I asked for a rum and Coke.

"Can I see some ID?"

"I keep my wallet in my car," I told him.

"So where's your car?"

"I keep it in my wallet."

"He's eighteen," Christina told him.

"So he doesn't qualify for senior discounts," Tom said, scribbling in his pad. "Corona and a Cuba libre."

He went to get our drinks. Left me with a smirking Christina, who was clearly pleased with herself. "See what a little truth can get you?"

"You trying to make an honest man out of me?"

"Honest man? You can't even get a rum and Coke without my help, I'll be impressed if I can make an honest *boy* out of you."

I pulled out a cigarette, threw the pack on the table. "It's not lying that bothers you, is it?"

Christina took a moment to consider this. I lit my cigarette and she slid the ashtray over my way. Watched me through the smoke. Absently tonguing the corner of her mouth. "No."

"So tell me."

"There are some people who just shouldn't lie."

"Like who?"

Tom was back with our drinks. Corona for Christina. Rum and Coke for me. Probably sensed an interruption and disappeared without taking any orders. Let us tend to our drinks. Christina removed the lime from her beer and handed it to me. I took it without a word, dropped it in my glass. Welcomed sips as we found the way back to our conversation.

"Like who?" I repeated.

"People like you."

"How do you know I'm people like me?"

"I'm very good at this kind of thing."

"Show me."

"Well . . ." Christina picked up her own drink. Took a large swallow of beer, licked her lips. "First of all, you're far too certain of every last thing you do. You act like the front man of a small-town band, oblivious to anything outside your tiny, little fan base—"

"Christina—"

"Oh, and don't even try to deny it, Jeremy." Christina took another swallow. "You're so full of yourself, grandeur has delusions of *you*."

"Ouch. You just come up with that?"

"No, been wanting to use it for a while."

"I wasn't going to deny anything. . . ." I put out my cigarette. Took down half of my drink, playing catch-up. "But if you want to really impress me, you're going to have to do better."

"I suppose *you* could do better?"

"I know I could."

"Tom!" Christina shouted across the restaurant. A few people at the bar glanced up, then remembered their contract with cool. Tom had no such luxury and he hurried over. No opportunity to inquire, Christina already pointing her finger at me. "Tom, this kid's twelve years old. He has no business drinking alcohol."

"So, two more, then?" Tom asked.

"Chop-chop."

I wasn't entirely prepared for her new incarnation. Unsure of how a playful Christina fit into the general scheme of the cosmos. Enjoying it nonetheless. Drifting further and further away from my problems. Back burners on high. Making up for missed moments as Christina leaned forward, crossed her arms, and smiled.

"All right, then, Dr. Joyce Brothers. You tell me about me. I dare you."

"Too easy."

"Oh, but now I'm curious."

"Too bad." I lit another cigarette. "I want a clean slate."

Christina held my challenging stare. Arms still crossed on the thick, wooden table. Deliberating. Gathering information before putting me to the test. "That guy, at the bar."

I didn't look away. Eyes locked with hers. "Red sneakers, black leather jacket?"

"What can you tell me about him?"

"What do you want to know?"

"Let's start with what *you* know."

"He's put himself together very deliberately," I told Christina. "Slicked-back hair. Clean-cut, I can almost smell the aftershave from here. Flashy watch. Shoes without a smudge or scuff. Hasn't even taken off his leather jacket. But it doesn't cover how antsy he is in his own skin. Peeling the label off his beer. Snubbing out his cigarette before it's done, because he can't think of anything else to do with it. . . ."

"I'm not sold," Christina said. "If he's so into how he looks, how come his pants are ripped?"

"They're not," I retorted. "He's got gaps in his jeans, but not a single loose strand hanging anywhere. Especially down by the cuffs, that's where wear and tear starts. He put the holes there himself, it's called tear and wear. It's all planned out."

"So how come he forgot to wear his belt?"

joaquin dorfman

"He's drinking a Bud Light."

Christina's face became one sarcastic revelation: "I am enlightened, Master Dōgen."

"May I continue?"

"All right." Christina got off her horse and rejoined me. "So he's drinking a Bud Light."

"And he's been eyeballing the snacks nonstop. Hasn't reached for a single one, though. The guy's resisting. On a diet, and his belt just hasn't caught up. Not that he's obese. Poor guy could possibly manage one or two notches, but that's even more embarrassing than not wearing a belt at all. Probably just broke up with his girlfriend. Everyone leaves a relationship fatter than when they came in."

Tom stopped by with fresh drinks.

Christina eagerly started in on hers, ready to engage. "Has it occurred to you, even once, that *best-dressed* is perfectly acceptable if he's waiting for his date?"

"He's not waiting for anyone," I told Christina. "Not for anyone in particular, at least. If he were, he'd be randomly looking over to the entrance. Wondering when she's going to show up. As it stands, he's looking over only when someone walks through it. Checking out the action. He's waiting for someone, but that someone is anyone. And he wants to look his best when she walks through that random door."

"Maybe he's expecting a buddy," Christina speculated. "His wingman."

"Hasn't checked his watch once."

"Maybe our guy just got here."

"Check this out. . . ."

Christina shifted her eyes. Watched on the sly as our en-

242

tertainment signaled for another beer. One more bottle opened, and the bartender served it up. Placed it in front of him and knocked on the counter, twice.

"See that?" I helped myself to another hit of my drink. "Buyback. Nobody gets a drink on the house unless they've had at least three."

"Our guy could be a regular, favorite of the bartender's."

"He's got cash on the bar. A regular would have a tab running, wouldn't even need to ask."

"So he's had a few." Christina sucked back the rest of her drink. "Doesn't mean he's looking for action. Could be here to watch the game."

I laughed. "What game? Bartender's changed the channel eight times and not a peep from this guy. Plenty of surfing to be found on the beach, that's not why he's here. He's lonely. He's scared. And he's hoping to cure one condition so he won't have to worry about the other."

Christina tried to play it off. "I guess we'll never know. . . ."

I took it as victory and leaned back. "If that's the case, then how could you ever know the first thing about me?"

"All I said was that people like you shouldn't lie."

"And I remember asking what kind of people I was."

"And now I'm telling you"—Christina's voice dropped to a more sober register—"that people like you shouldn't lie, because people like you can get away with it."

I nodded, took it under consideration. "How do you know I can get away with it?"

"Because I don't believe you've lied to me once since we've met. . . ."

I stared into my ashtray. Tapped cinders into the beggar's

glass palm, looked back up. "Then how can you ever be certain about me?"

Christina's eyes maintained their gravity. "By getting to know you better."

"How's that working out for you so far?"

All I was given was a taste of guarded anticipation. "Sara's not your girlfriend?"

"No."

"Promise?"

I paused. Turned my glass around on the table. Clockwise, counterclockwise. Safecracker. "I only met Sara around a month or so ago. I'd see her in the hallways, she'd see me. A few words here and there, not much. She came to me with a problem, and I did everything I could to help her. Still am, in fact. . . ."

Thoughts of Sara continued to surface, words forming a first-time confession to both Christina and me.

"But she's such a great girl, somehow more real than what you usually get in high school. I don't know how, but she's ended up meaning a lot to me. . . ."

I shook my head. Thought back to what seemed like someone else's recollection.

"The night before I came here, she showed up at my house. She tried to kiss me. Well, actually, she did kiss me, but . . . for all the affection I felt, I couldn't deny that all I ever really wanted to do was help her. I feel like there should be more to it, but there wasn't. . . ."

I looked up. Surprised to see Christina wearing an expression of solemn understanding. Close to empathy.

"Sara's not my girlfriend," I told her. "It'd be nice, I know it would, but she's not the one. . . ."

Christina nodded slowly. "Is there anything else you haven't told me?"

"No."

I watched her sigh, lean back in her seat. Reach for her Corona, finish it off. She put the empty back on the table and regarded it. I kept my lips locked. Unfamiliar with these moments, distinctly aware of a slow emergence. None too sure what it was, or if it even had a name. Turning words over in my head. Recognizing nothing apart from our silence as it settled over us. . . .

Christina looked over at the bar.

Gave our red-sneaker friend the once-over.

Looked back at me and raised an eyebrow. "So is there anything I should know about me?"

I touched up my face with a smile and replied, "You enjoy having wine with dinner."

Christina picked up the drink menu and offered it to me. "It's just possible you really know what you're doing after all."

I accepted my task without a word. Opened the wine list and searched for a proper selection. Eyes scanning over bottles of red and white. By the glass, by the bottle. Four hundred dollars in my pocket, and the prices were no match for my ill-gotten gains.

40. Interlude IV

Way I heard it from Dromio was this. . . .

The day had taken them from sailing, to the Blue Paradise, to a bowling alley near Topsail Island. Dromio and Jeremy versus Nancy and Matilda. Strikes and seven-ten splits, sodas and snacks amid the clatter of pins, spontaneous cheers, and low-end gutter balls.

Jeremy had just come through with his first strike of the evening. First strike of his life, in fact, and Dromio's cry of triumph echoed over all thirty lanes. The women shook their heads as the men gave each other high fives. Even scores on both sides, an unexpected comeback in the making.

"How about that!?" Dromio did a bit of a victory dance in front of his wife. "That is what we, in the industry, call a strike!"

"No way!" Matilda yelled back. "There's no way this is Sebastian's first time bowling!"

"Yeah!" Nancy agreed, downing her drink with a grin. "Bastian's just another cheap hustler!"

"A cheap hustler in very good company!" Dromio announced, putting an arm around Jeremy.

"That's right!" Jeremy beat his chest with a solid fist. "This is Illegitimate Son Number Two, right here!"

"They're everywhere!" Nancy screeched, drawing attention from several other bowlers.

Matilda collected their empty bottles and paper plates. Announced that she was going to get more drinks. Nancy followed her on tipsy feet, leaving Dromio to total up the score. Bending over, scratching out arithmetic across the overhead projector. Didn't notice that Jeremy had sat down across from him. Not until Dromio put down his pen, looked up, and saw him staring.

"Something wrong, Sebastian?"

Jeremy gave his lower lip a bite. "I was just thinking about Jeremy."

"Don't worry about him." Dromio sat down next to Jeremy and lit a cigarette. "I think spending time with an older woman's going to do a lot for that kid."

"Wasn't worried about him," Jeremy assured him sullenly. "Just thinking."

"What about?"

"About what happens if things work out between you two."

"Why wouldn't things work out between us?"

Jeremy stared off into the next lane. Watched a large, barrel-chested man roll a perfect strike. Raise his thick arms above his head. Bulging sandbag muscles, psychotically gleeful eyes. The conquering hero striding back to his woman and planting a large kiss on her neck. . . .

"You can't always know what a person's about," Jeremy said. "You can try, but the moment you think you do, that's the moment something changes. Sometimes that's the moment everything changes."

Dromio nodded, contemplating. "Took me several lifetimes to figure that out."

"So things change . . . and come tomorrow, there's more change. And more change waiting after that. It only seems like a matter of time before someone's going to find out something they don't like."

Dromio sighed. Flicked some ash off his shorts. Curled and uncurled his toes, the back of his sandal smacking repeatedly against his heel. "You know, Sebastian . . . When I got Jeremy's telegram, my brain tripped itself up just how you're describing it. I'm a different man than the Dromio who left Brenda King to the wolves. Hell, not even Brenda King. Just poor, defenseless Brenda. And when I had to come face to face with that part of me, all I could think was . . . I have to tell Nancy. I have to tell Matilda. I drag this old Dromio back out of the closet and throw his ass down on the mercy of the court."

Jeremy kept his eyes on the nearby bowler.

Secretly hung on to every last detail of his father's admission.

"But it finally didn't have anything to do with them," Dromio continued. "Every last emotion turned out to be purely about me. I was the one who had to come to grips with this. This was *my* past, *my* dirty little secret. And its only real power was the fact that it was, indeed, a secret."

Dromio turned to Jeremy, who remained straight-faced. "My son and I will always have newer challenges to deal with, despite the fact that things have *already* worked out between us. Just like you said, every day more and more change. . . . This is what we do when we step into battle."

Jeremy gave up a small, uncertain laugh. "I'd say *battle* is a little overdramatic."

"And I'd say *battle* is giving us all the best of it."

As if on cue, the conversation was pierced by a yelp and the sound of bottles breaking.

Neither of them saw just how Nancy had lost her grip on the bottles. All of a sudden, she was on the floor. On her ass, surrounded by a liquid moat of beer and soda pop. Shards of glass baring their teeth at the feet of the bowler with the sandbag muscles. Already shouting as he stared down at the wet patches on his pants, minute drops that had sprayed over his girlfriend's legs. Towering over Nancy, veins dangerously close to making their escape.

Matilda standing to one side, rooted to the spot.

Jeremy was out of his seat in a heartbeat. Already in character. Method living as he stepped up to bat.

Got right into the gorilla's face. "Watch your mouth, pal!"

"Your mom here needs to watch her damn step!"

"I slipped," Nancy managed, a bit disoriented.

"Back off!" Jeremy ordered the gorilla. "It was an accident!"

"What damn difference does that make?" The gorilla was having trouble deciding who to focus on. "Look at my pants, the woman's got me looking like an asshole!"

"You don't need her to make you look like an asshole, asshole!"

"Better watch *your* mouth, boy. I'll make you eat your *teeth*!"

"Well, come on!"

In the midst of all this, Dromio rushed to Nancy's side. Helped her to her feet and told her to take Matilda aside. Grabbed ahold of Jeremy just before fireworks turned to dynamite. Pulled him away, past lane after lane of gawking players. Gave a nod to the manager as he marched Jeremy through the front door and a few steps out into the parking lot. Let him go abruptly. Gave Jeremy a moment under the building's neon glow.

Jeremy waited, fists balled up. Face defiant, trying to project his rage anyplace that would take it.

"That was real big of you, Sebastian," Dromio told him. Hands out, soothing gestures. "Thank you for defending Nancy. I appreciate it. But I think you might have flown a little off the handle, there."

"I should have kicked his ass," Jeremy muttered.

"That guy in there outweighs you by several thousand elephants!"

"I'm not afraid of him."

"Well, you should be!" Dromio insisted. "A drunken monster like that can send you to the hospital with a shattered nose or a broken jaw! You ever seen a guy with his jaw wired shut?"

Jeremy shook his head.

"Well, it *sucks*." Dromio paused momentarily. Didn't elaborate. Exhaled loudly, then continued. Reserved now, emotions back in the toy box. "You don't have to leap buildings in a single bound, Bastian. You don't have to be more powerful than a locomotive to do what's right. This is kid stuff."

"Hey, look!" Jeremy was indignant with conflicting instincts. "I wasn't about to let that jerk get away with what he said!"

"And while you were busy not letting him get away with it, *I* was the one helping Nancy to her feet. Making sure *she* was all right. You get in this guy's face, suddenly *I'm* forced to defend *you*, and the guy kills us both. This is all far too sensible for you to not get it, Bastian. So tell me, please. . . . How long have you been doing this macho vigilante crap?"

Jeremy's mouth opened. He licked his lips and shook his head. Hands plunging into his pockets as he searched the parking lot. Eyes sweeping license plates in hopes of unscrambling what to say next. Dyslexic emotions unable to come up with anything other than:

"Since Saturday . . ." Jeremy sighed. Glanced down at his rented bowling shoes. Ground his toe into the asphalt. "Since I got here."

"You and self-consciousness have built quite a home together," Dromio said.

Jeremy nodded.

"A little out of step with the world around you."

"Yes."

"Putting a cautious foot forward in any and all situations."

"How do you—"

"Doesn't take a genius to figure out. Most everyone out there is a polar opposite of how they present themselves. The genuine article is a thing of the past. Gone the way of the Big Bopper and five-card stud. . . ." Dromio smiled affectionately. "You went a little overboard with the tough-guy act, that's all.

I was sure of it from the minute you threatened to break that guy's legs at the Blue Paradise."

"Yeah?"

"What I'm not sure about is *why now?* Why all of a sudden this act?"

Every last part of Jeremy's body looked as though it wanted to be somewhere else. Even his hair, lifted by a passing breeze, seemed to be looking for a means of escape. Eyes glued to his shoelaces as he eked out:

"I wanted . . . I wanted, at the very least, to be your equal."

Dromio waited. Let Jeremy tread water on his own.

"I came here—" Jeremy corrected himself, restarted. "When I got here . . . you were at the center of all things, and I thought . . . I thought maybe you needed certain things from people. Certain signs of strength. And I guess I thought it was now or never. Now's the time to start being strong, but . . . I guess it turns out I'm not as strong as I'd like to be."

Dromio nodded: "You ever say anything like this to anyone else?"

Jeremy hung his head farther, betrayed a slight exhaustion. "No."

"Look what being strong can get you. . . ." Dromio put a hand on Jeremy's shoulder. "I like *this* kind of strength. I think being yourself suits you better than you think. But don't think you have to put on a show for my sake, or anyone else's. If you like us it's because we're good people. And being good people, we're always ready to accept, Bastian. Myself, I wouldn't care if you were a televangelist pirate."

Jeremy didn't look up, tried to hold back a grin. "It'd actually be kind of cool if I was."

"You're goddamn right it would," Dromio agreed. "Hell, some of my best friends are televangelist pirates. Whatever. I welcomed you into my family and I meant it. But if you want in, and if you've decided to accept us . . . to accept me . . . then do me a favor, Bastian. . . . Please, just stop hiding."

Jeremy lifted his chin.

Face to face with Dromio now.

Bathed in red neon, far removed from the Blue Paradise.

Jeremy opened his mouth to speak when . . .

"Hey, you little bastard!"

The pair turned to see the gorilla striding toward them.

Incubated rage fueling his every move.

Dromio had seen it a thousand times from a thousand others.

No room for diplomacy and he readied himself.

"Bastian?"

"Yes?"

"Keep your face away from his fists, and kick him in the balls if it means saving your own skin. . . ."

Jeremy barely had time to nod.

And it took three or four guys to pull them all apart. . . .

At least, that's the way I heard it from Dromio.

41. Fulfillment

The best part about dinner wasn't the food.

Wasn't the wine, either.

Wasn't even the conversation, though it came a very close second. Easygoing and never once falling back on boredom or apathy. Relaxed words between bites of New York strip steak and angel hair pasta. Agile and effortless. Uncharacteristically friendly disagreements around the corner from every subject, no longer testing the waters for unpleasant surprises. Caught up in our own exchanges, ideas, and ever-broadening smiles . . .

Christina.

That's what made it all work. Something new after so long. Stepping out onto the beach for the first time. First time jumping into a pile of leaves. First lunar eclipse or meteor shower. First time in a movie theater as the lights dim. First pet, first kiss, first roller coaster ride, all these forgotten sensations coming back to me now. Manifesting themselves, refusing to let my eyes drift from Christina's any longer than necessary. Keeping tabs on each of her movements, every detail clocking in at half its normal speed.

Braver, newer world.

Like walking on the moon . . .

The dishes were lifted, check paid.

A hefty tip for Tom, and he asked us to stick around.

Have a drink at the bar.

Our friend with the red sneakers had long since stumbled out. I took his place, and Christina sat next to me. Both of us commanding a fleet of rum and Cokes. Leaning sideways against the bar. Heads propped with a little help from elbows and arms. Discussions winding round each other, dipping into lower decibels as our knees touched. Shins rubbing together. Hands occasionally wandering into personal space.

Palm to palm at one point.

A fascinated Christina comparing finger lengths.

"Wow . . ." She leaned in close to make absolutely sure of her findings. "You have got some small hands there, sailor."

"Well, I'm not a very tall man."

Christina leaned to the side and stuck out her tongue. Fished for the red plastic straw in her drink. Got hold of it and took a lengthy sip. "Does Sebastian have smaller hands than you?"

"You know, Sebastian is a good two inches taller than me."

"No."

"Yes, very much so."

"Well, you'd never know it."

"Yeah . . ." I threw her a lopsided grin. "I mean, not unless you measured us or something."

"I've just always thought of him as your little brother."

"He also happens to be older than me by a good couple of months."

"Mm."

We kept our hands together for a bit.

"Do you have any brothers?" I asked. "Sisters?"

"I had a sister...." Christina withdrew her hand and crossed her arms on the bar. "Older sister. She died after a very risky surgical procedure. Which is interesting, because when you think of high-risk surgery, the first thing that comes to anybody's mind is *miraculous recovery*."

It was strange, the way she talked about it.

Sadness hardly visible behind her acceptance.

Christina looked up from her drink and must have sensed my sympathy. "It was a good six years ago. Bad six years ago, whatever. Either way, I'm about as close to *at peace* as I think I'm going to get." She looked back into her drink. Toyed with the straw. Just us two seated at the bar, but three seemed to be a more appropriate number. "She was a good sister. Good person, a social worker. Helped a lot of people, did a lot of good for a lot of people. That's why I do this. That's how it is that I'm sitting in front of you, right now, instead of some other me."

"Guilt?"

"Oh, not at all." Christina shook her head, swiveled her chair to face me. "I love what I do. And I loved my sister. Memories make this better, not worse. You've got me all wrong."

I decided it was all right to smile. Raise my glass, even. "Here's to me being wrong."

"Had to happen sometime," Christina agreed, joining me in a drink. "Now what about you?"

"I told you, I don't have any brothers or—"

"I mean about the helping. Why do you do it?"

"No reason."

"Anybody with an act also has a backstage."

"You'd think that anybody who wears glasses has impaired vision but—"

"Jeremy—"

"Has it ever occurred to you that some people just are who they are?"

"It occurred to Ralph Waldo Emerson once."

"Also Edgar Allan Poe, but they both got the idea from me." I held up my hand to stop Christina before she could retaliate. "Maybe this just is who I am. Not just my role, but my life. I can't even remember what I was like before I started helping people."

"What do you get out of it?"

"I get . . ." I trailed off. Searching for an answer, not finding one. Aware that nothing was going to turn up. Almost appalled with the void staring back at me. Wandering the surface of the bar with my eyes, looking for an explanation among the coasters, empties, and scattered peanuts.

Christina was staring. Expectant, leaning forward. Propped up, cheek resting in her palm.

"I don't know," I told her.

She kept staring.

"What do you get out of it?" I asked.

"Me?"

"Yes."

"Fulfillment."

"I don't get that," I told her. Unable to keep the wonder out of my voice.

"Hey . . ." Christina waded in with a comforting tone. "Don't worry about it."

"Not much a chance of that now."

"You know, I don't think Dromio gets fulfillment from his self-appointed mission, either. But he's got Nancy and Matilda. And now he's got you, that's where he gets his . . . you know, the thing that gives him balance. They're his absolutes. And that's got to help you, finding your father . . ."

I sighed. Unable to continue talking without giving it all away. The bartender walked up, placed fresh drinks in front of us. Knocked on the bar twice. I reached for mine, took out the straw, and tossed it in the ashtray.

"Jeremy." Christina gave me an affectionate punch on the arm. Wobbled a little bit. "How is it that you don't have a girlfriend? You're smart, resourceful, on occasion you're even funny—"

"Don't forget good-looking." I smirked. "I believe someone called me good-looking the other day."

"Good-looking, yes. A girlfriend might do you some good, you think?"

"Wouldn't know. Never had one."

"You've never had a girlfriend?"

I instantly regretted it. Reached for my cigarettes. "Not as such."

Christina was evaluating my face. Probing for what I was trying to hide, but the rum was having its way with me. I found myself resorting to amateur techniques. Avoiding eye contact, feigning a deep interest in my lighter. Faking the same interest in the smoke curling from my mouth, and suddenly Christina had struck oil:

"So if you've never had a girlfriend, ever . . . then have you . . . ever . . ."

"I'll give you three guesses."

Her eyes and mouth became gaping spheres. Achieved planetary status, and it must have taken superhuman strength for her to ask, "You're a virgin?"

I sighed. "Yes. Yes, I'm a virgin."

"Wow."

"But I only attribute it to the fact that I haven't had sex yet."

"That'll do it."

"I'm a virgin by choice."

"Women choose not to have sex with you?"

"Clever you."

"Wow."

"Yes."

"What are you, a mutant?"

"No, but I'm *real* popular on islands with active volcanoes."

"It's just hard to believe, coming from a Johansson. Your old man must've scored with half the women in Chicago."

I nodded. "It's an idea I've been kicking around in my head since I got here."

"Wanna know how Dromio and your mother met?"

"You know?"

259

"You interested?"

"Might help change the subject," I said, suddenly a shade more sober.

Christina smiled. Took a swallow of Cuba libre, smacked her lips together, and reached back into the past. . . . "Your mother was working at a Safeway in Chicago. This guy walks in and goes to the gourmet section. He starts filling his cart, piling up around five hundred dollars' worth of food. As he does, he wanders around. Trying assorted fruits, eating some bread, a cup of yogurt, even opening packets of cold cuts. Nobody notices, all because he's pushing around this cart filled to the brim. Big spenders can do what they want, but your mother did notice this. Almost immediately . . ."

I crossed my arms on the bar. Rested my chin there, listening.

"Now, she's watching this guy the whole time. Still watching him, in fact, as he abandons the cart in a secluded aisle and walks out of the store. Having eaten his fill without paying a cent. She rushes after him, out into the parking lot. Stops him and gets straight to the point. This guy makes no bones about being caught, either. Just smiles ruefully and admits it's his favorite scam. Does it just about three times every day. And your mother started to laugh."

Christina paused.

"And?" I asked.

"And the rest is history."

I nodded, stored all the details. "Christina?"

"Yeah."

I stared at the bottles across from me as something began to form in my head. "Did Dromio ever do any time?"

Christina didn't answer.

I tilted my head up to get a better look at her. "I want to know, Christina."

"Look, it's no big deal. . . ." Christina crossed her own arms on the bar. Lowered herself down to my level. On her cheek, facing me. Elbow to elbow. "He was caught doing that little grocery scam a couple of times."

Shoplifting. "Four times?"

Christina blinked. "Yes. How did you—"

"Lucky guess," I told her, off the cuff. "My lucky number, actually."

"Well, it was four, yes. But he never went to jail."

Each sentence collaborating with the conversation between me and my mother. About my father, details of his brushes with the law forming a bigger picture. "Charmed the judge into letting him walk?"

"You are on *fire* tonight."

A smile spread across my face. Both sides of a drunken, internal dialogue slowly coming to an agreement. "Well, I know things about people."

"You're pleased."

"I am merely revitalized."

"Hmm."

"Thank you."

Christina gave an unexpected giggle. Even surprised herself as she stopped, cleared her throat, and asked, "For what?"

"For existing, I suppose."

"Well, I believe you can thank my parents for that."

I didn't reply. Kept staring into Christina's eyes. She didn't look away, what few sounds were left dissolving around us. Restaurant fading as Christina reached out, stroked my face. Moved up and stroked the back of my neck. I extended a finger and touched the tip of her right index.

We stayed that way for a while.

Finally, Christina broke the silence. "You were right about the betta fish."

"I know."

"Problem is . . . How do betta fish reproduce?"

"Excuse me?"

"You told me betta fish tear each other to pieces if they're put in the same tank. If that's true, then how do betta fish . . ." She gave a demure smile. "How do betta fish . . . do it?"

My throat went dry. "When I told you about the betta fish, I wasn't talking about you and me."

"What makes you so sure I'm talking about us right now?"

"I know things about people."

"As you've proven time and time again."

Christina shifted her eyes to the clock over the bar. Shifted back to mine. "You want to go to my place?"

"Should you be driving?"

"We'll call a taxi."

"Should the cabbie be driving?"

"We'll find out after he does or doesn't run us into a tree."

"How are we going to get your car—"

"Jeremy . . ." She put a silencing finger to my lips. "Do you want to go back to my place?"

I took a breath. Hoped it didn't feel too shaky against her fingertip. I nodded.

"You can say yes," Christina whispered.
"Yes."
"Good."
Christina called the cab.
I got the check.
Tipped big, and the two of us left the bar.
Arm in arm.

42. That Which Is Truly Significant

Christina's apartment was on the second floor. Third door on the right. We made it up the steps without too much trouble, holding on to each other for support. Off-balanced legs nearly sending us back to the bottom. Another challenge presented by the door. Searching for keys, trying to get a perfect match in the darkened hallway. When the door finally gave, we went stumbling through. I was sent flying, slipped, and landed on my ass. Christina laughed and helped me up.

"This is the living room," she told me.

"I know, it just attacked me."

Christina closed the door. Apologized for the mess of papers, folders, and notepads littering the area. Nowhere to sit, and Christina took care of that by leading me to her bedroom. Much tidier and there was a bed to sit on. Christina took my jacket and sat down next to me. I remained seated. Hands in my lap, feet flat on the floor. Perfect posture. Looking around the room, paying far too much attention to every last detail.

"Is there a single poster on this wall that isn't socially committed?" I managed to ask.

Christina twisted her torso around and pointed behind us.

I did the same. Saw a large poster of Albert Einstein staring back. Trademark hair and bushy mustache. Eyes wide and playful, tongue sticking out. Brilliant mind taking a backseat to a moment of pure, ridiculous fun.

"There's the perfect sentiment, right there," I told her.

"I know a better one," she said.

"What?"

"Go read what it says under the picture. . . ."

I crawled across the bed.

Christina joined me as I stood up.

Looked down at the printed words as I began to read: "As for the search of truth, I know from my own painful searching . . . how hard it is to take a reliable step, be it ever so small . . . toward the understanding—"

"Of that which is truly significant," Christina finished, arms around my body as she drew me in for a deep, bottomless kiss. Not a fleeting hesitation as I kissed her back. Holding her close in a tight embrace, an almost maddening display of light flashing under closed eyelids. We fell back against the wall. Pressed up against the face of a scientific revolution, as Christina tried her best to disengage my shirt. It got stuck around my head and she kissed me through the material. Finally managed to untangle me, and whispered, "God, you're skinny."

"Don't call me God, you'll ruin the moment."

She laughed into my mouth and the two of us were at it

again. Intense kisses overwhelming everything else, taking me further and further from my mind. Or deeper into my mind. Taking me somewhere I wanted to be, was all I knew. The one and only thing there was left to be certain of.

Three timid knocks from the living room.

Christina and I stopped. Breath heavy, both of us listening.

I, for one, hoping that it was just imagination.

It wasn't, and the next set of knocks was even louder.

"Don't answer that," I said.

"What if it's an emergency?"

"We already got one of those."

"I should probably answer that," Christina said. Bent down and picked up her shirt, which had somehow found its way to the floor.

"If it's your ex-boyfriend, can I beat him up?"

"Depends on whether or not this is happening in your dreams."

"Point taken."

"Wait here." Christina slipped her shirt on as I quietly said goodbye to her bra. She walked across the room. Paused at the door and turned around. "Don't think this means that I like you."

I gave a polite nod. "Didn't cross my mind for a second."

Three more knocks. Even louder this time.

"I'll be right back," she told me.

Closed the door behind her.

Alone in the room, and I had to refrain from doing a little dance. Leaned against the wall instead. Enjoying the flush in my cheeks. Heat pumping pure elation. Stomach filled to capacity with sexually aroused butterflies. I closed my eyes and let myself go with every sensation.

Then I heard Christina's voice. "Oh my God!"

My blood went from a hundred and three degrees to absolute zero in one paralyzing instant.

"Jeremy! Get in here, quick!"

I jumped from the wall and charged across the bed. Into the living room, where I stopped short.

Christina was trying to guide a small Mexican woman to the couch. Jeans, gray hooded sweater, and—

A horrified ball lodged in my throat.

The woman's face was bruised and scraped. A complete mess beneath her hood. Both lips busted open. One eye gone black, the other practically swollen shut. Large gash on her cheek. Blood had dried on her face and escaped down her neck, turning half the sweater into a nauseating rust color.

She was talking at a fast clip, Spanish bursting through her tattered lips.

Christina sat her down, turned to me. "Jeremy, ask her what happened."

My voice got caught somewhere in my lungs.

"Jeremy!" Christina barked. "Get it together, ask her what happened!"

I managed to force out the question. Tried to follow as she rattled off her reply, missing every other word as I translated: "She says that she got home . . . and her husband . . . he'd been drinking, and . . . Oh, Christ, he came at her with an iron."

"Where is he now?" Christina asked.

I translated, got the reply, and flipped it again. "She

doesn't know. . . . She says she ran out on him. . . . He chased her, but he was too drunk. . . . Christina, she walked all the way over here."

"Comfort her," Christina told me.

"What?"

"Come over here and comfort her!"

I made my way over. Sat down on the coffee table and told the woman she was safe now, that we were going to take care of her. Not knowing if any of it was true. Just doing what I could, which seemed like less and less with every passing word. Reaching out to touch her arm, and she pulled back with a wince.

Christina rolled up the woman's sleeve.

Revealed a wrist jutting at a grotesque angle from her arm.

Christina must have sensed my impending cry and cut me off. "Don't yell, Jeremy. Don't yell, she can't see us any more scared than we are."

I held back, noticed something else, and felt my stomach give me a sinister kick. "Christina, her hood."

Christina looked and saw the blood on the back of the woman's hood.

Reached for it.

"All right, Jeremy," she said, breathing in and out. Under control, all struggles hidden. . . . "Try to keep cool. This isn't going to be pretty."

The hood was off.

Blood had plastered half her hair to the back of her skull.

Sticky red, matted, and clumped.

I couldn't help a small whisper escaping my throat. "Oh, God."

"Tell her we're taking her to the hospital," Christina told me.

The woman must have recognized the word *hospital* and her eyes went from shocked to horrified. Standing up suddenly. An outpouring of fragmented protests.

"Jeremy . . ." Christina rose and steadied the woman. "Tell her that doctors are required to help her, and required by law not to tell anyone about her status in this country."

"She says her husband says that the hospital will—"

"Tell her!"

I did as I was told. Saw some of the fear ebb as she allowed a frightened nod.

"I'm going to help her downstairs," Christina said. "Call for a cab and meet me outside."

"Where's your phone book?"

"Screw it, I'll call the cab. Get your shirt on and get Maria downstairs."

I ran into the bedroom. Searched around frantically under the ecstatic image of Albert Einstein. Came up short and grabbed my jacket off the floor. Put it on, zipped up, and ran back into the living room.

"Watch out for her arm," Christina ordered. "Try to stay a step below her. If she starts to fall, you catch her. If you both start to fall, make sure *she* falls on you. Not you on her, and not her on the floor, got it?"

I nodded.

"And keep talking to her!" Christina called over her shoulder as she raced into the kitchen.

I put my arm around Maria and guided her out the door. Held on to her as we approached the steps, blood-encrusted sweater rubbing against me. Took it one step at a time. I kept the words going all the way down to the bottom.

A door opened across to our right and a large woman stepped out. Polka-dotted nightgown and a shower cap over her meaty head. Southern accent slanting her words. "Who the hell are you?"

"A friend of Christina's," I told her, still shuffling toward the front door.

"It's eleven-thirty, for Christ's sake!"

"I've got a dying woman here!" I shouted at her.

"Jeremy!" Christina was down the steps and by my side. Blanket in her left hand. Addressing the fat woman, every bit the diplomat. "I'm sorry, Mrs. Banes. We just need to get her to a hospital—"

"It's eleven-thirty at night!"

"I know—"

"I'm not running a hotel!"

I was already out the door and making my way down another set of steps.

Christina was by my side, ears sealed as Mrs. Banes called after us, "This is the last time, Miss Michaels! I'm tired of all these goddamn criminals coming into my house! You hear me? This is the last time!"

I heard the screen door slam shut, and we were by the curb.

Chilly night reflecting what had been an overcast day.

Waiting for the cab to show.

"When the driver gets here," Christina instructed me, "I need you to get in the backseat with Maria. I'm going to get

in front of the car and make sure he doesn't take off without us."

"Why would he do that?" I asked.

"You know how cabs don't stop for black people in New
York?"

"Yeah?"

"Same principle. Keep talking to her."

Christina wrapped the blanket around Maria, and I continued to use my voice. Nothing else to do but talk. A proper
selection of words can work wonders, I had always believed
that. Hard to hold fast to that belief, though. Shivering on the
abandoned streets, miles from the hospital, light-years away
from the truth, and nowhere close to the understanding of
that which was truly significant.

43. All the Pain and Misery in the World

It was heading toward one in the morning.

Only a few others were seated in the waiting room of Cape Fear Hospital. Partners in misfortune, tired faces battling worry. One or two mothers with sleeping children draped over them. Uniform lighting from overhead turning the room into a pasty, surreal experience.

I sat hunched over. Elbows on my knees, hands together. Staring at the floor. Right knee bouncing rapidly. At least that was one thing the real Jeremy would have done. Occasional glances here and there. Random urges to pick up a magazine dulled by the plastic grins of couples enjoying high-priced dinners, highballs, and yachting across crystal-blue waters.

Not a doctor in sight.

A sleeping baby woke up. Began to cry.

I looked over.

Looked away as it started to breast-feed.

A pair of feet stepped in front of me.

I glanced up and saw Christina. Calm face giving little away, and I almost didn't want to know.

"She's going to be all right," Christina said, voice clinging to lower registers.

Hospital voice.

"Her head?" I asked, matching her volume.

"Very mild concussion. The blood stopped long before she got to my place, and they're stitching her up right now. Reset her arm, gave her a nice little cast. The bruises, swelling . . . that's going to have to heal on its own. Painkillers should see her through that nicely, though."

I sighed. "Good."

"Not a lot more we can do here, Jeremy."

"And this is what fulfills you?"

"Every good fight carries with it a very sad question."

"Which is?"

"What kind of a world would allow a fight like this to even be necessary?"

The floor drew my attention again. I stared at the white tile, my own fuzzy reflection staring right back. Didn't respond when Christina asked if I was all right. Everything past eleven in the evening gnawing at me. Chewing through layer after layer of reality. Second time this week I found myself mixing help with hospitals. Not nearly the same this time around, though. My stunt outside the abortion clinic finding no common ground with this experience four days later.

Christina put her arm on my shoulder.

I snapped to and saw she had sat down next to me.

"You did good, Jeremy," she said. "Every step of the way, you were outstanding. You did a good thing for someone tonight. And all the pain and misery in the world won't change that."

"He beat her with an iron."

"I know."

"What if it was something I said to him?"

Christina frowned. "To who?"

"Her husband . . ." I tried to hold Christina's eyes with mine. "When we were out in the fields, maybe I said something wrong. Or didn't say enough, and when she came home—"

"Her husband wasn't there. That's not how I know her."

"It's not?"

"Maria works at the Blue Paradise, Jeremy."

I opened my mouth. Closed it again. Wasn't sure what I was feeling. Too much going on, inside and out. Knowing damn well that none of this had anything to do with Dromio, but my grip was slipping. Going in circles, blindfolded. Waving my stick around, just trying to get even a piece of the piñata.

"Look, Jeremy . . ." Christina sounded tired. We didn't have a lot more left in us, but she moved ahead anyway. "None of this changes the fact that he pays all the migrant workers in his kitchen the same going salary as anyone else. Doesn't change the fact that if Maria had gone to him tonight, he would be here right now, instead of us. In his own way, your father's a good man."

I gave a weak laugh. "You drag me through a thousand arguments about how much you hate Dromio, only to conclude that he's a good man?"

"When something like this happens, it forces me to put things in perspective."

"I'm tired."

Christina nodded. "Let's go pick up my car and head to the beach house."

"You're not drunk anymore?"

"Are you?"

"I've never been less drunk in my entire life."

"There's a good reason they say reality can be sobering."

"Yeah."

"Come on."

We stood up, and I immediately wrapped my arms around Christina.

She returned the favor.

The two of us pressed closer together.

One a.m. in the waiting room of Cape Fear Hospital. Awash with fluorescent lights and the sad fact that late-night emergencies were never ending. On and on, even while the rest of the world slept. Closed lids in darkened bedrooms. Alarm clocks set for whatever hour had been deemed best to wake up.

44. Good Night, Jeremy

Christina turned off the light and slipped under the sheets. Curled up next to me, arms wrapping my body with much-needed warmth. Legs entwined with mine. Lips resting against the back of my neck. Both of us falling together, down into the waiting embrace of unscripted dreams.

One last effort from Christina as she whispered in my ear.
"Good night, Jeremy."
Ocean sounds accompanying our last moments awake.
The pair of us fading into one large, singular heartbeat.

PART SIX

TUESDAY

45. What If Nobody Gives Up?

Sleep was made easy with Christina by my side.

Waking up proved just as easy, if not sweeter than sleep.

Sunlight streaming in through the windows. Nightstand clock putting the day at half-past one in the afternoon. Ocean wind outside along with the cry of seagulls. All those things certainly helped.

Opening my eyes, though.

Opening my eyes and seeing Christina's face, first thing.

Made everything else seem like God's afterthoughts.

I didn't move. Stayed just as I was, lying on my side. Christina's lips inches from mine. Watching her sleep, following the rise and fall of her body with every breath. Five minutes turned into ten minutes. Ten into fifteen. Would've been happy to let fifteen spread out over the rest of my life, but she woke up at eighteen. Flutter of the eyelids, and we were both looking at each other.

She smiled. "Feeling any better?"

"Yes."

"Good."

I hesitated.

Christina saw it and gave me an inquiring look.

"I was just thinking that it must have been you," I managed.

"What was me?"

"I fell asleep with all this weight," I explained. "And now it's gone. I think that was you."

Christina graced my face with her fingertips. "That's sweet."

"You sucked the pain right out of me."

"See, that's not nearly as sweet."

"It's true."

"You do understand that medical advancements have rendered leeches obsolete?"

"Okay, sorry about the *sucking* remark." I drew a bit closer. "I've never woken up next to anybody before. This is kind of new to me."

"So you want me to tell you what happens now?"

"What happens now?"

Christina drew her face close to mine. "We kiss. . . ." This was followed by a kiss. "Then we kiss some more. . . ." This was followed by a few more kisses. Longer this time. "Then we keep kissing. . . ." Kept kissing. "We keep kissing until one of us gives up and tells the other to brush their teeth. . . ."

A long, winding kiss followed.

"What if nobody gives up?" I asked, barely able to get the question out.

"How would you like to find out?" she whispered, and pulled me closer still.

There was no knock at the door this time.

Because they say lightning never strikes twice.

Because Jeremy didn't bother to knock. Just burst right in with a wild look on his face and the kitchen phone in his hand. "Hey, wake up, your—OH, SHIT!"

Christina and I disengaged with a synchronized cry of surprise.

"Christ, Sebastian!" she shrieked. Wrapped the sheets around her despite being fully clothed. "Don't you ever knock!?"

"Not as long as doorknobs still exist," Jeremy told her. Turned to me with clenched teeth and slow, deliberate words. "Phone call for you, *Jeremy*. It's your *mother*."

And having Christina around was once again an undeniable curse.

I clenched my own teeth and asked for clarification. "You mean *my* mother, or *your* mother?"

"*Your* mother!"

Christina raised her hand. "Is there something wrong with you two?"

"Oh, nothing's wrong with either of us," Jeremy replied, practically singing to cover his irritated state. "It's just that Jeremy's mother is here in Wilmington. At the Hilton."

"Bastian, what happened to your face?" Christina asked.

I had noticed the bruise and split lip as well. Didn't have the time or concern to chat about it. Leaped out of bed and snatched the phone from Jeremy. Put it to my ear and strode down the hall, dressed from the waist down. Doing everything I could not to break into a sprint.

"Mom!" There was no further sense in playing it cool. "What are you doing at the Hilton?"

"Why aren't *you* at the Hilton?"

"Why aren't you at work?" I countered, buying time. Heading downstairs, taking the steps two at a time.

"I'm not at work because I'm here," she told me. "And I'm here because something is rotten as *hell* in the state of Denmark, young man."

Young man, that was never a good sign.

"How did you get this number?" I asked, walking into the living room.

"I told the manager that I was your girlfriend."

"And he *believed* you?"

"Bastian, I could easily pass for twenty-six!"

"You just called me *young man*, you couldn't pass for King Tut!"

"Oh, you are in *so* much trouble!" she fumed, telephone poles all along the coast trembling with fear. "Give me your address. I'm coming over there to smack your face!"

"No, I'm coming to the Hilton, you can smack my face there."

"Bastian—"

"One hour, main lobby," I instructed and hung up.

Jeremy was down the stairs and in the living room, talking straight, no chaser. "All right, playtime's over, Baz. The wheels are coming off the wagon. We tell them now."

"You gave me until tonight," I told him. Rushed over to the door, slipped on my shoes. "Until tonight, you *promised*."

"I didn't promise anything—"

"I gave you your day with Dromio!" I whispered harshly. "Now you stay out of this, *Bastian*, they're my family, too!"

"Oh, man . . ." Jeremy shook his head, hands balled into

fists. "You have no idea how deep you just dug your own grave."

Christina walked onto the stage, followed by the Johansson women.

The battle between us on hold as Nancy decided to further complicate things. "Jeremy, your mother's in town?"

"I'm taking care of it," I told her.

"Look . . ." Nancy sat down in one of the easy chairs, rubbed her face. "Why don't I go with you? The two of us can sit down with your mother, tell her what's happened. She's going to find out anyway, so . . . I think the time has come for a family reunion."

"Just what I was thinking," I concurred. Took my jacket off the coatrack and walked back into the middle of the room. "Look, all of you, the whole family . . . Let's meet at the Blue Paradise tonight at six-thirty, and we will settle this. Will you be there?"

I ignored the obvious agreements and turned to Jeremy.

Knowing full well this was my last shot.

"It's almost over," I told him. Knew my eyes were pleading with him. "I promise, Sebastian."

Jeremy stared me down.

The rest of them oblivious to what was really happening.

"We'll be there," Jeremy said. "Six-thirty."

I threw on my jacket and rushed out the door. Took the outside steps two at a time, cleared the last five with a mighty leap. Heard Christina follow me down the steps, calling my name.

She reached me just as I was opening the car door. "Jeremy, where are you going?"

"Christina, are you sure about my father?"

"What?"

"Dromio," I insisted, talking fast. "Are you sure that's how he met my mother, pulling that scam in the grocery store?"

Christina looked caught in a hurricane. "Yeah, but—"

I jumped in my car. Started the engine and put her in reverse. Smashed the gas, gravel flying as I backed up. Put it in drive and catapulted myself toward Wilmington.

Didn't even think to say goodbye to Christina.

Didn't occur to me, because the clock was ticking.

Minutes falling like dominos, and it would all be over in a few hours, anyway.

46. How Else Would I Know?

Two-thirty, and daylight was already starting to lose interest in me.

I screeched to a halt in the parking lot of the Hilton.

Jumped out of my car and jogged up the steps.

My mother was waiting for me by the front desk. She caught sight of me and walked over. Long strides on high heels, power strides. Met me in the middle of the lobby, and I was swiftly reminded of our previous conversation as her palm struck out against my left cheek.

"*That's* for the King Tut remark," she informed me.

I rubbed my face and nodded. "Fair's fair."

"And you can avoid further punishment by telling me exactly what's going on. And no lies, Sebastian. The truth."

"The truth," I agreed. "I'll tell you the truth, I *want* to tell you the truth. But you've got to promise to keep the questions to a minimum and do exactly what I tell you. I need you to trust me for a bit."

"Any reason why I should?"

"I'd get down on my knees, but then both of us would just feel weird."

My mother sighed. "All right, it's a deal. What's going on?"

"Not here," I told her. Motioned with my head, and she followed me across the lobby. Into the bar and over to a table by the window overlooking the Cape Fear River. I signaled a waitress and ordered a couple of coffees. Once she was gone, my mother reached across the table. Got hold of my jacket zipper and pulled.

Leaned back with a disbelieving look. "Any particular reason you're not wearing a shirt under there?"

"Quite a few reasons." I zipped up my jacket.

"You slept in your clothes."

"Yes."

"Please tell me you're sleeping in a bed, in a house—"

"I'm doing both those things."

"Where?"

I didn't answer right away. Caught sight of a large boat making its way down the river. Navigating through shimmering waters. Clouds steering clear of the sun. Cotton-ball wisps watching from afar, and I tentatively put my best foot forward.

"Mom, I'm in love."

My mother was rendered temporarily speechless. Our coffees arrived along with a refreshingly clueless smile from the waitress. I thanked her, saw that my mother was still rebooting. Thanked the waitress again and reached for the sugar. Two packets. Looked across the table. . . .

"Mom?"

"Hmm?"

"Cream?"

"You're in love?"

"Yes."

My mother reached up and covered her eyes. "You got her pregnant and you want me to—"

"No, Mom, no." I stirred my coffee, trying to appear casual. "So far, I'm only in love."

"Give me the cream."

I slid the silver pitcher across the table. She picked it up and poured. Did some of her own stirring, lost in whirlpool thoughts. She began shaking her head, slowly. Sighed and looked up. "I gotta tell you, Bastian, I'm . . . a little disappointed in you."

"Disappointed?"

"More than a little disappointed, in fact."

"I thought you'd be happy."

"Hard to get happy about what you're going to say to Sara when she finds out—"

"Mom . . ." It was something I hadn't planned on, but there was no way around it. "I don't know how to tell you this but . . . I'm still a virgin. I didn't get Sara pregnant."

My mother went slack-jawed for an instant before crying out, "Then who the hell did?"

In my defense, I only had half a second to come up with an answer that would justify why I needed her help in the first place. Not so much in my defense, I probably could have done better than *Jeremy*.

"Jeremy!?"

"Mom, inside voice."

My mom toned it down, leaned close. "I could have got-ten in a lot of trouble."

"I know, and I'm sorry. But you didn't."

"Why didn't Brenda King just sign the damn papers herself?"

"She didn't know. And even if she had, you're the one who can do forgeries."

"Well, you can thank your father for that little bit of expertise."

Bingo.

I moved in for the kill.

"Forger, shoplifter . . ." I gave what I believed to be an ironic smile. "Quite a guy, this long-lost father of mine."

"Well, you learn something new every day." My mother picked up her coffee and took a sip.

"You remember when you told me about his favorite scam?"

"Huh?"

"You know the thing with the grocery store . . ."

"You mean at the Safeway? The free meal and the cart full of food?" Another sip of coffee. "I don't remember telling you about that."

"You must have," I told her. The room seemed to ex-pand. Windows letting in twice the light, a saturated thrill sending me into an euphoric tailspin. One hundred and eighty degrees turning three-sixty, going all the way around again, and I had to do everything in my power to keep a straight face as I insisted, "You must have told me, Mom. . . . How else would I know it?"

And suddenly, there was champagne.

Along with a waiter. Tall and mustached, holding a pail filled with ice and a bottle of Dom.

"Madam, this is from the young man over by the bar."

My mother looked past me. A confused smile on her face as she spotted her benefactor. "A little young, I suppose, but definitely a hottie."

I turned in my seat. Focused and tried to hide a wince. None too thrilled to see Olaf sitting at the bar. Wide grin on his face as he waved and went back to his drink. I went back to my mother and told her to tell the waiter to send back the champagne.

"Keep it on ice for me," she instructed.

"Mom, that guy's trying to get you drunk at three in the afternoon, do *not* talk to him."

"What's with you?"

"I have something to take care of," I told her. Got up out of my chair. Reflexively reached for my jacket, then remembered it was already on. "Meantime, you meet me at the Blue Paradise tonight for dinner. Get there at seven."

"The Blue Paradise?"

"Best restaurant in town. Seven on the dot, not before."

"Hey . . ."

My mother reached into her purse. Pulled out an envelope and handed it to me. I looked down, saw it was sealed and taped shut. Duct-taped. Turned it over and saw the words TOP-SECRET scrawled over the front. In red Magic Marker.

I looked up. "When did we become secret agents?"

"It's from Paul."

"Is it a suicide note?"

"If it is, then it's a very top-secret one."

"I swear to God, I don't have time for this. . . ." Shoved the note in my pocket, and gave my mother a quick kiss on the forehead. An added reminder of dinner, when and where. Strode out of the room. Past Olaf, not even a half-glance in his direction. Halfway through the lobby when I heard my mother calling after me. I let the wind out of my sails, turned. She walked up, holding a small piece of paper. Waved it in front of me.

In all seriousness. "What do you want me to do with this check?"

"What?"

"The check you told me not to deposit. What to do with it?"

I shrugged. "Save your money."

"Yes, that's why it's called a savings account. You got a better way to pay for college?"

"As a matter of fact, yes. . . ." I winked. "Blue Paradise. Seven o'clock."

"Not before."

"It's going to be one hell of a night."

I was out the door and into the streets.

On my way to withdraw twenty-five grand from the bank.

Whistling, with a little bounce to my step. No calculator necessary to crunch the numbers. The sum of all parts showing that twenty-five thousand was a small price to pay for what I was getting in return.

47. Nobody Ever Gets Away Clean

It took a bit longer than I had anticipated. The nearest First Union branch was a half-hour drive from Wilmington. Any withdrawal over ten thousand required several security checks. Plus, there wasn't enough left in my account to leave it open. The bank manager informed me that I would have to close out the whole thing. I did not have a problem with that and ended up walking out of the bank with the full twenty-six thousand six hundred and thirteen dollars. Put twenty-five large into a black tote bag, threw it in the trunk. Drove half an hour back to the Blue Paradise, almost six when I parked outside. Walked in and made a reservation with Chaucer for Dromio's usual table. Took a cue from Olaf and had him chill two bottles of champagne for me. When Chaucer asked, I only revealed that there were any number of surprises in store. He took it in stride, got it done.

I walked back out to my car.

Looked across the street and saw Olaf.

Parked half a block away. Keeping an eye out through the windshield of a Big Niko delivery car. Locking eyes with mine. I nodded and got into my car. Unspoken understanding, and when Olaf drove off, I followed him. Same as he'd been following me all day. To and from the Hilton, and now right back, too. Up four concrete ramps to the top floor of the parking deck.

Parked and got out.

Went to the trunk and got the tote bag.

Walked across the empty expanse toward Olaf's car.

Little time to appreciate my view of the Cape Fear River. Ships and luxury yachts turned into bath toys from my fifth-story perspective. Waning sunlight turning the waters orange, buildings purple. Surrounding rooftops free of life and activity. Far removed from the rest of Wilmington as Olaf got out of his car. Walked a few paces toward me and stopped.

Pulled out a Schimmelpenninck.

Was blowing exhaust by the time I made it over.

The two of us stood ten feet apart and faced off.

Not a word coming around, all negotiations over and done with.

Olaf took a drag of his cigar. Took it out of his mouth and contemplated it.

Looked over at me. "You sure you don't want one of these?"

"Schimmelpenninck?"

"Admit it, you like saying the name."

I looked around. "Tell you what. I'll buy one from you. Twenty-five thousand sound good?"

"Music to my ears."

Olaf pulled out the tin of cigars. Took out a Schimmelpenninck and tossed it over. Perfect throw. Graceful trajectory landing right in my outstretched hand. Put it in my mouth and lit it. Not a taste I wanted on my tongue, not by a long shot. I blew out exhaust and returned his stare.

Olaf extended his hand. "My money?"

I held my ground for a moment. Took another drag, then went ahead. "How do I know this is the last of it? How do I know that two months from now you won't show up at my door? Out of cash and looking for another handout? What guarantee do I have?"

Olaf dropped his arm. "Well, frankly, you have nothing more to give me."

"My mother's got a bit of stake in this, too."

"She doesn't have a whole lot to spare. Can't get water from a stone."

"Sara?"

"Her mother's the rich one," Olaf rationalized. "And I know what you're thinking, so don't even worry about me going to Esther Shaw. She finds out her daughter had an abortion, and she'll gladly send you and your mother to jail. And what good would that do us?"

"Thanks for the thought."

"It's just college, Sebastian. I never had the means to go, either, and that's just the way it is."

I suddenly found myself very angry with Olaf. The money no longer an issue, I could now truly feel the knife twisting in my gut. The sickening knowledge that I had been violated turning into unadulterated rage. Barely able to contain it, no way to stop the words that were suddenly pouring from my mouth.

"You know, my father grew up without any money. Not a

chance in hell, same as you. Went to college on a basketball scholarship. Lost that and was back on the streets. But he didn't stay there. He got out. He got out and now he's able to feed and clothe his family without a problem. Because growing up isn't something that happens to you. It's a choice *you* make."

"It's a choice that incredibly privileged people can talk about," Olaf sneered. "What your old man isn't telling you is that before he *decided* to grow up, life had long since given him no other choice. You want to survive in this country, you have to bite and chew, claw your way out of the grave you were born in. Don't tell me what a great man your father is on this fine day, years later. He was once just like me, Sebastian . . . And nobody ever gets away clean."

"That's *not* an excuse!" I yelled.

"I'm not making excuses," Olaf told me. Cool and unperturbed. "I am, however, the only one here who hasn't lied to everyone, so please, *Your Honor*, get off the bench, give me my *money*, and I'll do you the honor of *not* going to your old man, whoever the hell this guy is."

It was over.

A bird landed on the parking deck. Looked around and took off again.

Olaf extended his arm.

I tossed the bag, and it landed at his feet.

Olaf picked it up.

Opened it, very pleased with what he saw.

Zipped it close and turned away.

Back to his ride, and I imagined that car wouldn't be finding its way back to Big Niko's anytime soon. Olaf opened the front door, and I called out one last time. "How did you get the information?"

Olaf regarded me with a perfectly reasonable look. "If you didn't get Sara pregnant, then who did?"

I nodded. Understood. "I guess you'll never know."

"And you get no answers, either, so welcome to the party."

Olaf got into his car and closed the door. I watched as the engine came to life. Backed out of the spot. Turned in a sweeping arc and headed for the ramp. Down the ramp and the sounds of the motor faded.

I walked over to the edge of the parking deck.

Looked down and saw him drive out onto the streets. Going the speed limit. Obeying all stop signs, considerate of all pedestrian activity. Slowing down to let a group of children cross in front of him. Pausing at a red light. Signaling a left turn with his blinker. Around a corner, and then he was gone.

Out of sight.

"Enjoy it, you son of a bitch," I whispered. "I've got more for myself than a nobody like you will ever have."

I checked my watch and saw that it was almost time.

Let it go, and prepared myself for the final act.

48. Family Reunion

I had to circle around several times.

Almost a half hour before finding a spot near the water-front.

Didn't have the opportunity to change clothes. Same pants from the day before. Same socks, same underwear. Just a jacket between my bare skin and the evening air. No spare items in the trunk or backseat. No time to buy something nice before rushing off to the Blue Paradise. Telling myself not to worry about it. Gearing up, my curtain call less than a block away.

Seven on the dot as I rounded the corner.

A long line snaking toward me. It was going to be a capacity crowd at the Blue Paradise.

Caught sight of my mother bringing up the rear.

Walked up to her and pulled her from the line. "Come with me, Mom."

"Hey, wait . . ." She trotted alongside me with hurried steps. "I just lost my place in line."

"Don't worry about it. I own this place."

"What?"

We passed by Chaucer. Clipboard in hand, searching the roll call for the next party. He glanced up and nodded. "They're all here, Jeremy."

"Good looking out, Chaucer."

"All right, Bastian, what is going—" My mother stopped short. Feet doing the same, bringing us to a halt in front of the Paradise doors. "Hold on . . . *Jeremy?*"

I put a reassuring hand on her shoulder. "Only for another minute or so."

"After which I should start calling you what?"

"All questions are about to be answered," I assured her. "Now, when we go in there, I'm going to need you to roll with a few punches. And promise me this one last thing."

"What?"

"Count to ten. No matter what happens in there, promise me you'll count to ten before saying anything."

"Do I have a choice?"

My only answer was to take her by the arm. Lead her through the entrance and into the Blue Paradise.

A packed house greeted us. Every last table taken. Bar overflowing with patrons, waiters rushing every which way. Maximum volume on all voices. Jukebox cranked, feeding off the energy and excitement of Dromio's smoky restaurant.

A quick glance across the room revealed Jeremy and the rest sitting at the master table. I caught Dromio's eye and knew it was time. Didn't even stop to wonder why his nose was bandaged like a post-fight heavyweight. Took a deep breath. Lungs filling, head pulsing with a rush of adrenaline. Air rushing out, cleansing me of every last hesitation. Every last trace of fear expelled as I strode over to the bar. Distributed a few quick and silent greetings to the O'Neill brothers, Chief Hunt, Chaucer's wife. . . .

I told the bartender to cut the jukebox.

Planted my left foot on an empty bar stool.

Hoisted myself up, right foot on the bar.

Both feet steady as I faced the restaurant and called out over hill and dale:

"EXCUSE ME, LADIES AND GENTLEMEN! CAN I HAVE YOUR ATTENTION, PLEASE?"

I saw everyone at Dromio's table stand abruptly. Alarmed, as people slowly let go of their conversations. Forks and knives laid by the wayside. Jukebox cutting out. Dromio, Jeremy, Nancy, and Matilda all making their way toward me with slow, alarmed steps. Christina just a few feet behind. Confused expression, and, suddenly, all eyes were on me.

Not a sound other than shifting seats.

A muffled cough or two.

"Thank you!" I gave myself a few seconds before continuing. "For those of you who don't know me, thank you for your attention! And for those who think you do, I would just like to say that tonight marks a monumental, even life-altering milestone in my life. For eighteen years now, I have been an incomplete person. Just me and my mother, who did such a wonderful job raising me that I never even realized there was anything missing. But it was always there, somewhere in the back of my mind. Crawling around on nights sitting alone in my room, waiting for the phone to ring or trying . . . trying to finish that last paragraph for a school midterm. Wondering about my father, secretly dreaming that one day I might find him. Not dead, as my mother always said he was, but resurrected by some fantastic miracle. . . ."

I paused for effect. Feeling out the crowd, every last one of them eating from the palm of my hand. "You know . . . I didn't come to Wilmington here with any expectations other than to help my best friend do what I always wanted to do, what I never could do. But now, finally, I can say . . ."

I looked down at my mother, staring up at me with apprehensive eyes.

Dromio slowly approaching her, the pair now side by side.

"I can finally say, *Mom . . . it's time for a family reunion.*" I looked out over the wide-open ocean of faces. Let my proclamation ring out over the loyal subjects of the Blue Paradise. "My name is Sebastian Montero, and this"—I gestured to Dromio—"is my father."

Long silence after that.

Shocked looks from both Dromio and my mother, who cleared her throat. "One, two, three . . ."

Jeremy approached the bar. "Sebastian, it's over."

Nancy and Matilda burst out of their shell shock simultaneously: "Sebastian!?"

"That's right," Dromio said, a pained trepidation creeping into his eyes. "He's Sebastian, and this is Jeremy. They switched identities."

"I couldn't keep lying to my father," Jeremy told me. "So I came clean. Told him everything this morning, Baz. Everything. It's over."

"Jeremy." I hopped down from the bar. Practically skipped over to him. "You don't understand. Dromio is my father, too. We're brothers!"

"Have you all gone insane?" Nancy cried out.

". . . Nine, ten." My mother was done counting. "Sebastian! This is not your father."

"Mom, come on!"

"Bastian—"

"He can't have changed that much, just look at him!"

"Bastian . . ." She paced her words to the beat of a hostage negotiator. "I have never seen this man before in my life."

"Dromio!" A desperate edge was slipping into my words. "Dromio, tell her!"

"Bastian . . ." Hearing my own name from his lips sent the first true streak of doubt through me. "This is the first time I've ever seen this woman. I take it she's your mother."

"Hey, stop it, both of you!" I cried out. Losing my cool, stares of Blue Paradise clientele starting to eat away at me. Sinister eyes now, a thousand unconvinced jurors. "Stop all the bullshit! Act like adults, for Christ's sake! I don't care what happened all those years ago. I need you both!"

"Bastian . . ." That tone was back in my mother's voice, trying to coax me off a rooftop, talking down to me. "What can I say to convince you that this man is *not* your father?"

"You can start by explaining why I'm just like him!"

"Bastian—"

"Not good enough?" I was sick of hearing my name like I was holding a gun in my hand. "How come Dromio played for the same basketball team as my dad? Blue Hawk through and through, you said it yourself! How is it that you knew Dromio's favorite scam, the cart full of groceries? Apprehended four times for shoplifting, charmed his way out of lockup every time? Everything fits, damn it!"

My mother was done with shock. A look of absolute horror had found residence on her face. "Can we please talk about this someplace else?"

"No, Mom."

"Please—"

"No, you've got to face up to the truth."

She took another deep breath. "Truth is, your father's dead."

"We're past that now. He's standing right next to you."

"No, he is dead. Very dead. . . ." My mother lowered her voice, though it made little difference in the arena of faces around us. "He died in jail. He was convicted for forgery nearly six months before you were born."

I balked for a minute. Regrouped, came right back. "So what about the stories? Everything you've told me. How come Dromio's just like him?"

There was something in her hesitation that gave it all away. Something in the surrounding silence that brought a wounded understanding to her face. They say the truth will set you free, but there was nothing remotely liberating about the choke hold tightening around my neck as my mother sent the world crashing down around me.

"The truth is . . ." She took a breath. "Your father died in jail. He wasn't just a forger, either, he . . . He wasn't a good man, he would have been a worse father, and I was . . . ashamed that I had been . . . I didn't want you to know about him, so I made him up. I needed somebody real, a model, and

Brenda King gave me that model. I took as much as I could from Jeremy's long-lost father to compensate for the worst in yours. I was the only person other than Brenda who knew about it, and I never thought . . . I never thought she would tell Jeremy. I never thought he would go looking for him, and I never thought it mattered so much to you. . . ." My mother's expression changed to one of irrefutable guilt. "I'm so sorry, Bastian. I thought I was safe."

Mortified silence followed.

The hand around my throat was joined by its cousin, reaching into my stomach. Tightening around organs I didn't know I had. A bilious sensation growing, spreading. Not just in my throat, but legs, arms, fingers, every last part of my body looking for a means to vomit. Scream out, rail against what I had just heard, what I had been hearing from my mother for my entire life. But it felt as though my cries would have torn that place apart. Ripped down walls and dropped the roof onto mute, staring customers. There was no dignified way out of it, no way to reasonably pack it all up and accept what now could only be described as fate. The past few days unraveled. Yard after yard of fabrications and quiet deliberation coming to rest at my feet. Spilling out of me like the exit wound of a gut-shot animal.

Nothing left to proclaim.

Not a lot to be said, though I turned to Dromio, tried. "I'm really . . ." I stopped, gave it another go. "I really don't know what to say. . . ."

"Well, I do!" Christina's voice punctured the silence. Striding toward me with a mouth contorted by outrage. "I gave you a chance last night! You could have said something at any point, I *gave* you that chance!"

My mother cleared her throat again. . . . "I take it this is your girlfriend."

Christina came to a stop in front of me, and I did everything I could to look past those eyes. Deny what was happening, even as it happened. "Every last thing about you is a lie."

A slap would have been better.

A slap would have been a hell of a lot better.

Instead, Christina turned her back. Shouldering her bag as she walked away, through restaurant doors that instantly slammed shut behind her.

Not nearly enough activity to get the ball rolling, and the Blue Paradise remained one motionless coliseum. Stayed that way for a while, had me trapped. Wanting to move on, afraid of what might happen if I did. Time-capsule reflections as I looked over everyone's face. The O'Neill brothers, Chief Hunt, Matilda, Nancy, Dromio, and my mother.

Hell is where the heart is, and I straightened myself.

Gathered what little poise I could manage and spoke in the most reasonable tone I believe I have ever managed.

"My apologies . . ."

I walked past Dromio and my mother. Past Jeremy, avoiding eye contact. Staring straight at the Blue Paradise doors, the first goal of many. The first step to wherever I was headed. Head held high for no other reason than it was all I really knew how to do.

Out the doors and into the streets, where I finally dropped the act.

Turned right and started to run.

49. I'm Sorry About Your Father

Injury rarely travels without its longtime companion. Insult joined the festivities in the form of an empty parking space.

No car, just a fire hydrant.

Looked up and down the street, as though my ride might just be hiding.

Playing a little joke.

Not the case.

Still numb, and it didn't quite register. My car had been towed, and all it was, was just another thing. An event. Something that happened.

I honored the occasion by simply walking away, and soon I was just wandering.

Walking along the waterfront, not paying attention to my surroundings.

Unaware that Historic Wilmington covered a much smaller radius than I thought.

Blind to the broken-down buildings and factories sprouting around me.

Not registering the footsteps behind me.

Though it clearly stood to reason as I was grabbed from behind. Numerous hands, arms, dragging me into an alley. Nothing but my senses and a nearby streetlight informing me of the sudden ambush. Suddenly I was free, standing in front of a group of people. People with pastel polo shirts. One of them standing out, angry eyes decorating a savage grin.

"Hey, there, Bradley . . ."

Bradley nodded, the very act somehow flexing his biceps. "About time you learned my name, Johansson."

"Yeah, about that . . ." My patience was at an end, despite the empty space growing inside me by the second. "Whatever it is you've got against me, let's take care of it right now. And if we're going to take care of it, how about we make it you and me? Leave the rest of these losers out of it. You're the only real fighter in the group, anyway, am I right?"

Bradley stepped up, once again reminding me of my five-nine height.

"You really think you can take me?"

"No," I replied. "Now give me your best shot, if you think that'll do it."

I didn't see his fist so much as feel it.

A blinding pain spreading across my cheek, summoning starlight in front of my eyes.

Not more than a few seconds to realize that while there are only twelve rules in boxing, that's thirteen more than just about anything outside the ring. No rounds, no timers, no referees. Fights turned out to be unscripted, unscrupulous, and faster than a hummingbird's heartbeat. No ballet, not even close to the Charleston. Nowhere near the realm of anything choreographed. Just blind fury in the form of seeing how many times a person's body could be pummeled. Veins bursting beneath the skin until someone was down on the ground.

And maybe it was genetic. Maybe it was a skill I never realized I had. Maybe it was just that the floodgates opened. Shock and tired depression giving birth to a sudden rage. Blinded by the hopes and spectacular failure of the past few days, a screaming heat that seemed to come from directly behind my eyes, fueling fists I'd never used. Each mistake and misstep sending solid hits to Bradley's jaw, right eye, chin, an explosion for each and every blow landed. Bradley's punches making their mark somewhere in there, but there was no pain. Hardly anything for my vision to account for, just blurred colors coupling with searing streaks of light. Nothing concrete for my memory to latch onto, because one second, Bradley was rending my face useless. The next, I was standing over him. Several of my knuckles split open. Lips in bad shape. No way to assess the damage to the rest of the face, but I suspected there would be bruises come sunrise.

White streetlight shining down on Bradley's battered face.

Nose gushing blood.

Teeth turned red.

All his boys staring, abashed by whatever had just happened.

Probably as new to the fight game as I was. Standing over Bradley's landlocked body in the same way that people wait for a bus.

A clear victory, but hardly an important one.

Rage subsiding, dropping faster than a diabetic's blood sugar.

Not a thing resolved, nothing altered.

Not one recognizable change in those few seconds of fight.

"Bradley . . ." My breath was coming out in steep measures. Chest heaving, blood coating my lips. "Bradley, what have I ever done to you?"

"Your father . . ." Bradley heaved, spat out some blood. Rolled over, managed to get up on all fours. "I've had to work since I was seventeen just to help keep my family going, thanks to your goddamn father."

I glanced up.

Saw a group of privileged, unbelieving faces bearing witness.

Looked back down and saw that Bradley had managed to sit up. His broken face stared up at me, eyes defiant. Exhaling through mouth wide open. "Blue Paradise was their restaurant. Both of them, my father and yours. Your father forced mine out of partnership, didn't even bother to buy him out. . . . Head under water ever since, Johansson. Any idea what that's like?"

"I'm not Dromio's son," I told him.

Bradley could barely manage to choke out his confusion. "What?"

"It was all a mistake," I said. "I'm not Dromio Johansson's son. My name is Sebastian Montero."

"Why—"

"Because Dromio has a son. A son named Jeremy. And Jeremy's not responsible for what his father has done. Same as your father's not responsible for beating me up tonight. And I want you to remember that when you finally meet

Jeremy Johansson. I want you to bear all of this in mind,
Bradley. . . ."

I offered him my hand.

He batted it away, and sad to say, I understood.

I turned and walked away.

Stopped and turned.

Bradley had found his way back on both feet.

"I'm sorry about your father, Bradley," I said. "Trust me,
I really am."

And this time I did walk away. Out of the alley and into
the industrialized streets, as clouds gathered.

And it started to rain. . . .

50. The Man with the Plan

I found myself in front of Christina's apartment building.

The front door was locked.

I stood there for a bit. Went back down the steps, out onto the sidewalk. Looked up and saw her light was off.

The rain had been light and steady. Predictable until then. But suddenly downpour became the new language of the night, and fat drops of water made it clear that I was not welcome. Slamming against me, soaking into my hair, clothes, shoes. Just another thing that happened, and I ignored the gurgling sounds of ravenous gutters.

I called out Christina's name. Shouted out against the gale. Waited in the pouring rain for what turned out to be her landlady.

"Get the hell away from here!" she yelled from the porch. "Get off of my property before I call the police! Christina's not here!"

Technically, I wasn't on her property, and I called out again.

"Get out of here!" Mrs. Banes screamed.

I probably would have kept on. Not caring about consequences, screaming out loud until circumstance decided to end it all.

Stopped by two headlights approaching.

Slowing.

The window of a BMW rolling down, and a familiar voice calling out. "Bastian?"

I turned away from Christina's house. Blinking rapidly, eyelids forcing the water out of my eyes. Squinted. . . . "Cesar?"

"Hey, Bastian!" Cesar called out.

"Whose car is this?" I sputtered.

"Nicole's! Get the hell in here, there's rain outside!"

I went ahead and did as I was told. Opened the passenger door and flopped onto the leather interior. Water gushing from every possible place, garnering a laugh from Cesar as he began to drive.

"What the hell happened to you?"

I had forgotten about my face, and I gave him some kind of clever answer.

"Heard you were going to be in Wilmington." He smiled. "Knew it was only a matter of time before we ran into each other."

I gave some kind of agreement.

"Hey, where are you headed?"

"Could you possibly take me to Wrightsville Beach?"

"Bit out of my way, but considering how things went between Nicole and me . . ."

I figured the conversation would end at that. Nothing other than windshield wiper sounds to guide us home.

"You want to know how well things went?" he asked.

"How well did things go, Cesar?" I managed.

"I cannot believe the week I've had so far!" Cesar yelled. Nothing but happy thoughts reverberating off the windows. "Good God, Sebastian, you are so much the man, it hurts! Nicole and me . . . it's like something out of a movie, when love really works out, you know? Actual, real-life romance! And we owe it all to you, Bastian. Man with the plan. Oh, and you should know that Hamilton got a call from Mr. Wallace, congratulating him on one of the best essays ever. Hamilton told me he didn't have a single word written before class on Friday, now how the hell did you pull that one off?"

At first I didn't know what the hell he was talking about. Took me a few seconds before I finally remembered sitting in Big Niko's. With Jeremy, going over our brilliant plan. *My* brilliant plan to keep him safe from his own father. Photographs of Jeremy's new family and full reports covering the table as we prepared for the future.

And Hamilton had approached. One of many who occasionally came 'round for a little help. Not a single word written for his Mr. Wallace's British lit midterm. Desperate pleas for me to save his ass.

Seemed far enough in the past to have earned its own BC. A date buried under so many layers of history, it hardly seemed important anymore. . . .

But I sensed Cesar waiting for the details.

So I looked up, watched passing lights play over the ceiling. . . .

"It's an old trick," I said flatly. One hundred percent monotone. . . . "I only tell one or two people about it every year.

You're late for a deadline. Not a thing written. You know your thesis, your opening argument. So you imagine your closing argument. Hamilton's thesis was *What if Shakespeare were a woman?* The final line of his essay, I told him, was *In summary, Othella would not have been one heck of a fella."*

I paused, not really caring about what I was saying.

"And?" Cesar asked, taking a left.

"And you type the last sentence of your essay on the top of a page. Label it page nine at the bottom and put two staple holes through the top. When everyone passes up their essays at the start of class, slip that sheet in the pile along with everyone else's. By the time the teacher goes through all the papers, all they find is your last page, and they generally assume the other pieces of paper came unstapled. By the time they call you to confirm that they need you to turn in your paper again, you've already written it with the extra time the scam bought you. . . ."

My words trickled down into silence. Didn't bother to punctuate the explanation with anything dramatic. I could tell Cesar was waiting for it. Leaning forward, both hands on the steering wheel.

I asked him for a cigarette instead.

Cesar didn't smoke, suggested a pit stop.

I told him not to worry about it. Soaking wet, my brain running on a dull, aching loop. More than ready to spend the rest of the ride in silence. Instead, I got Cesar showering me with praise. Giving me reports of other people I'd helped, other success stories. Always falling back on how good things had turned out between him and Nicole. I greeted his words with polite nods and sent them on their way. Wasn't until we were driving over the bridge to Wrightsville that he mentioned Sara.

"What are you talking about?" I asked.

"I think maybe she's run away from home," Cesar told me. "From what I understand, Sara told her mother that she was spending the night at a friend's house. Today, Sara's friend says she didn't know anything about it. And nobody's heard from her since."

"That's all?" I asked. Noticing that the rain had failed to reach Wrightsville Beach. Noticing something in my pocket where cigarettes should have been . . .

"That's all I know," Cesar admitted.

From out of my jacket came an envelope.

Almost entirely undamaged by the rain. Covered in strips of duct tape. The words TOP-SECRET written out in black Magic Marker.

"You should give Sara's mother a call," Cesar recommended as I stared at the envelope. "I heard she was looking for you. And your mother, too. Guess she's pretty bent out of shape."

I tore at the paper. Ripped it open and read over the enclosed letter.

Didn't need to read it twice.

Sighed and pointed out Dromio's house in the distance.

"Wow, Bastian." Cesar was sufficiently impressed. Pulled into the driveway, bending his neck to take in the entire building. "Looks like both of us lucked out for spring break."

"Yeah," I said. Opened the door and stepped out. "I'll see you, Cesar."

"Be good, Bastian. . . ."

I was about to close the door. Leaned down instead. "Hey, Cesar?"

Cesar killed the ignition. "Yeah?"

"Was it your mother or father who crossed the border from Mexico?"

"My mother."

"Mm."

"What's up?"

Truth was, I didn't know why I had asked. "I was just thinking, lots of people really do take mothers for granted."

Cesar thought about it. Finally came through with a nod.

I sent one right back in his direction and closed the car door.

Heard him start it up as I made my way up the stairs.

Walked into the empty house along with a gust of lonely, salt-scented wind.

51. Atta Boy

I did call Esther Shaw. First thing after changing out of my clothes, and it was around a quarter to ten when she picked up on the other end. Sick with worry. A complete wreck, probably a teardrop for every word. I calmed her down. Told her my mother was staying at the Hilton in Wilmington, but not to bother calling her. Told her to call the police, tell them to search for a twenty-five-year-old Caucasian male by the name of Olaf Stevenson. Have them call Big Niko, he would probably have a good deal of information on him.

Find Olaf, I told her, *and you'll find Sara.*

Cut off further questions by telling Esther I would be back tomorrow.

Hung up and looked down at Paul Inverso's letter.

Number scrawled in the bottom right corner.

I dialed. Listened to the phone ring. Looked around the kitchen, trying hard to remember what my own looked like. Back in Durham. Back where it turns out I belonged.

I heard an answering machine pick up. Telling me that I had reached Paul's phone, and to keep it simple.

Only halfway through my first sentence when he picked up.

"Christ, Sebastian." Paul sounded worried, a little upset as well. "Where the hell have you been?"

"Wilmington," I replied.

"Yeah, I know that." Worry ebbed, and irritation began to take over. "I'm just saying that I've been trying to get in contact with you for around four days now."

"I know. I apologize. Believe me, I'm sorry."

"Did you get my letter?"

"Yeah . . ." I looked down again. Unfortunate facts staring right back up at me. "How did you find this out?"

"When we went to the clinic," Paul told me. "After Sara dressed up in the courier outfit and left, one of the nurses . . . Well, I think she was kind of flirting with me. So I stopped by on Friday to see her. We made a date for Saturday, and that's when she asked me about Sara. I told her the situation, and she told me it must have been a hysterical pregnancy."

"Hysterical pregnancy."

"When a woman believes beyond a shadow of a doubt that she's pregnant."

I sighed. "Only that wasn't it, was it?"

"That's right. According to the nurse, Sara had walked in and simply sat in the waiting room. Said that she was waiting for someone. Certainly didn't have an appointment for an abortion, not even an examination. Sara knew she wasn't pregnant, and I can't figure—"

"It's all right," I told Paul. "Nothing left to figure. Don't worry about it."

"Sebastian, do you even know how parental consent works in North Carolina?"

I balked. "Parental consent?"

"Did you really think that just a signed piece of paper would do the trick?" Paul asked. Somber words pushing my head down into my shoulders. "A parent has to verify their consent before the practicing physician, and their consent has to be *written as well as signed* by the parent. There *are* no forms like the ones Sara gave you, not in the state of North Carolina, probably not in *any* state. Did you even bother to check this out?"

I closed my eyes and pressed my face against the wall. Thought about Sara's innocent features, eyes that left doubt out by the roadside.

Sure that I would someday be able to laugh about none of this.

"Bastian, are you there?"

"Yeah, Paul. Do yourself a favor. . . ." I sniffed, collected myself. "Don't tell anyone about this. What you know, how you know. Things are going to get real ugly in Durham, and I don't want you stuck in the middle of all this."

"Look, Bastian." Paul was now irrefutably mad. "Don't blow me off like this."

"I'm not blowing you off," I told him. Opened a kitchen drawer and found a pack of cigarettes. "I was before, I didn't think that you . . . What difference does it make? You did good, Paul." I lit a cigarette and threw the match into the sink. "Seriously, well done. You should be very proud of yourself."

Paul didn't answer.

I thought maybe the line had gone dead, maybe he had hung up.

Then, in a low voice, I heard Paul say, "Thank you."

"Thank *you*."

"Is everything going to be all right with Sara and—"

"Trust me, Paul. You don't want any part of this. And this conversation never happened."

Brief silence before Paul finally asked, "What conversation?"

I tried to smile, couldn't against the cuts on my lip. . . . "Atta boy."

I hung up the phone. Put it back in its receiver and wandered into the middle of the living room. Surrounding luxury now just a collection of unfriendly commodities. Plush couches, white rug, and entertainment center turning their backs on me. I went over to the glass doors. Slid one open and stepped out onto the veranda. Up to the railing, figured at least the moon could always use company.

Stared out across the horizon.

Six hundred and thirteen dollars in my pocket.

All that remained of my future.

Bruises and frayed knuckles starting to beg for my attention.

Distant thoughts of Olaf and Sara.

Asking myself where they were right now.

Hard not to admire how beautifully they had played me.

Wondering just how long the pair of them had been planning it.

playing it cool

Knowing that I couldn't refuse to help.

That I wouldn't ask questions, that I could do anything.

That I simply was who I was. . . .

The tide was coming in now, and I eventually got to thinking about Dromio.

52. Final Interlude

Way I heard it from Dromio was this. . . .

Past closing time, same familiar scene.

Dromio and the family having a few drinks at their table. Chaucer behind the bar, counting up receipts. Taking inventory. A few Mexican workers mopping up, clocking out. Turns out nobody had thought to turn the jukebox back on after I left, and the faint sounds of a Latin radio station could be heard from the kitchen. Salsa and samba rhythms not having any effect on my mother. Not a single finger bothering to tap along to the beat as she sat at the bar. Drink in hand, lost in thought.

Didn't notice Dromio sitting next to her until he spoke up. "You all right, Anita?"

She took a sip of her drink, smacked her lips. "I'm not the one you should be worried about."

"He'll be fine," Dromio said, lightly touching the bandage over his nose. "Bastian's a trouper."

"Bastian is eighteen."

"Look, I know things got out of hand—"

"They didn't have to." My mother confronted him. "You say you knew the whole time they had switched identities? Chaucer got you a complete file on both of them, photos and all?"

"Two strangers contact me out of nowhere? You *bet* I knew what was going on."

"Yes, but how were Jeremy and Sebastian supposed to know you knew unless you *told* them?"

"They weren't doing it just for kicks, Anita," Dromio replied, kept his voice from finding its way across the room. "They had their motives, and mine involved making sure I didn't scare my son away."

"And what about *my* son?"

"I'm sure he'll have learned his lesson before too long."

My mother practically coughed out her drink. "Lesson?"

"What?" Dromio asked, handing her a napkin. "You never sent Sebastian to his room without supper?"

"That's punishment," she informed him, ignoring his offer. "You punished my boy for trying to pull the wool over your eyes. That is retribution. Don't dress it up as a lesson you had the right to teach him. No matter what he might have thought, you are not his father."

"And where could he have possibly gotten that idea?"

My mother took down the rest of her drink. Set it aside and got out of her chair abruptly.

"What do I owe you for dinner?"

"Twenty-five cents."

"Bill my office," she told him. Scooted her seat back under the bar. "What about the drinks?"

"On the house."

"They damn well better be." She looked across the room, past upended chairs perched on bare tables. Called out to Jeremy, "When you see Bastian, let him know he's still got his old room back home."

That said, she walked away.

Tried the door, remembered it was locked.

Chaucer was there in a heartbeat. A jingle of keys, and she was ushered out into the night.

Leaving Jeremy with his new family, and Dromio standing by the bar.

Another night in the life of the Blue Paradise very nearly done with.

At least, that's the way I heard it from Dromio.

53. Certainly Not Done

Someone draped a blanket over me, and I came to.

Shrouded moon in the sky telling me it was approaching midnight. Sticky skin, thanks to unusually high beachfront humidity. Plastic straps of a reclined beach chair pressing into my back, Dromio sitting at the foot. Offering me a bottle of water. I accepted, took a sizable gulp. Placed it next to me and retracted my arms back beneath the blanket.

A few minutes went by.

Both of us allowing the ocean to talk.

A light turned on in one of the windows above us.

Turned off.

"Didn't see your car in the driveway," Dromio said.

"Got towed in Wilmington," I said.

"How'd you get here?"

I shrugged. "My guess is you probably already know."

"How's that?"

"Just got to thinking tonight."

"About?"

"Scotch," I told him. "I seem to remember someone at

the Paradise telling me to be thankful for what I had, that sometimes all it takes is a week to lose it all. Using scotch as a nice little metaphor for what was going to happen to me. I remember asking him if he could read palms, and he laughed it off. I suppose I must have known it then, somehow, but . . . only now, in retrospect, am I really sure about it. Man of your influence, ex-detective in charge of your restaurant, a kid from out of the blue claiming to be your son . . ."

"Ah . . ." Dromio wandered over to the railing. Turned to face me. "So you've figured me out?"

"I did the same thing. Got a full report on you and your family, photographs and everything. I guess I didn't expect you to also be so . . . the way you are."

"Prepared."

"Stands to reason."

"That's what I told your mother."

I drew my legs up to my chest. "She mad at me?"

"Are you mad at her?"

"Yes . . ." I listened to the sounds around me, searching for more than the arrival of recurring waves. "But I suppose you couldn't swing a dead cat around this town without hitting someone who's guilty. Maybe Christina, though . . . Christina was definitely a casualty."

"Casualties aren't just reserved for the innocent."

"What happened to your nose?"

"I was about to ask you about your face."

"Had a run-in with Bradley."

"Oh . . ."

"Yeah, seems you ran his father out of some kind of joint venture called the Blue Paradise."

"He stole," Dromio said. Plainspoken words free of regret or apology. "He embezzled money, and if I hadn't caught him, he would have gone to jail. Didn't want that to happen, didn't want him as my partner anymore. Certainly wasn't about to buy him out after what he did to me, so I quietly showed him the door. . . . It's the nature of business, not everyone can end up with what they want."

"Interesting words from a man who runs a socialist restaurant."

Dromio gave me a look, "You see a sign outside my restaurant with the words '*Red* Paradise'? This is a business, Sebastian. Plain and simple. I pay my waiters a steady salary to make sure they don't have to rely on anybody but themselves for their earnings. My profits have gotten me a house on Wrightsville Beach, three cars, sound investments, a trust fund for my daughter's education, and now one for my son. Show me a socialist spends his money any differently than me, and maybe then I'll start looking for a residence in utopia."

"I couldn't care less about your politics," I informed him. "Capitalism versus altruism. Self-interest versus selflessness. I don't care that your restaurant is a cash cow all dressed up as Sherwood Forest. I don't have any problems with you hiring illegal immigrants long as you pay them well. And if Bradley wants to blame you instead of *the nature of business,* then that's his problem." I swung my legs off the reclined chair and sat up. "I've been anything but a straight shooter for many years now. I'll admit that without any apologies—"

"None?"

"What could you have possibly gained from playing me like this?" I demanded.

"A son."

"Don't give me that. You had him after the first day, and you knew it. You could have stopped this, and it had nothing to do with gaining a son."

"I had Jeremy after the first day, and you knew it, too. You could have stopped this, but you wanted a father. So don't dance circles around me, Bastian. What's all this really about?"

And Dromio and I were like strangers on a train. Four straight days under the same roof, nowhere closer to knowing each other than we were before meeting. I felt like nothing more than a guest in Dromio's hotel. Dromio was nothing more than a manager. Four straight days getting to know each other, and it all seemed to be nothing more than the imaginary bond between customer and client.

Nobody ever gets away clean.

It was enough to send the heart packing. Turn my life inside out and my thoughts putrid.

"You didn't have to be so accommodating," I managed. Voice dragging on the wooden planks beneath my feet. "You didn't have to talk to me the way you did at the Blue Paradise. You didn't have to treat me like I was really your son."

Dromio nodded.

And it might have been my mistake, a misread sign in the darkness, but I could have sworn he was on the verge of saying something else before telling me, "I don't expect you to understand all of it right this minute."

"This whole time . . . is there anything you've said to me that wasn't a lie? Am I walking away from this with even a scrap of truth?"

"Truth . . ." Dromio sighed and looked up at the passing clouds. *"An ingenious compound of desirability and appearance."*

"Is there anyone in this town who *can't* quote Ambrose Bierce?"

"Truth is far more intangible than something you can walk away with," Dromio said, almost forcefully. Displaying something very close to faith. A certainty that bordered on passion. "And that's where lies come in. They fit right there in the palm of your hand, you can almost taste them. It's what's presented in order to keep the world going. It's what people like us do."

"People like us?"

"Said it yourself, Bastian. You and I are exactly alike."

"Uh-uh, forget it," I said as clouds in the sky began to part. Stood up from my seat, blanket falling around my feet. "Forget it, Dromio. There's no chance I'm going to live like that."

"Like what?"

I paused, though I didn't really need to think about it.

Just say it. . . .

"Like you."

"Then you're going to have to change, Bastian. Because let me tell you something . . . like it or not, that's who's standing in front of me right now."

"Like you changed after you left Jeremy's mother? That *big event* you said forced you to grow up so you could feel better about yourself with your twenty-twenty hindsight? So you've settled down, raised a family. You don't scam grocery stores, you smooth-talk customers. You don't play around with other women, but you play around with everyone around you. Honestly, Dromio, can you point to a single fundamental change in your personality eighteen years later?"

It hadn't been my intention to take it there. And upon seeing Dromio's expression melt the way it did, I can't say I felt very much like retracting it. All cards on the table. No point in bluffing anymore. Standing over Dromio, watching him face the facts. Face the facts, no matter how veiled they were by time and distance alike.

A tremendous wave came crashing onto the beach as Dromio simply looked up at me with a satisfied smile. "And I did change, Bastian. . . . I did." He stood, hiked up his shorts. "But I'm certainly not done. And, by the way, neither are you."

Dromio went one-eighty and headed for the door.

Stopped at the threshold.

Back still turned.

"And might I also add," he concluded, "there's nothing that says this is going to be our last conversation."

"Is that a promise or a threat?"

"Who knows?" Dromio mused. Raised his arm and knocked on the wooden frame just above him. "I guess we'll have to find out when we do."

"Yeah."

"Be sure and lock up after you come in. . . ."

Exit, stage left.

And I stayed behind.

Stayed behind with Thursday, Friday, Saturday, Sunday, Monday, Tuesday, and the approaching Wednesday as my only companions. Moonlight fading in accordance with the timeless institution of cycles. Humid wind picking up the pace, challenging dune-grass roots. A distant lighthouse flash-ing its warning for all those out at sea. Rows of houses up and down the coast like mountain-range teeth, presiding over an empty beach waiting to be filled.

I was miles away from home.

Vastly unsure of what would be waiting on my return.

Stubborn mistakes that had no interest in being rectified.

Thinking that *Perhaps next time, I'll do better.*

I stayed behind.

Just long enough to see if the sand crabs needed anything before saying good night, and heading inside to pack all that I had brought with me to the coast of North Carolina.

Epilogue

And although I was done, everything was far from over.

My welcome home took the form of two plainclothes-men, waiting for me in the kitchen. The drive back from Wilmington had offered substantial time alone. Miles of interstate worth of rehearsal space. My resolve to tell the truth conveniently on hold, trying to keep Dromio's face at bay. Slipped back into character for the sake of survival. Gave the police a believable story about Sara and Olaf: how I could have possibly known about it, why I didn't alert anyone beforehand, all questions handled with the nervous tendencies of the innocent.

Not a word regarding abortions or blackmail.

The police warned of further questioning, but word spread quickly. Fast and far, and I wasn't exactly shocked when Dromio called me a few days later to let me know that Chief Hunt had called the DPD.

Put in a good word for me.

They won't be bothering you again, Dromio told me.

The resulting conversation with Dromio had me confessing

what really happened with Sara and Olaf. The abortion that never happened, the blackmail, everything I had left out in my statement to the police.

Every last bit of money I'd saved for college lost.

An agreement was reached, and for a while after, we talked about our time in Wilmington. I revealed select moments from my side, and Dromio filled in a few blanks for me. Almost casually, nothing but a distant relative of our last conversation, out on the balcony. Nothing more than a few formalities capped off by a goodbye that neither explained nor concluded anything.

And that night my mother and I sat down for a chat.

Cleared the air as best we could.

My mistakes in exchange for the lies about my father.

It was as good a place as any to start.

Jeremy, on the other hand, offered no such possibility. Nearly two weeks passed before we would even greet each other in the hallway. Even then, all traces of things past were wiped clean. Replaced, finally, with what had always been there. Never really brothers, never really friends, and the chain had ultimately snapped in Wilmington. Nothing left to say, because it had already been said. That Monday morning in the bathroom. Our final negotiations, the illusion of friendship sacrificed for our own ends and desires. All there was to know about Jeremy officially reaching me once or twice a week from third-party sources. Far more time to myself, a glimpse of things to come.

I slowly curtailed my services to those who asked for them.

Inevitable collapses followed. The house of cards I had

built on favors for others came crashing down, one by one. And with every bad turn of events for others, things for me continued to move forward with precious little fanfare. Big Niko was finally caught cheating, and I took the SAT. Cesar and Nicole broke up, and my college applications were sent out to every corner of the United States. Brenda and Peter King finally had it out and opted for a temporary separation. Meantime, I wrapped up my finals. Sara Shaw and Olaf Stevenson were eventually tracked down in Florida. The money hadn't lasted, and Olaf was busted after applying for a job at a pizza parlor. He was charged with the transportation of a minor over state lines. Esther Shaw, as predicted by my mother, grounded her daughter for less than a month before seeking family counseling.

I found all this out at my graduation.

A strangely somber day for me.

I don't recall the procession. Guest speakers, valedictorian, all of it lost to me. I do remember my mother smiling through uncharacteristic tears. People keeping their distance from me, with the exception of Mr. Wallace. Proud and welcoming despite Olaf's negligence resulting in the death of one of his dogs. He had simply smiled. Crushed my hand with a five-finger embrace and offered his warmest congratulations. Never once mentioning what had happened in Wilmington.

Just one of those boxes that never gets unlocked.

Summertime came, and it was time to gracefully wedge myself under Dromio's thumb. Four straight summers of working Blue Paradise nights in exchange for tuition.

I knew it wouldn't be enough to pay him back. There would be more to come, other favors called in. I made whatever extra money I could, was set up rent-free in the attic of another link in Dromio's chain.

Days and evenings spent taking food orders. Late nights under a low network of wooden beams, lying on a bed crammed between a rickety desk and a North Star sewing machine from 1872. Late nights with plenty of time to think, oftentimes about Dromio. Analyzing our conversations, start to finish, kind words and advice he'd been under no obligation to give. The story Nancy had told me about Dromio and his old neighborhood, how he had cried in the front seat of their car, telling her that he never wanted to go back.

I don't ever want to be that again.

It got me to thinking about the path I had forged for myself before any of this happened. Where that path might have led if I hadn't met Dromio. No way to tell, but I had to wonder if he might have sensed where I was headed. Seen me, decades from eighteen years old, face buried in my hands. Tears spilling in anguish over a misspent youth. Because he must have known, at some point during my stay with him, that the switch would blow up in my face. He must have been preparing, fostering every chance to make my defeat all the more crippling. Perhaps not from the very beginning, but by the time of our last confrontation, when I asked him, *What could you have possibly gained from playing me like this?*

A question he had elegantly sidestepped by asking, *What's all this really about?*

You didn't have to treat me like I was really your son.

And Dromio's only reply had been, *I don't expect you to understand all of it right this minute.* . . .

But he had been about to say something else. I grew more certain of it with every time I projected back. Not just a dramatic pause before speaking, but an indisputable hesitation before leading me down the page. Laying bare his manifesto on the subject of lies. A necessary tool for *people like us*, and he must have known. Must have recognized my displeasure, must have known that I would never allow myself to become like him. To become the man who had baited me. Hooked me, dragged me onto his boat before throwing me back in the water with a scar that would always remind me. . . .

And hadn't I done exactly that?

No more helping, no more lying, denouncing every last part of me that I had come to know as Sebastian Montero. No more favors, enough time now to lie on my back, late at night, and realize that anything I had been headed toward before meeting Dromio would always remain speculation.

Another one of those boxes that would never be unlocked.

I was now just a waiter at the Blue Paradise, and everything had changed. Trying to fit in as many shifts as I could, never once relating to Dromio as anything other than my boss. Occasions arising when I would wait on him, Nancy, and Matilda. And Jeremy, whose preferences I had down by mid-June. No avoiding the spectacular heartache of taking their orders. Setting food down in front of each one, seat assignments remaining the same, day in and day out. Week after week, it was just something that had to be dealt with. Nancy kept drinking screwdrivers, Matilda would smile and slip me two dollars every now and then, but none of it made a difference. By the end of summer, their faces had become those of familiar strangers. Rediscovered, rewritten as customers who lived well, and tipped graciously.

The Johansson table . . .

Fall semester found me in Minnesota.

Last on my list of colleges, but cabin fever had become a pastime for me. Snow-covered isolation and a respectable economics department, not too shabby. Granted, I had no plans to study economics. I actually had no plans at all. No major in mind, no sense of where I was going. Definitely no intention of taking any part in student activities. My first visit to a college party lasted ten minutes and half a Cuba libre. My first time attending the student council didn't go past opening remarks. My first basketball game didn't even see me to the first time-out.

And damned if I was going to join a fraternity.

I went to class instead.

Went to the library.

Tackled my essays on the day of their assignment. Tried to keep residence in my soothing chrysalis, despite the fact that there was still the last paragraph to be dealt with. Unable to finish unless I absolutely had to. A leftover quirk that had never really been habit, hours before due dates spent typing out rows of 3s and lowercase q's. Unwilling to finish what I had started. Watching the snow gather outside my window, hiding detail and giving life to temporary serenity.

Last paragraph.

Which is unavoidable.

As conclusions always are.

Which finally brings me back to you, Christina.

You and me, and the last time I saw you. Rushing out of the Blue Paradise, doors opening and streets swallowing you whole. Extinguished lights looking down at me from your apartment as I stood outside, in the rain. I picture you running out. Some forged and optimistic memory where you throw your arms around me. Water rushing around us, and the skies saying *let it rain*. I imagine phone calls and letters. I take this past summer, force your presence into my free nights. Pretend that you weren't conveniently working out of state. Replay conversations, extensions of our first and only nondate. Time spent together past the few days we had, and I do everything I can to stop these thoughts. Refrain from giving them any serious consideration.

Summoning all my strength to keep you right where events placed you.

Aware that I haven't done a thing to change.

That I don't know how to, yet.

At best, I've just stopped. Turned around, and contented myself with looking backward.

And I truly do believe we have Dromio to thank for that.

But none of this is good enough.

Simple isn't good enough.

I want my shirt back, Christina.

And, while this is the way you've heard it from me, I think you should take a moment. Take a few days, take the months before spring turns to summer to consider that every last word of this is finally the truth.

If the need should arise, you'll know where to find me.

playing it cool

Smiling widely and tending to the endless requests of needy customers.

Taking care of business.

Order after order, until closing time says otherwise.

Playing it cool and doing time at the Blue Paradise.

Acknowledgments

Special shout-outs are in order for all of the following and in no particular order:

To Hank, for all the prowling.

To Jim and Nick, for catching the kinks.

To Rodrigo Dorfman, for the excellent Web site.

To my father, who, all those years ago, took the time to believe in a young man by the name of Sebastian Montero.

About the Author

Joaquin Dorfman was born in Amsterdam in 1979. Though the bedrock of his fan base is in the Iberian Peninsula, he currently resides in Durham, North Carolina, where he suffers from insomnia and an aversion to commitment. He co-wrote the novel *Burning City* with his presumed father, Ariel Dorfman.

Although Joaquin claims authorship of *Oliver Twist*, Plato's *Republic*, and the book of Deuteronomy, *Playing It Cool* is his "official" solo debut.

His awards include a gum wrapper he found on the street last winter.

Visit Joaquin at www.joaquindorfman.com.

9/16/06